Praise for Sheri Lewis Wohl

Scarlet Revenge

"Vampire stories have been written by hundreds of authors, but this is probably one of the few times that you will actually see one who works at the Library of Congress…With the setting of the story, it almost gives the feel of *National Treasure* meets paranormal."—*American Library Association's GLBT Round Table*

Vermilion Justice

"It's probably impossible to read this book and not come across a character who reminds you of someone you actually know. Wohl takes something as fictional as vampires and makes them feel real. Highly recommended."—*American Library Association's GLBT Round Table*

Necromantia

"This is one of the most sensational and thrilling books I have read in a long time. From the stirring opening scenes to the dramatic and exhilarating conclusion, this novel keeps the reader completely engrossed."—*Inked Rainbow Reviews*

By the Author

Spiritus Group Series

Crimson Vengeance

Burgundy Betrayal

Scarlet Revenge

Vermilion Justice

Reluctant Psychic Series

Twisted Echoes

Twisted Whispers

Twisted Screams

Necromantia

She Wolf

Walking through Shadows

Visit us at www.boldstrokesbooks.com

WALKING THROUGH SHADOWS

by

Sheri Lewis Wohl

2017

WALKING THROUGH SHADOWS
© 2017 By Sheri Lewis Wohl. All Rights Reserved.

ISBN 13: 978-1-62639-968-6

This Trade Paperback Original Is Published By
Bold Strokes Books, Inc.
P.O. Box 249
Valley Falls, NY 12185

First Edition: September 2017

CREDITS
EDITOR: SHELLEY THRASHER
PRODUCTION DESIGN: STACIA SEAMAN
COVER DESIGN BY SHERI (GRAPHICARTIST2020@HOTMAIL.COM)

In Memory of
Loba & Falco

As you crossed the Rainbow Bridge
you took a part of my heart with you.
I find solace in the knowledge
you left behind a world just a little better
because you were in it.

"If Satan's kingdome be divided
against it selfe,
how shall it stand?"

The Discovery of Witches
Matthew Hopkins, Witch-Finder
M.DC.XLVII.

PROLOGUE

Along the Columbia River, 1836

The pounding hooves finally stopped. The pounding of Hannah's heart did not. Outside, the storm raged, and rain pelted the roof as the wind howled. Chills raised the skin on her arms, and water dripped onto the rough floor from the hem of her dress. Had there been light inside the small space, she would have seen the water did not run clear. Instead, it stained the floor red as it saturated the wood.

Hannah clutched the book tight to her chest and looked wildly about, trying to see in the veil of darkness. Her eyes adjusted, and she was finally able to make out a bit of detail. The room was small, with only two windows, one with a broken corner where the wind pushed through, bringing a spray of rain with it to dampen her face and spot the leather binding of the book she held.

Time had run out. She had hoped and prayed the gods would give her more, and now she understood it was not to be. Just as had happened to so many of her sisters as they had pressed westward in the hope of finding safe haven, she had failed. Her powers could no longer aid her, and soon her spirit would be set free from the restraints of this earth. She would join those who had gone before her. She looked forward to gazing upon faces she had not seen for many years. She ached for what she would leave behind. Now she prayed only that her daughter would remain safe. Deep in her heart she had to believe what she'd done would carry her precious daughter to a long life.

Leaving her beautiful, trusting daughter outside the gates of the fort was risky, but she had to take that chance. All they had built, all they had sought rested solely in the hope of the child of her heart.

She held the vision of her little girl's face in her mind and the book close to her body. How many had died to protect the wisdom between its pages? It would do her no good to think of that now. As the last, she had to protect the knowledge it contained. Perhaps in the future the gods would lead her descendant to it. She had written her words to the child she prayed would one day be born and walk the same path as she.

A flash of lightning lit up the cabin, and though she had spent many days and nights in this room, it was the first time she noticed the space between the boards of the floor. Dropping to her knees, she laid the book next to her and began to work at the crack with her fingertips. As she pried, slivers from the edges of the floorboards dug into her skin. Blood dripped as she clawed at the boards until she had loosened two of them enough she could pull them free. Her blood soaked into the leather of the book as she maneuvered it through the opening. At last it lay flat on the ground below. She had created it herself and hoped the attention she had given it would keep it safe and intact. After she replaced the boards, she kneeled on them and began to chant, holding her arms out at her sides, palms toward the heavens. Her words were low, drowned by the raging storm outside. No one would hear them anyway, save the gods she prayed to.

As her words trailed away, she heard the sound of approaching hoofbeats. They had found her trail again and were tracking her as if she were a deer fleeing from the slaughter. She pressed her bloody fingers against her lips to stop the scream that threatened to burst forth. A metallic taste filled her mouth.

She sagged to the floor, and the pain began to push at her spirit. On the shelves at the walls hung herbs she could use to help ease her discomfort. She did not move. It did not matter any longer if she was in pain. It did not matter if they found her. It would be useless to run; she had nowhere left to hide, and she lacked the will to even try. Curling into a ball, she closed her eyes, and calm settled over her. Her daughter was safe, which gave her peace. So too did the knowledge that a time would come, had to come, once more for the power of the book to be released.

It was not this night. She had left what little magic she could summon with the book and the spell to keep it hidden at least for a little while. It had to be enough.

The door slammed against the wall, and a gush of wind and rain poured through the opening. A spray of cold rain water whipped across her face, only to slide down her cheeks like the sobs she did not have the strength to produce. Rough hands grabbed her arms and dragged her back out into the storm, her blood surely leaving dark streaks across the wooden floor. She could barely feel their harsh touch or the wind or the rain.

CHAPTER ONE

Spokane, Washington
Present day

"No, no, no, and no." Molly Williams could hardly grasp a disaster of such proportions. She stepped back and ran her hands through her hair. Standing in the open door of the walk-in freezer, she stared at what was left of her week's work: piles of sodden cake, dripping decorations, and running colors. The fire that had started in one of her ovens overnight had turned her business into a huge wet and worthless mess, one that smelled nothing like its usual sweet scent of vanilla. Now it reeked like a nearly dead campfire.

The fire marshal stood behind her. "It's not a total loss, but we'll have to complete the investigation before you can move toward repairs."

Molly turned and stared at him. "Investigation?" It was a fire, plain and simple. Button it up and let her get back to business. How hard could that be? Then it hit her. "You think I did this?" She waved her arms to encompass the mess that less than twelve hours ago had been a shining operation filled with wonderful baked goods and prize-winning cakes.

His neutral expression didn't change, and she suspected he was quite experienced at dealing with distraught victims. And she *was* a victim, regardless of what he thought. "Ms. Williams, you have to understand that it's routine procedure to trace the source of any fire. I'm not saying you did or didn't do anything. The fire will tell us the full story. It always does."

All right, she actually did understand. It was just hard to stand in the middle of the charred shell of her dream and not want to stomp her feet and throw a childish tantrum. It wasn't fair. It had taken ten long years to make this place a success, and now it all, literally, had gone up in smoke. She'd given up so much to make a go of it, including a personal life. Now she had nothing. No business. No one to go home to.

Her shoulders dropped and she sighed. She blinked, though she told herself it was against the smoke that rose from the still-smoldering remnants of her business and not because she was close to tears. "I understand. How long?"

"We'll have our part done in a week or two. Once your insurance company has our report, you'll work with an adjuster to restore your business. Hard to estimate how long that will take."

She looked around and shook her head. "What do I do in the meantime?" She wasn't really asking him, but herself.

He shot her a sympathetic look, and she sensed he didn't believe she would torch her own business to collect on insurance money. He'd be right. She would never, ever destroy what she'd worked hard to build, and she found a little solace that he did consider her innocent. "Take some time off," he suggested. "We'll do what we can as soon as we can."

She shook his hand. "Thank you." Looking down at the soot she'd transferred from her hand to his, she added, "Sorry."

He shrugged. "Not to worry, Ms. Williams. It's an occupational hazard."

A pair of arms wrapped around her from behind, and she jumped. Winnie. She'd recognize the scent of her perfume anywhere, even standing in this mess, and it was a lovely thing to smell right now. She turned and embraced her friend, no longer able to hold her tears in check, and they flowed down her cheeks. "It's gone. It's all gone." She choked, sounding like one of those wounded heroines in a sappy romantic movie. The day was just getting better and better.

Winnie kissed her cheek and then turned her toward the front door. At least it was still intact, so she could pretty well button up the place while the fire department did its investigation. "Not all gone," Winnie countered. "Temporarily out of commission. Come on. Let's get out of this furnace. It's depressing."

"You think?" If it depressed Winnie, how did she think Molly felt?

Her sarcasm didn't even faze her best friend. "Absolutely. Come on." Holding Molly's arm, Winnie led her outside where the air was clear, though the lingering scent of fire wafted out behind them. She shivered, and tears welled in her eyes again. She longed for it to all be a nightmare that she would wake up from any minute.

Using her sleeve to wipe away her tears, she stood a little taller. She refused to make a spectacle of herself out on the street. Darn it, she had her pride even if she didn't have a shop. "I don't know what I'm going to do."

Winnie, as usual, didn't miss a beat. "I do. Come on, this way. Let's have a little coffee while I explain your game plan." She couldn't imagine what Winnie had in mind, given that Molly had called her only an hour ago to relay the bad news.

At the coffee shop half a block down—the same small shop that bought her baked goods every day to sell with their specialty beverages—she sank into one of the chairs on the outside patio. "I'm glad you have a plan because I'm completely lost." Lost seemed like a very inadequate word for what she felt. It was just the best her brain could come up with at the moment.

"Sit tight," Winnie commanded her as she pushed open the shop's door and disappeared inside. Less than five minutes later she returned with two lattes. One she set in front of Molly and one she held on to. "Okay. Now let's talk about what we're going to do."

Molly turned the warm cup between her hands. "We? This is my mess. You have a job to get back to." They'd picked different paths after they finished culinary school. Molly had turned her love of baking into a successful bakery, while Winnie became the executive chef in one of the most successful restaurants in the city. So successful, she opened a second one last year. Both were doing fantastic.

Winnie sat up straighter and smiled. "Well now, here's the kicker. I'm on vacation for two glorious weeks." She leaned back in her chair, turned her face to the sky, and spread her arms. "Two weeks." She lowered her arms and looked at Molly once more. "So, this is what's going down. You, me, and Angus are going on a walkabout."

She was taking a sip of the latte and almost spit it out. "A what?"

"We're heading south and doing some day hikes along the Umatilla and Columbia rivers. We'll spend a night or two in cool places like Hood River and probably even Portland. It'll be a blast."

"And I would want to do that why?" Winnie was way more adventurous than Molly and way more impulsive too. Molly was too often conservative, and her friend was about the only one who could get her out of her comfort zone. Sometimes it was pretty sweet. Sometimes not so much. Like right now, when all she really felt like doing was going home, opening a bottle of wine, and polishing it off while she felt sorry for herself.

"Because it will get your mind off all of this. By the time we get back, the fire department will have their report submitted, your insurance company can help you start rebuilding, and you'll be a hundred times more relaxed."

"I'm not going to be a third wheel. Besides, I have to think about Loba." Her valid objection was twofold. Trotting along behind Winnie and her honey would totally suck. She also didn't want to stick her beautiful German shepherd in a kennel. Loba was sensitive and would pick up right away on the mood this fire had brought on. It wouldn't be fair.

Winnie waved her hand dismissively. "Trust me, you'll be a welcome addition to this adventure. Angus is doing some hands-on research about the trails, tribal lands, and history of the area. I told him I'd tag along, and now you and Loba are going too. It's a win-win for all of us."

"Research?" For some reason that was what jumped out at her.

Winnie nodded. "He has a keen interest in the history of the Pacific Northwest and has been working on a book. He wants to hike around, make some notes, and take a few pictures. So, what do you think? It'll be fun."

"I didn't even know Angus was a writer." If Winnie had told her before, she'd forgotten.

"He's a man of many talents. Now, come on. What do you say? Up for a little adventure?"

She took a breath and started to argue some more, then changed her mind. Winnie might have a good point. If she stayed here, she'd just sit around moping and probably drink way more wine than was good for her. At least if she was hiking along the river, she'd be busy, and the endorphin release would help make her feel less depressed without needing alcoholic intervention. "All right, third wheel it is."

Winnie's smile lit up her face. "That a girl. Trust me, it'll be fun."

Now that she'd had a few minutes away from the catastrophe, she could put things more into perspective and realized what she had to do if she was to leave town for a stretch of time. She finished off the last sip of latte and set the cup on the table. "Before we go, I want to walk back to the store."

Winnie rolled her eyes. She knew exactly why Molly wanted to go back to the bakery. When friends were as close as they were, they couldn't hide much from each other. "Come on. You know that stuff is just fantasy."

Molly wasn't offended. She understood where Winnie was coming from. Few believed in the power of her birthright. It had taken her a lifetime to even begin to understand a tiny bit of it, and she still didn't know it all—just that the powers were passed from mother to daughter and continued generation after generation. As the most recent of the witches in her line, she felt it important to leave a blessing on her bakery before she walked away. Her powers were far from established yet, though her family assured her that they would come in time. Right now, she did what she could with what she had. In this moment of extreme powerlessness, it made her feel as though she could take back a little.

She put a hand on Winnie's and smiled for the first time since the call had come in from the fire department. "Humor me."

❖

Winnie stood in the bedroom doorway and watched Angus fold clothes and tuck them into the dark-green pack. God, he was beautiful. Not that she'd ever tell him. He'd hate it, but there it was. His thick black hair and hypnotic green eyes had sucked her in the first time they met. It wasn't his looks that had locked up her heart though. Lots of pretty-boys were around and were plenty shallow enough to think that was what mattered. Not to Winnie. She was far more attracted to his brains and his courage and his passion. Not long after they'd met, she'd realized she was hooked. He was the one her soul spoke to.

That was her blessing and her curse. She knew what he meant to her but didn't have a clue what she meant to him. Maybe that's why she'd jumped so quickly on the idea of Molly coming with them on this adventure. She was afraid. It was easy to tell Molly what to do and how to do it, all while sounding supremely confident. It was entirely different when it came to her own life.

"You're sure it's okay for Molly to come along? I really should have called you first." She'd worried about it all night, and now in the morning sunlight, she was still second-guessing her invitation. In hindsight she'd realized what she'd done could be a major faux pas. This was his trip, and to not ask him first was just plain rude.

Angus looked up and smiled, the crinkles at the corners of his eyes so appealing. "Babe, I've told you, it's fine. The more the merrier. We'll have fun, and it will get her mind off the fire." He walked over and put a hand on her cheek. "It was so kind of you to do this for your friend."

She smiled as the warmth of both his words and his touch flowed through her. His open heart always amazed her. She'd never met anyone like him. "I know you wanted some time alone together."

"We'll have time together, but there's always room for a friend in need." He kissed the tip of her nose.

"How did I ever end up with someone like you?" It wasn't an idle question. He was more than she'd dreamed of, a bright, shining light compared to her dim bulb.

His smile grew and he winked. "Just lucky, I guess. Now get your arse in gear, and let's see if that pack of yours is ready to go."

She might be a dim bulb, but she was his dim bulb. Her smile matched his, but instead of leaving to get ready, she wrapped her arms around his neck and pulled him close for a kiss. "In good time." She had her own fire burning, and he was just the one to put it out.

An hour later they loaded their two packs into the back of the dusty SUV Angus loved as much as if it had been a million-dollar sports car. She didn't see the appeal. Her little hybrid was perfect for just about everything, not to mention quiet and fuel efficient. "Are we missing anything?" he asked as he tucked several gallon bottles of water in beside the packs. Of course, considering all he was putting in the SUV, maybe her hybrid wasn't quite as perfect as she liked to believe.

She tilted her head and laughed. "Really? You're asking me? I'm counting on you to lead the charge on this one. If you want a fabulous dinner for six, I'm your go-to woman, but this," she pointed to the gear in the back of the SUV, "this is your call."

He slung an arm around her shoulders and stared at what they'd piled in. "You do have a point, my lovely. I should undoubtedly double-check my Mistress of the Kitchen's gear."

"Yeah. Good plan."

He did it too and, after several minutes of inspection, told her, "Yes. I believe we're ready to set sail. Molly has a pack?"

"She said she did. I think she does a little hiking around here with Loba, although I don't really know what that means in terms of gear."

"No worries. I'll give the contents of hers a look-over too," he said as he crawled behind the wheel. "Then we'll get this party started."

Winnie leaned back against the seat and smiled. She was ready for an adventure. It had been a long time since she'd taken any days off, and spending it now with the two people she loved the most was perfect. The sun was just beginning to peek over the mountains, filling the morning with a beautiful glow. It was a fantastic way to start a vacation.

Molly was sitting on the front porch at her house, a light-blue pack at her side, waiting for them. It looked brand-new. Maybe her hiking with Loba was a bit more casual than Winnie thought. Oh well. If Angus could get her squared away, he could do the same for Molly.

Angus jumped out and jogged over to the step. "Mind if I check that over before we take off?" He inclined his head toward the pack.

Molly yawned, stretched her arms over her head, and nodded. "Probably a good idea. I haven't hiked much more than an hour or two at a time. I included what I thought we might need, along with food and water for Loba. Let me know what else I should take. You know I'm used to getting up before dawn to go to work. I don't usually put together a pack this early in the morning."

He rummaged in it and then straightened up, smiling. "Fine job, my dear Molly." He patted her shoulder. "We're ready to go." Angus put the pack alongside theirs, and as Molly crawled into the back passenger seat, Loba jumped up beside her.

"All right, scout leader, where are we going?" Molly asked.

Angus put an arm on the back of the seat and turned to face her. "How are you?"

She blew out a long breath. "To be honest, Angus, I'm not sure. My life just went up in smoke. I don't know if I should dig deep and be strong or say screw it and go find a regular job. Let somebody else worry about the business while all I do is bake."

He nodded. "Been there, my lady. But," he turned to Winnie and smiled, "I say dig deep. You never know what's waiting for you on the other side. If you give up, you'll never know."

Winnie's heart swelled. It was no big mystery why she loved this witty, adventurous man, though she continued to hold back and not tell him. Fear always blocked her. She couldn't risk him rejecting her love. All the what-ifs cascaded in on her any time she gave it serious consideration.

It was easy enough to advise others, like Molly, but when it came to herself, she was a coward. Maybe she had the strength and just hadn't uncovered it yet. Or maybe she didn't. She was too chicken to find out. She opted instead to live for the moment, satisfied with the tenderness he shared in words like these. It was enough.

She returned his smile with a sincere one. "He's right, you know, Molly. It looks pretty bleak right now, and yesterday was a very bad day. By this time next week, though, I'm betting things will be very different."

"Lord, I hope so."

Winnie reached back and took her hand. "It will, I promise, and we'll be right at your side."

Molly squeezed her hand, and a small smile did wonders for her face. "I'm going to hold you to it."

"Deal."

It was about three hours before they reached Umatilla, Oregon. Angus muttered that they would have gotten here quicker if they hadn't stopped in Kennewick for coffee. As far as Winnie was concerned, it was no big deal. After all, it wasn't like they had a schedule to keep. The day was young and all theirs to do as they pleased. Now that they were here, they would hike the trail along the Umatilla River for an hour or two, let Angus take his pictures, and then pile back into the SUV to head farther down the highway to the Columbia River.

They'd have enough time to hike a little bit there too before they would find a hotel for the night. Tomorrow, they'd start all over again—travel along the river and hike a new trail. It would be a grand adventure that would hopefully take Molly's mind off the fire. Or at least take some of the sting out of the tragedy.

This should be an interesting trip for all of them—challenging for her and Molly, given they were not the types to get out and enjoy nature on a regular basis. And challenging for Angus as he herded two non-nature women. Loba, well, Winnie figured, she could roll with anything. It was going to be fun.

CHAPTER TWO

1837

Aquene felt the change the moment the spirit entered her, and she knew what she must do. Tiloukaikt also understood the journey she was compelled to take, and he gave her his blessing. The Great Spirit had bestowed an honor upon her, and she would do everything in her power to live up to it. For Tiloukaikt it did not matter that she was not one of his warriors. He embraced the spiritual journey as deeply as he did the way of the warrior, only one of the reasons he would one day become a powerful leader of her people.

Nearby, Tilla stood patiently waiting. She was a good horse, a beautiful horse, with her pale hair and black mane. She had been Aquene's since she was a colt trying to stand on unsteady legs, and they had grown up, becoming equal partners. Now was no different, for they would discover the path of enlightenment together just as they had experienced life together. She could not picture a world where she did not share each step with Tilla. When her horse was with her, Aquene was never alone.

In her pouch she placed dried salmon, fresh and dried berries, a smaller bag with dried herbs, and the beads her mother had worn before she traveled on to the spirit world. Around her neck hung a small leather bag filled with what she knew not and did not need to, for it was a gift of protection that gave her great comfort. She would not require much else, for she was skilled at many things. Had she been born male, she would have been a warrior. She did not care that she was not a man. The Great Spirit had seen fit to make her as she was, and she found no shame in that. Though she did not fully understand what she was to discover at the end of her quest, she knew it would be the thing that would fulfill her destiny.

"Must you go?" Alumpum stood patting Tilla, a frown on her face. Tilla snorted, and Aquene smiled. She sometimes believed that Tilla was jealous of Alumpum, thinking she loved her more.

As with Tilla, Aquene had grown up with Alumpum. Side by side they had learned to make the knee-high moccasins each of them wore now. Their mothers had taught them to weave the mats that, as one, they could use to build a house and just as easily take it back down. They could dry the salmon caught along the banks of the river, dig rich roots, and pick the berries so wonderfully sweet. Together they had learned the magic of the herbs that could make powerful medicines. It was as if they had been born of one mother rather than two.

Now the universe was taking them in different directions. Soon Alumpum would join Ouray, and they would share their lives until their days were done. It made Aquene happy for her sister-friend. She thought of her with children and knew what a good mother Alumpum was meant to become.

But it was not to be for her. Many young men had made clear their interest in Aquene, and though she tried to feel happiness in their offers, she could not find it within herself. She did not experience the joy inside that she could see on Alumpum's face each time she gazed upon Ouray. Her heart did not capture the sunshine that lived inside her friend. She did not believe it ever could.

She put a hand on Alumpum's shoulder. "I must go. The Great Spirit," she looked out over the horizon, "tells me I must follow the wind. Out there my destiny is waiting for me. I can almost hear it calling." It was what she felt deeply inside her. A will that seemed to come from somewhere magical pushed her forward, away from the place she called home and the people she loved. Fear did not hold her back, for she was ready to take the first step.

"Why can you not stay? Wynono looks at you with longing. He would give you strong children and much happiness. He would treat you well. You would live a good life together." The pleading in her voice touched a warm place inside her.

Aquene smiled. She knew of the look in Wynono's eyes. Many times she had seen it, and her heart was sad for him. She could not return to him what he offered her so freely. It could never be, and she did not desire to give him false hope. She would not do that to him or any other man of her people. She must stay true to her heart and her calling. With this journey even Wynono would at last see and understand that her path was away from him and not to him. He would find another and, with her, the happiness she would deny him.

Aquene leaned into Tilla, inhaling the unique, musky smell of the horse. It soothed her, as did the feel of her coat against Aquene's cheek. In a moment, she pulled away and looked over at Alumpum. "He would, my sister, and yet I will not take from him what I cannot return to him. My heart is not his. It will never be."

Alumpum put her hand on Aquene's face, her eyes dark and soulful. For a long breath her friend stared into her face. At last a calm expression crossed her features, and she nodded slowly. "Your heart belongs to no man, my sister. I believe I have always known and did not speak of it, for I wanted you to be as I am. You are not, and that is as it should be."

Her friend at last understood what many of her people yet did not. She knew of Aquene's deepest desire and did not judge her because of it. Her friend was forever faithful to her, and it made her heart full. "You speak the truth."

The smile that turned up the corner of Alumpum's mouth made her eyes light up. "You are true and kind, wise and powerful. You are destined to make the Liksiyu the most powerful of all people. I feel the truth of it right here." She placed her hand over her heart.

Of this, Aquene was not as certain. Nothing about this journey was clear to her except that she was compelled to go without company from any other. The path was hers alone to take, save for Tilla. Out there waiting for her was enlightenment and, most exciting, the future. It was important in ways she did not fully understand and, in reality, did not need to on this day. It was enough, for she had learned to be very patient.

Tiloukaikt joined Aquene and Alumpum. His faced was lined, his hair long and held back with a leather tie. His dark eyes could be cold and ferocious when they needed to be. They did not need to be so on this day. As he gazed into her face, his eyes soft and kind, it warmed her. Yes, one day he would certainly be a most powerful and wonderful leader. "You are ready?" His voice was deep and rich. She had always loved listening to him as he spoke in the language of their people. Like

Aquene, he too could speak in the tongue of those who came to their land, but it was a language that did not hold the beauty and melody of their own.

She nodded and smiled. His visible belief in her made her even stronger. "I am ready." Tears pooled in Alumpum's eyes. Aquene's were dry.

He put one hand on her head and stared deeply into her eyes. "There is power inside you, special one, and you must use it to survive what awaits you beyond the horizon. You will be challenged. You will be hunted. No man and no beast will harm you, for you carry within you the power of the Liksiyu. Always remember."

To hear such praise from the man who was destined for greatness made her heart strong. She witnessed the might in him grow day by day. She felt power gather around him like storm clouds collecting in the sky. Like Aquene, he would soon realize his destiny, and she was sad that she would not be there to see it. She could not say why she knew this to be true, only that she did. His words made her believe that he too knew the truth of her journey. This was the last time they would gaze upon each other.

"I will do my best to seek the knowledge of the universe and bring it home." Even as she spoke the words, they felt strange.

Tiloukaikt stared into her eyes for a long time, then slowly shook his head. "I know the Great Spirit will not bring you home to us. I see it in your eyes, and I hear it on the wind."

Fear whispered through her for the first time. It was one thing to feel the tremors of change in her own mind, but to have one such as Tiloukaikt echo her thoughts back to her sent the winter breeze into her heart. "I will return." Her words sounded hollow even to her.

His eyes turned sad as he said to her, "Your feet will touch this ground once more, but we shall not gaze upon each other again. Go, with the hearts of our people, and know that we are always with you."

His words were not a mystery as she shared the wisdom behind them. Yet though she knew them to be true, she did not understand why. She longed to see the whole story, but it had not been shown to her. One day it would all become clear. She would cling to that faith in order to have the strength to leave her home.

The sky above was clear and blue, the few clouds wispy white and beautiful. Grasses swayed in the gentle breeze that brought with it the familiar sounds and smells of her home: cooking fish, curing meats, and women's laughter. How could she leave and never return? How could she not follow her destiny? Each pulled at her, equally strong.

She mounted Tilla and reached out one last time to link her fingers with Alumpum. If what Tiloukaikt said was true, and she knew it was, she would never see or touch her sister-friend again. She wanted to remember her face and feel her warmth. After a moment, she let go and straightened up. It was time to go.

Then she looked to the west and began to ride. She did not look back.

❖

Perhaps it was time to leave this place. Matthew Hopkins stood in the open window of the small room in the Oregon City home of missionary Tobias Seed and stared. He saw nothing and heard only the familiar sounds of the morning. Above him the sky was clear and blue, the sun beginning its trek across the horizon. All was calm, yet he sensed stirrings of the kind that called for his expertise.

Turning his head, Matthew studied the small book lying on the petite table. Bound in smooth, rich leather, it was beautiful and expensive in contrast to the rough top it lay on, which was very unlike the polished wood of his own furniture. Out here, he had grown accustomed to the lack of civilized surroundings, though he did not enjoy sitting at this table and in this tiny, drafty room. At the moment, it was the best he could do, so he ignored its crude nature.

He held his hand over the book as he thought about what he must add to it. His writings included all he had learned while walking this path. The knowledge the centuries had given him was valuable and his work much more complete than when he had written his first book. Short and concise, it had been filled with the important lessons he had learned during his career. Now he had little to impart to the latest volume, which was most aggrieving. Staying here could add nothing more to his most important work; he should leave.

Yet he could not. His writings were detailed with the teachings of this century, so why did he feel he had not completed the job? His thoughts returned to a night a year past. As the fire consumed her body, his work should have been finished. Still he was unable to leave behind this wild and unsettled place. In his heart, he knew why, though he was unable to let the words pass his lips. She was the one who left him feeling this way, for she had defied him even in death. She had bested him by leaving behind traces of her evil for another to discover and use. Until he righted that wrong, he could not leave this hell.

He had been following her and her kind since before his title and the delivery of his first masterpiece to the people. He had seen his destiny before his twentieth year and, with his father's blessing, had embarked upon his most important journey. At the time he had not realized the extent to which his calling and fate would take him.

Unlike those he hunted, he had believed himself to be of mortal stock. After all, he had been there in 1634 when his father's life ended and he was united with God in the Kingdom of Heaven. Holding his father's hand as he made that crossing had filled Matthew with the glory that he felt awaited him once he fulfilled his own mission on earth. He had understood with perfect clarity that he was sent to cleanse the world of those who sought to spread their evil amongst the good and honorable people he offered his life to protect. Once his job was completed, he would join his father at God's right hand.

The years had flowed by like an endless sea that brought new, creative ways of trying to disguise their evil. The witches he sought were clever but underestimated him each and every time. He was smarter than they and had the power of heaven behind him. One day soon, he would be victorious and his mission would end. First, he had to find the grimoire that she had managed to hide. As much as he wanted to move on, he could not, at least not until he found the book. He sensed that her magic was the strongest he had encountered thus far and that it would call to others. In fact, he knew it would.

He had destroyed her but had not, he feared, destroyed her power. Others would come, and he would need to be ever on guard for the signs that would tell him who was pure and who was wicked. Glancing out the window again, he decided it was most assuredly time to leave Oregon City and return to the cabin in the woods. He had missed something, he was convinced of it. He would return, he would find it, and he would end whatever evil she had brought to this land of great rivers and endless fields of wild grasses.

"Witch-Finder General?"

He smiled at the title. Even after all these years, all these centuries, he still never tired of the honorific. It was true that Parliament had never confirmed his claim to the title, but that was a petty detail. As far as he was concerned, God had conferred it upon him, a much higher council than the humans of Parliament. Thus, he had carried it with him year after year, never growing weary of the sound of it upon the lips of others, particularly when those lips were rosy and lovely.

"Miss Seed. How may I help you?" Prudence Seed was quite pretty, with her dark hair tucked beneath her white cap, her cheeks glowing with a touch of pink, and those very kissable lips. The familiar twinges assailed him.

She dipped her chin and could not quite hide her smile. He would like to flatter himself and say he appealed to her because he was a virile young man, but out here in the West, cultured men like himself were rare. This was an untamed land yet, and she saw few who were not crude explorers who wore the same clothes for months on end, did not shave their faces, and smelled worse than the animals they hunted. Someone like him, who embodied the best of refinement, was a treat, and even more so, she responded to his mysterious allure.

"Come sit with me." He held out his hand and led her to the chair pulled close to the fire. For a woman who willingly gave up her life in the city for an unknown future in undeveloped lands, she maintained a grace and dignity that spoke loudly about her character. She enchanted him, and he longed to hold her in his arms and give of himself freely. That she was a maiden did not concern him. Out here in the wilds, the rules of polite society no longer mattered, at least not to him.

Her response to him seemed to match his own. She did not hesitate at his invitation to enter his private room and willingly put her small, warm hand in his. What he liked the most was her purity and her righteous heart. She was the kind of woman he had dedicated his life to protect.

As she sat in the chair with the firelight flickering over her beautiful face, he ran his hand down her neck. Her skin was smooth and soft and…what? He jerked his hand away. It could not be, not this beautiful, loving soul, yet his touch was skilled, and he knew the marks when he saw them…when he felt them.

She screamed when he jerked her head to the side, baring a long stretch of her pale neck. There it was as if mocking him by its very presence on one he had believed to be pure and with whom he had contemplated sharing his body: the mark of the witch. Against otherwise smooth flesh, it was raised ever so slightly, a splash of crimson that gave irrefutable proof that the devil himself had laid his fingers to her body. Disgust made his stomach lurch.

Her screams continued as he tore the hat from her head and the dress from her shoulders. They were alone in the house, for her brother had left on horseback before dawn on a journey to save the souls of the wild people who lived in the hills. He would not return for several days.

As her torn clothing fell away his worst fears were confirmed. Yet another mark marred the skin on her back. Such a bright future vanished in a breath. He knew of one way to save her soul, and he was the only one to do it. He put his hands around her neck and squeezed. Once, long ago, he would have used the water or the walking to wring forth her confession. No longer, for his skill in detection was divine. His diligence and prowess were sufficient to understand the horribleness of her sin and to issue the only judgment possible against her. He was inquisitor, jury, and judge. He came to cleanse the land, and so he would.

When her struggles ceased and her body at last fell limp, he picked her up and carried her from the room. With her draped across the back of his horse, he rode away from the Seed home and into the morning. The tree rose out of the stand clustered far from the house, strong and thick. Yes, it would do. He dismounted and took the rope from his saddle. It took only a bit of time before all was readied.

The heat of the blaze followed him as he rode away, the flames engulfing her as she hung from the tree visible for a long time. But he didn't look back.

CHAPTER THREE

Near the John Day Dam
Present day

Molly was having second thoughts about the grand plan now that they were here. They'd spent a couple of hours outside of Umatilla hiking the river there and stopping every so often so Angus could take pictures. Then they'd piled back into his SUV, and at first she figured they would drive the Oregon side of the river as though they were headed to Portland. He surprised her when he went back over the river and into Washington once again. Heading west, he piloted them in the direction of Goldendale and the John Day Dam. She thought he would stop at Goldendale, but instead he chose a place called Cliffs Park. Though Molly was a lifelong Washington resident, she'd never even heard of Cliffs Park. Angus had made the journey from across the pond as an adult, and here he was full of more trivia and history about the place than she would ever be able to pull out of her head. She obviously needed to get out more.

She had to admit, the scenery was pretty. Usually if she was driving to Portland, she chose the Oregon side with its wide-open spaces and ubiquitous wind turbines. Not that this side didn't host its share of turbines, but it still had groupings of trees that gave it a much different look and feel. She rather liked it and wondered why she'd never bothered to come this way before. Actually, she knew why. Speed was an issue because she was always in a hurry, and the Oregon side was faster. She never took the time to slow down and enjoy the view.

Out of the car, she stood and stretched her arms up over her head. The John Day Dam below them served as a barrier between the Columbia River and Lake Umatilla. Impressive, yet she wasn't quite sure of Angus's choice in hiking areas. She was used to heavily wooded areas that blanketed the mountains and embraced the streams and lakes. In other words, lots and lots of pine trees. This was quite different. Oh, it was hilly enough, and the Columbia River was pretty damned impressive. It was just so different with its open spaces dotted by clustered stands of trees and sagebrush-peppered rolling hills. The effects of glaciers thousands of years earlier were impossible to miss. It was very cool and quite unique.

Apparently, Angus actually did have a plan, even if it wasn't clear to her. She now knew he was working on a book about the people who originally called this area home and wanted to get an up-close and personal feel for the area. In her humble opinion, the Children of the Sun, or the Spokane Tribe, would be more interesting, but that was just her. She was, after all, born and raised in Spokane, so why not study the indigenous people of her own area? Winnie had told her he'd decided to make Spokane his home partially because of its history. It fascinated Angus, and when he wasn't working as a voice-over artist, he was writing his nonfiction books. Perhaps he'd already completed his research on the Children of the Sun, and this was his next chapter. What did it matter anyway? She was just along for the ride.

With hands on hips, Molly looked to the south. While the view was stunning, it didn't look like a very exciting hiking prospect. Near the river, the landscape featured lots of rolling hills, punctuated by rock cliffs, and as far as she could see, full of weeds, brush, and wildflowers. She kind of liked the low-lying brush, which put off a faint sage-like odor that smelled a little like the kitchen.

Though the landscape didn't have the vast spread of trees so common in the Spokane region, this area had some trees and plenty of basalt rock cliffs. Thank you, prehistoric glaciers. While Angus might want to get a good feel for the early inhabitants and initial explorers, like Lewis and Clark, if he thought she was going to climb those rock cliffs or jump in a canoe to cross the river, he could jolly well think again. She appreciated the majesty that was represented here. She also respected it. The wide Columbia did not appeal to her sense of adventure, as she knew all too well about the currents that tore beneath the calm surface. Only a fool would challenge those waters. And the cliffs? Those babies were steep, creepy, and if folks were to be believed, home to plenty of snakes, as in rattlesnakes. No thank you, Angus.

Before she opened her big mouth, she stopped. What did she have to lose? Or that she hadn't lost already anyway. It wasn't like she could turn around, go home, and start baking for her loyal customer base. As it was, she'd had to turn over the projects she committed to for the next couple of weeks to her friend, Kristin, aka Tasty Cakes. She might never get those accounts back either, but she had to do what was best for her customers, given she was out of business temporarily. That left her here and with two choices: go home and be depressed about a situation totally out of her control, or stay here and accept Angus's grand plan, and maybe, if she got lucky, have a little fun. This forced-vacation thing was a pain in the butt. Not that she had control issues or anything like that. Nope. Not her.

She decided to continue to hang with Winnie and Angus, and hope for that fun thing. She'd stay, but she still didn't intend to climb to the top of any damn cliff. Angus would have to dangle a whole lobster tail and a big bottle of pinot before she'd even think about it, and the chance he had either of those things in his pack was pretty slim. She'd hike a while longer, sure, along the lovely rolling-hills sections with nice grass and trees. She'd breathe in the pleasant scent of sage and let it whisper soothingly along her senses. When they were done, they'd find a motel in Goldendale or maybe cross the river and hit one of the hotels in Hood River. She'd order wine from room service and then take a hot bath while Loba snoozed on the bed. Now, that was an awesome plan.

"Ladies." Angus stood at the open back hatch holding their packs. He handed Molly hers and she slipped it on. "Water?" He seemed to have a mental list and was ticking off each item. Nobody was leaving either until he checked off each item.

She patted the side pocket of her pack. "Loaded up." She might be a baker, but she wasn't totally lost when it came to hiking. Granted, this area was a little more remote than her typical hike and, so far, a few hours longer than normal for her and Loba, but hey, she still knew water was the number-one item to keep plenty of in her pack. In her case, she had to carry double so both she and Loba had enough. Like most dog lovers, she'd even go without water if she had to in order to make certain Loba had what she needed.

"Good girl." He smiled, taking the edge off the *girl*, which he knew she hated yet still loved to tease her with. As much as she liked Angus, he had a definite wicked streak. Actually it made her like him more.

"Thanks, *boy*," she said softly as she slipped her arms into the straps of her pack.

His smile grew. Another thing she liked about him. He could take it as easily as he dished it out. He turned his attention to Winnie, who was still sitting in the passenger's seat changing into her boots. "Come on, pokey," he said around the side of the car. "Molly and I are ready to go. Kick it up."

"Just hold your horses," Winnie said. "Flip-flops aren't exactly hiking footwear of choice, you know."

He rolled his eyes as he looked at Molly. Probably a good thing Winnie didn't see him do that. "That's my woman," he said under his breath. Then he peered up toward where Winnie sat with her legs sticking out of the open door. "Hey, babe, why exactly did you bother to change out of your boots when we left Umatilla?" Actually, Molly had been wondering the same thing.

Now Winnie rolled her eyes. "Because I wanted to. Got a problem with that?" That was Winnie. She did, as the saying went, go to the beat of a different drummer and, in her case, without any kind of apology.

He saluted her. "No, ma'am. Just asking."

"Good. Then leave me in peace and let me get ready." She returned her attention to the long laces of her tan boots. Looking at their newness, Molly had a pretty good idea why Winnie had shucked her boots so quickly. She hoped that if she was right, Winnie didn't get blisters so bad she couldn't walk. Been there, done that, and she didn't want to go there again. Nor did she wish that kind of misery on her best friend.

Molly smiled when Angus went up and helped Winnie with her footwear. She loved the way these two were together—their teasing, their laughter, and their caring for each other. All the little things said so much without uttering a single word.

Throughout the years, she'd met all of Winnie's boyfriends. Most she'd liked, which said quite a lot about Winnie's taste in men. A few, however, not so much, and thankfully they'd faded away without a great deal of fanfare. Angus, well, he was, in her opinion, a keeper. She was pretty sure Winnie thought so too, which left her with only one question. When would the two of them meet on that page? From the outside looking in, it was hard to tell who the holdout was: Angus or Winnie?

If Molly weren't here, maybe they'd finally be able to answer that question for themselves. With her along, they'd be at their best, and likely most conservative, behavior. Neither was bound to tip their hand with her and Loba traipsing along behind. She supposed they would sort it out in good time, and she hoped they decided to do it together. They were a perfect match.

When Winnie was finally booted up and, like Angus and Molly, had her pack on her back, Angus led them away from the locked vehicle. The day had grown progressively warmer in a pleasant and comfortable way. The sun on her face felt good, and the air was fresh and clear.

The Umatilla River ran strong as it merged with the Columbia River, and the sight was incredibly beautiful. With each step, she thought more and more that Winnie had been right. This was exactly what she needed to smooth out the rough edges the shocking fire had caused. A couple of days of this kind of exercise and communing with nature, and she'd be ready to tackle the mess back at the bakery. In fact, as she thought about it, she realized it could be an opportunity to make the changes she'd been wanting to for months. She would come back better and stronger.

An hour or so into their second hike, they stopped at a sunny spot near the river to eat. Boulders made great seats, and even better, the stones were warm from the sun's heat. Kind of like her nice heated seat in her car back home. Loba dropped to a patch of grass and stretched out. She appeared to be enjoying their adventure as much as Molly was.

Slipping the pack off her shoulders, she dropped it to the ground, amazed at how light she felt now. It hadn't seemed that heavy while they were walking. Only now when it was off her body did she realize how much effort it took to carry the pack. Sweat from the humid weather made her shirt stick to her back. After she shrugged to loosen the shirt from her body, she dug the folding water bowl out of her pack and filled it for Loba, who jumped up from her resting spot and quickly began to drink. When Loba was done, she returned to her grassy bed to sprawl out once more and close her eyes. Molly envied her ability to relax anywhere, anytime. More than once she wished she could do the same thing.

"Ladies?" Angus held up a bottle of wine he had miraculously pulled out of his pack. "Libations for the weary?" His grin spread across his handsome face. Wasn't hard to see why Winnie was so drawn to him. Molly's spidey senses detected that he had a fine soul. Right now, looking at that bottle of wine, she could switch sides and keep that man forever.

"Count me in." She smiled. Now, this was her idea of relaxation. In fact, she could kick back on this comfy rock—well, as comfy as a rock got, anyway—and spend the rest of the afternoon imbibing as she watched the sun set. Loba might get bored after she woke up from her impromptu nap, but Molly was pretty sure she could make a day of it.

"Oh yeah, baby," Winnie said on a laugh. "Now, this is a man who knows how to lead a hike."

As she nodded and watched, Angus pulled a multi-tool from his pocket and uncorked the bottle. His acts of magic continued as he began to pour wine into collapsible silicone cups that, like the wine, appeared from his backpack. What other treasures did he have tucked away in there? A little brie? A loaf of crusty bread? She watched, but nothing else delectable came out of the pack. Darn.

They sat in the sunshine sipping the fresh white wine, which was lovely. Who needed French bread and brie when they had a wine that danced on the tongue? No drugstore, cheapo purchase here. This was the good stuff. She looked up to see Angus studying her, his head tilted.

"What?" She could almost see his mind whirling with some unasked question.

"Tell me about about the Old Ways."

Well, that was a surprise, and for a second she remained silent. Molly rarely shared her heritage, and few people asked even if they knew of her background. Even fewer knew their language. Most people were familiar with the terms "witchcraft" and "Wicca." Not many used the term "Old Ways." She was a little impressed, though equally wary. For hundreds of years her family had been hunted and many destroyed for no other reason than because of what they were. Being a witch was rarely a matter of life and death these days, but still a social stigma lingered. Molly and others like her were very cautious when it came to sharing. She wrapped her normal life around her like a shield protecting her from a world that had too often failed her family. It was hard to let go of that shield.

Out here in the beautiful daylight, listening to the sounds of the water rushing by, she felt an unfamiliar desire to talk about her family and her life. Though she would be hard-pressed to explain why, she trusted Angus. "What do you want to know?"

He shrugged. "Anything? Everything? I grew up with stories of the paranormal and of the witches who could do both good and bad. The stories were meant to scare us into being good and to let us know about the presence of forces out there that could also protect us. The thing is, you're the first real witch I've actually met. Or at least that I know I've met. You fascinate me, and I kind of like you a little bit too."

She smiled. Lots of people shared her world, many friends old and new, yet none of them besides a select few had any idea what she was. That sounded kind of ominous, but most people wouldn't understand. Oh, they'd catch the references to Wicca if she were to reveal to them her heritage. She could almost picture the smiles and the nods they'd give her. They'd think she was just a little out there and searching for some alternate way to express herself. Eccentric. Harmless. They'd be wrong. Not that she was a threat to anyone. That wasn't the way it worked.

Her powers were real and developed to extraordinary levels through generations of her family. Not strong enough to prevent her bakery from catching on fire, however. Apparently, precognition wasn't in her toolbox. Of course, her grandmother would point out that wasn't where her strengths lay. Each of them had their own special touch, though hers hadn't shown itself quite yet. It was frustrating because she was not-so-patiently waiting to discover her place in the universe. Right now, she was the only one in the family in flux. Or maybe, more likely, she was the only flunky in the family.

"Here's the deal," she said, deciding she wanted to share her history with Angus. "I'm what you call a hereditary witch. Nothing unusual for my family, as it goes back in my lineage for centuries. All the women in my family have powers, hence the hereditary. We're born with it."

"Wicked. So you can cast spells and vanquish bad guys?"

Molly was just taking a sip of wine and almost spat it out as she began to laugh. "You make it sound so cloak-and-dagger. Nothing quite that mystical or magical. Yes, I can do healing spells. Not as good as the rest of my family, mind you, but I've been taught the basic skills. I can't say I've ever been asked to vanquish a bad guy. Doubt I could, even if I was asked. We're healers, not executioners."

"Ah. I've heard stories from my granny about waving wands and disappearing creeps."

"Molly is pretty awesome," Winnie said. "She's kept me out of the emergency room more than once."

"Easy enough. Again, my family is all about healing and using what we've been gifted with to make things better. Besides, Winnie isn't prone to major injury, thank goodness, and honestly, that's less about magic and more about using what nature provides to heal. We've been utilizing our skills throughout the years to help others."

"Ah, that she is," Angus said, obviously referring to Winnie and her tendency to injure herself. "I've had occasion to dress a minor wound or two myself. For such an accomplished chef she's a wee bit dangerous with a knife."

Winnie's protest was quick. "You two make it sound like I'm accident-prone."

"Well, darlin', if the shoe fits." Angus turned a look on Winnie that warmed Molly's heart. She wished someone would gaze at her that way. Her own fault really. She'd spent all her time building her business and keeping her secrets safe. The only risk she'd ever taken in her life was starting the bakery. Financial risk she was willing to go for, emotional never. Pretty much a coward in that respect.

As she watched the interaction between Angus and Winnie, the feeling of isolation grew. She didn't want to be alone. Didn't want to turn into a crazy cat lady, and the way things were going, that's what might happen. As much as she liked cats, not exactly how she wanted to end up. Maybe after the fire damage was repaired and life was back to normal, she'd try to start dating. Wait, no, not try. She *would* start dating again. It was past time to let go of the fear.

"What's the coolest thing you can do?" The question broke into her silent planning. Angus, sitting on the rock leaning into Winnie in that comfortable way that spoke of two people in harmony, was watching her intently. She had a funny feeling he could almost read her thoughts. What kind of family did Angus come from? Perhaps a little magic in his blood too?

She started to answer that she couldn't really do anything cool and then stopped. For a moment, she stared up into the clear sky and gave the question serious thought. She'd learned to do some unique and wonderful things from the women in her family, yet even with all that education, she still didn't hold the special thing that would let her stand shoulder to shoulder with the elders of her family. It was a little like being a toddler and learning to walk while navigating between surfaces—from tile, to carpet, to hardwood.

Bringing her gaze back down from the blue sky, she stared over at Angus. "I don't know yet. My mother is a true healer. My grandmother, a precognitive. Me? Well, the universe hasn't seen fit to show me what my bit of talent is yet."

"Really?" Winnie asked. "You never told me that."

Molly shrugged. "No big deal. In time, I'm sure I'll find out. In the meantime, I'm good. Mom and Grandma were great teachers, and I've learned a lot throughout my life. I can do easy stuff, like the blessing I put on what's left of my shop. That's about it."

"Liar, liar, pants on fire." Winnie turned and looked at Angus. "Whenever she tells a lie she does that shrug thing. She'd totally suck at poker."

"I do not."

"Ah, yeah, you do. Let's play poker sometime. I'll wipe you out."

Well, maybe she did have a tell. Lying wasn't exactly her strong suit. Neither was poker. "Okay, so it is kind of a big deal. Apparently, I'm a late bloomer. Most women in my family develop their superpower, if you will, well before they're my age. I'm beginning to wonder if I'm the family's black sheep. Gran keeps telling me that it'll come to me when I need it most. I guess I just haven't needed it yet."

Angus tilted his head and studied her intently. "No," he said slowly. "You are no black sheep. I can feel the power in you just waiting to come out."

"You can feel the power in me?" For the first time, she looked at him closer. Much closer than simply as Winnie's boyfriend. "What are you?"

Winnie leaned away and stared at him too. "Yes, my handsome Irishman. What are you?"

His smile grew radiant. "A simple man from the green fields of Ireland. That's all."

Sure, she thought, and I'm a simple baker.

Though they'd been hiking again for at least an hour, Winnie kept mulling over their conversation as they drank the entire bottle of wine Angus had brought along. It was fun to sit in the sunshine and share the spirits, but she was a little unsettled by what they'd talked about. It wasn't so much the turn toward Molly's being a witch. She'd known that little secret for years.

What did surprise her was how quickly Molly had shared it with Angus. That wasn't like her. What made it even stranger was the vibe that rolled off Angus when she did. It threw Winnie off in an unexpected way. For heaven's sake, she'd been sleeping with the man for over a year, yet she'd never felt that wave of something she couldn't describe come over him. It sent chills down her arms. It was exciting and scary all at the same time. It made her wonder: Did she really know him at all? Did it really matter?

"What are you thinking about so hard, love?" Angus put an arm around her shoulders. His closeness felt as wonderful as always. Some things didn't change. "You're frowning on this glorious day. Have I not shown you, Molly, and Loba a wonderful time?"

Her first instinct was to say yes. But she gazed at the sky and suddenly questioned exactly how glorious it really was. It had nothing to do with Angus either. He was a pretty good team leader. It was less about Angus and more about Mother Nature making her question their adventure. An hour ago, it had been clear skies and sunshine. That was pretty much gone now. Dark clouds had moved in to push out the blue, and the air, so warm earlier, was taking on a chill. It sort of matched the mood settling on her.

"A good time? Yes, you have. That's not it."

"What is it then?"

She looked at him. "I'm thinking that parts of you are a mystery to me."

He leaned away with a surprised expression. "You know me better than anyone."

How true was that? This morning she would have said that she knew him well. Not now. "Do I?"

His green eyes mirrored his surprise. It might be her imagination, but she thought she glimpsed a bit of hurt along with it. "Indeed. Better than anyone. I don't understand, love. What's bothering you? What's brought on this change?"

She looked back to see Molly wandering to the water's edge with her phone up. She was intent on taking a picture of an eagle soaring over the river, presumably in search of a tasty salmon. For the moment, the two of them were alone.

Taking his face between her hands, she stared into his eyes. "Something you said back there, it changed you. It was an Angus I've never seen before."

He put his hands over hers. "Ah, the secret me," he said in his beautifully accented voice. Regardless of anything else, she didn't believe she'd ever get tired of listening to him.

"The secret you," she whispered. She felt left out somehow, and it hurt.

"I owe you an explanation."

"You think?" Please let him open his heart and his secrets to her.

He kissed her. "I do indeed think." He looked over her shoulder and then back at her. "Later, luv. You and I will talk. My secrets will be your secrets."

"You promise?"

His index finger drew made a cross against his chest. "Cross my heart and hope to die."

"Cross your heart, but please don't hope to die." Just the thought of it made her grow cold. Her world would never be right without him in it.

His smile returned and, with it, the twinkle in his green eyes. "Your wish is my command, my beautiful lady."

"Hey," Molly said as she walked up next to them. "Things aren't looking or sounding so good." Just as the words left her lips, thunder roared and lightning flashed. The storm was way too close. "I think we're going to get dumped on. Anyone bring a rain jacket?"

The question was barely out of her mouth when the sky opened up and rain began to pour. Great, just great. She was trying to show her friend a relaxing, good time to take her mind off the bakery, and what happened? Everything turned to crap. Her man morphed into mysterious. The weather soured. And to top it all off, she didn't have rain gear.

"This way," Angus shouted over the crashing thunder. "There's an old cabin up here where we can get inside for a few and wait out the rain." He ran from the open fields along the river and into the trees that stretched like a barrier wall to the north.

"How do you know about a cabin?"

He flashed a smile. "Not my first time here, luv. Now, come on, before we get drenched."

She should be surprised, but at this point, she wasn't. Apparently they had a lot of getting to know each other left to do. As he said, though, later. She was all for running for cover right now.

It was a great idea, at least until they burst through the trees and into a small clearing. She was hoping to see some kind of sturdy lodge-type structure. What she saw didn't come close to her expectation. The cabin wasn't much. It was blackened from age and disuse, and twenty feet from the drooping door stood what once, long ago, must have been a magnificent tree. Now it was battered, and on one side, it looked as though it must have suffered burns. There was no odor on the air. The fire had to have been a long time ago. Why hadn't nature repaired the damaged portion? Wasn't that what it usually did?

She didn't stop to give it any serious consideration because she was getting drenched. Getting under cover was a bigger priority than understanding nature's quirks. Angus opened the door to the screams of its stiff and rusted hinges and held it open as both she and Molly raced through. Clearly, nobody had been in here for a long time, and judging by its outward appearance, she had a good idea why. Hopefully it didn't crumble on top of their heads from the force of the storm.

Molly stopped just inside, pleading with Loba. "Come on, my good girl. Get inside. You're getting all wet."

Winnie turned as she shook out her hair, sending droplets of water in every direction. Angus was still holding the door open, but Loba remained outside. It was like an invisible barrier blocked her entry. "What's up with her?"

Molly dropped to her knees at the door. "Loba, come." The plea in her voice was tinged with concern. Winnie understood, because the two of them were always in sync. That Loba was hesitating to go inside with Molly didn't make a whole lot of sense, and it sent an uneasy feeling racing through Winnie. She'd never seen Loba hesitate at anything Molly asked of her. While Winnie didn't have a dog of her own right now, she'd grown up with them. One lesson she'd learned along the way: always trust your dog.

After a long pause, the beautiful dog, her head down and her eyes narrowed, gingerly stepped inside. A low growl came from deep in her throat.

CHAPTER FOUR

1837

Aquene rode along the Umatilla River until it became one with the Columbia. She and Tilla shared the clear water and drank until their thirst was quenched. At night, she slept beneath the stars and breathed in the air that filled her with life. She did not worry that she traveled alone, for she felt the Great Spirit with her always. The days were bright and the nights warm. The fish were plentiful and the grasses nourishing. Both she and Tilla were full of health and happiness. Every sign assured her that her quest was most certainly a gift of great importance.

Until now. Above them the skies grew sullen, and angry screams filled the air. Soon the rains would come, for that was the way of the darkness. Turning Tilla away from the river and the grassy shores, she rode toward the trees that grew thick, not far from the mighty waters. As she grew closer to the trees, the scent of burned wood filled her nose. It was not a fire of recent time, yet its scent lingered from many full moons past, as if to remind all who traveled by that destruction had visited here.

Breaking through into the clearing she was very familiar with, she slid from Tilla's back and studied the tree turned dark and sad. From a tall branch the remnants of a frayed and singed rope still dangled. The sight made her take a step back as she dropped her gaze to the ground. It was black and desolate; the ground had not yet healed. It remained barren, and she wondered if anything would ever grow there again. She was filled with sadness for what had happened here and for what never should have been lost.

The crack of thunder above her head made her move quickly. It would not do to linger and remember. The cabin offered welcome shelter from the approaching storm. She patted Tilla as she whispered in her ear, "Take cover." Tilla trotted under the boughs of some nearby trees while Aquene turned to the cabin. The door swung open easily, and she stepped inside just as the first of the rain began to fall.

She had not been inside long when the rain began to fall so furiously she feared the cabin would not stand. Raindrops fell through the roof in several places, and she removed the bag from her waist, setting it where it would stay dry. The light that filtered in from the windows was dim and getting darker as clouds moved in to turn the sky completely black. Wind blew through the missing piece of glass in the corner of one window. The rain did not seem to grow weaker. It was as if a war was being waged in the sky.

Wood was stacked next to the fireplace, dry and ready to use. She thought of the woman who had put the logs here, intending to make a fire to warm her home and her body. She was grateful for the wood, for it would bring her warmth during this storm. It also made her sad, for what had befallen her was wrong, and it distressed her still.

Aquene could not change the past and could not bring the woman back. As she held the logs she took from the pile, she whispered a prayer of thanks, for the fire she built with them chased away both the darkness and the chill beginning to flow through the one-room cabin. Though a small bed sat against one wall, and a table with two benches was near the fireplace, she chose to sit on the floor in front of the fire. She liked the way the waves of warmth washed over her. It made her feel part of the fire and part of the woman who had lived in this place. How nice it would be if they could sit beside each other now and talk. Sadness filled her once more, for it would never be.

The sounds of the storm grew softer, and at first she didn't understand why, for outside the window the rain still fell as if filled with fury. Slowly she turned and studied the room. She didn't see the shadows until they moved in a way she was unaccustomed to seeing nighttime spirits move.

Aquene stood and stared. It could not be, yet her eyes were good, her vision sharp. These were not simple shadows that danced from the light of the fire. The shapes were unmistakable—three people and one dog.

She watched for a heartbeat and then began to walk toward them. As the forms appeared to kneel on the floor, she stopped and watched. A flutter raced through her heart. The air seemed to shift, and the warmth that the fire had given to the room fled. A chill that had nothing to do with the disappearing heat from the fire crept through her as she watched one of the specters reach down, and its arm seemed to disappear into the floorboards.

Her curiosity made her move to the same spot in the room, where she noticed the darkened marks on the boards at her feet. It was hard to make them out in the dim light, though she believed them to be the size and shape of fingers. Aquene kneeled and touched the board. It moved against the pressure of her fingers, and she snapped her hand back. When she understood why, she once more touched her fingers to the board. It was loose. Removing it took only a moment, and once it was gone, the space below was revealed to her. So too was the book that lay beneath. She reached down and grasped it.

As her fingertips met the leather cover, a roar filled the cabin and everything went black.

Matthew studied himself in the mirror and tilted his head. The face that peered back at him was so unlike his normal countenance—more rugged and Western explorer than educated man of the world. He sighed and turned away. It was not the visage of his preference, for it did not speak to the divinity of his soul. Whatever persona he put forth for the world to see, his identity was true in his heart. His job was endless, or so it seemed, and thus he traveled to all corners of the world to do what he must. He endured the hardships, both of body and mind, as they came. He did not embrace discouragement, for he knew his heavenly father would one day bring him home for the godly deeds he had performed as he walked the earth.

He removed the kettle of boiling water from the fire and poured it over the tea in his cup. It was a delicate piece of china with minute blue flowers on it as well as the saucer. It seemed so discordant with this place where everything was rough and primitive. He allowed himself a tiny bit of time for one last moment of refinement before he returned to his mission. Only the crackle of the fire broke the silence around him, and it confirmed that his work in this place was done, and he could leave with a clear heart.

Out there, his true destiny waited. A vision had come to him and shown him what he must do. She had been devious, and he had almost fallen prey to her treachery. But she could never defeat him, and he would find the book she left behind to keep her black magic in the world.

Beyond the window, the sky was beginning to turn dark. It did so like to rain here, and for most that might be a deterrent. For Matthew, it was comforting, for it reminded him of home. He had left that home many years ago and had seen much that the world had to offer in that time. It still gave him comfort to think back on where he had come from, for what he had learned there was immeasurable.

Setting his empty cup back on the saucer, he sighed. Time was passing, and he dared not linger here much longer, regardless of how comfortable he was. Soon Tobias would ride back to Oregon City, and the questions about Prudence would be forthcoming. He did not have the desire to tell Tobias of his sister's betrayal, for he felt certain the young missionary possessed no knowledge of her bargain with the devil. The truth of his belief lay heavy on his heart, for neither did he understand her treachery until last night. Trickery had been a skill she employed well, for he was a master yet had not seen the signs until he had placed his hands on her. He had touched her with genuine passion while she had undoubtedly intended to dupe him. It hurt his pride to know she had deceived not just her brother, but him as well. For a short time, he had almost envisioned life as a normal man who could love a fine woman and raise a proud family of sons.

How wrong he had been. He knew better too, for he understood his path in this world, and its importance had not diminished in all these many years. Like any good man, he might enjoy carnal pleasures and indeed did so, on occasion, with women of willing hearts. But his pleasure had to be simple and not go beyond satisfaction of the flesh. A wife and family belonged to others and not to him. Ever.

From his pocket, he pulled the fine gold cross that had hung around Prudence's neck. Just looking at it again made his anger soar. It was an affront to God that she wore something so precious while mocking his goodness. After he had put the rope around her neck, he had taken the cross from her and slipped it into his pocket. He had destroyed her earthly body and sent her soul to hell, where it belonged. Her brother, who even at this moment was out doing God's work himself, deserved this token of divine love. He would leave it for Tobias, who was a good and honest man.

He understood how it would be for Tobias upon his return. At first, he would be confused by his sister's absence. He would search for her. They always did. In time, he would find her body, and though he might be upset by her ultimate fate, he would come to understand the truth and the wisdom of what Matthew had been compelled to do. He would know that it was God's will she be held accountable and, by that very accountability, that she was, in a way, saved. Had she been allowed to live longer, who knew what evil deeds she would have performed and how many innocent lives she would have destroyed. He had done Tobias and Prudence a beneficent service, and someday Tobias would realize and be grateful.

Matthew started to put the cross on the table and paused. He studied the fine gold piece as it lay in the palm of his hand. The gold was warm against his skin and reminded him of the warmth of Prudence's hand. In those few seconds, before he had realized what she was, peace and happiness had filled him. He had dared to dream.

He turned his palm this way and that, letting the firelight catch and sparkle on the gold. He sighed and slipped the necklace back into his pocket. Then he strode out the door, mounted his horse, and rode away into the night.

CHAPTER FIVE

Present day

Molly couldn't figure out what was wrong with Loba. Usually she was fearless and a perfect companion, and it never seemed to matter where they were. In fact, her sense of adventure often drew Molly in. It was hard to resist the joy of a German shepherd. Her behavior right now was so out of character that it sent chills up Molly's back. Nothing she said made a difference, nor did the lure of a good treat. Loba steadfastly refused to come any farther into the room than about three feet right in front of the door, as if she wanted to make certain she could make it back outside in a few seconds. Of course, given Loba's incredible sense of smell, she could be picking up some noxious odor that they as mere humans couldn't. For a second, Molly tried to give full rein to her own sense of smell, but honestly, she detected nothing beyond old wood, dust, and a lingering trace of a burned-out fire. This place might be just about ready to give up the ghost, but someone had built a fire in the rock fireplace recently enough that the scent was still detectable.

In short, nothing that would explain Loba's odd behavior. She gave up. For the moment, she didn't intend to worry about it. It had to be something she smelled that was putting her off, and if Loba was more comfortable hanging by the door, then let her. They weren't going to be here long anyway, she hoped.

The violent way the weather had turned from sunny and beautiful to black and stormy was as strange as Loba's behavior. She'd been enjoying their trek, and Angus had turned out to be a team leader extraordinaire. As many times as she'd driven to Portland, she should have been well acquainted with the landscape along the Umatilla and Columbia rivers. But after today, she had a completely new perspective. It had been loads of fun to hang with Winnie and listen to the interesting history lesson Angus gave as they hiked. The guy had some impressive hidden talents.

Yet now, as they huddled inside the old cabin waiting for the pouring rain to pass, she marveled at how fast the day had shifted. Damp weather wasn't all that unusual for the area, so she shouldn't be surprised. But the way the storm had washed away the beauty of the day made her uneasy.

Or perhaps it was something deeper. She couldn't discount her sensitive nature. Whatever was in the air here seemed to whisper along her skin, and obviously it did more than whisper to Loba, even though she still tried to convince herself Loba was reacting to a bad odor. Maybe that was why they were so close. Perhaps she and Loba were kindred spirits in a preternatural sense, a witch and her familiar. The thought made her smile, which was okay in this century. A few centuries past and just the thought of Loba being a familiar could have easily resulted in her death warrant.

Using the small flashlight she pulled out of her pocket, she began to study the little cabin. It was dim inside, as the storm had pushed away much of the day's sunlight. The beam of her light seemed to dance in the gloom, and as she watched she noticed the unusual shape of a shadow. It almost looked like a person. That might make sense if someone were standing there, but neither Angus nor Winnie was close. The day was definitely growing odd. Now she was seeing people inside shadows. It was becoming clearer by the second that she really did need a vacation. Then again, stressed as she was, she didn't have vision issues.

"Do you see that?" She couldn't be the only one, right?

Winnie turned from where she was standing at the window running her finger along a missing piece of glass in one corner, staring out at the unrelenting storm. "See what? Just watched a huge spike of lightning go across the sky. Pretty awesome, though it might mean we'll be stuck here for a while. Hope one of you has a lot of snacks in your pack. A girl needs to eat, you know."

"Shouldn't the chef in the group have the gourmet snacks in her pack?" Angus looked pointedly at Winnie. She shrugged.

Winnie pointed at Molly. "The baker could have whipped something up for us."

Molly was only sort of listening to the banter about food. "No. I don't have much for snacks, and no, I don't mean the lightning." She still watched the strange shadow as it walked…yes, walked. Absolutely nothing wrong with her eyes. "That." She pointed. Surely they could see it. The shadow was very distinct.

Both Angus and Winnie finally seemed to clue in on what she was trying to ask them and followed the direction she was pointing. "Well now, that is a bit odd," Angus said as he folded his arms across his chest.

"I don't know what you guys are talking about. I don't see a thing." Winnie turned back to the window. "That," she pointed to the sky where another bolt of lightning shot across the black clouds, "I see. Damn, that was a big one. Get ready for a sonic boom."

Thank God, at least Angus could see the shadow. In Molly's opinion, it was more than weird. She moved toward it and, as she did, heard a soft thud, as if the floorboard beneath her feet was hollow. Bouncing on her toes, she tested the board with her foot, confirming what she'd heard wasn't in her imagination. The board flexed as if it was quite loose. Not surprising in an old place like this, except that she hadn't noticed any of the other boards exhibiting such looseness. She kneeled and studied it in the beam of her flashlight. Not only did it sound and feel different, but it was definitely a little different from those around it.

"Hey. Take a look at this." The boom Winnie predicted hit, making the small cabin shake. None of them paid any attention.

Angus was already at her side, and Winnie left her spot by the window to join her on the floor. "What kind of place did you bring us to, Angus?" Winnie had an arm draped affectionately around his shoulders. "It's old, it's dark, it's creepy, and now it also appears to be falling apart. Another hit of thunder like the last one and we'll be lucky if we don't end up falling through these creaky old boards or have the whole roof cave in on us. God only knows what kind of dungeon is down there." She nodded toward the spot where Molly was kneeling.

He raised an eyebrow. "Well, it is a roof over your head, and I seriously doubt we'll find much of anything under this place besides dirt. You want to risk going out there?" He inclined his head toward the window, where rain still fell in a steady downpour. "I'm inclined to let the storm run its course while I stay pretty darned dry. What say you, my pretty maiden?"

"I don't know." Winnie was hedging. "Outside and wet might not be the worst thing. I mean, no offense, Angus, but this place is strange. Seriously," she pointed just beyond where Molly knelt, "I didn't see it before, but I do now. What the heck is with the creepy shadows?"

A few seconds ago, Molly had thought the play of dark and light inside the cabin was definitely freaky. But now it didn't seem all that important. Her focus had shifted. "Forget the shadows," Molly said as she stared down into the hole under the floorboard, her flashlight's beam illuminating the space. "Check it out. How in the world do you think this ended up here?"

She could hardly believe what she was looking at, but her eyes were pretty damned good even in this light. Most people would have a hard time putting a name to what she was staring at, but not Molly. Rocking back on her heels, she glanced out the window at the shadow of the burned tree before turning her gaze back to the exposed hiding spot. The significance of that tree now hit her with sickening clarity. She might expect to see something like it three hundred years ago on the East Coast. Here, never.

With a growing sense of dread, Molly reached into the space and wrapped her fingers around the cool leather of the grimoire. As she pulled it out, ice-cold air rushed over her, and the screech that filled the small cabin was so loud, she almost dropped the book in order to cover her ears with her hands. The last thing she heard before everything went black was the sound of her own screams.

The ground began to shake beneath Winnie's feet, and she nearly lost her footing. The dim light inside the cabin disappeared in the space of a breath, plunging them into a total blackout nowhere near natural. What was worse than the disconcerting descent into darkness were the sounds. This time it wasn't the crack of thunder. She was reminded of a cave echoing with the screams of twenty women. Only they weren't screams of surprise. They were the sounds of despair so deep and all-consuming that chills raced down her spine. She trembled.

She reached out, searching for Angus. He apparently was doing the same, for within a second her fingers touched his. The contact with his warm flesh was like a gift from God. Never before had she needed to feel him near her. Whatever happened next, she was not letting go of his hand.

"I've got you," he said as he pulled her close. "You're safe with me."

She couldn't see him, but she could feel him, which was good enough. "What's happening?" she said above the roar. "Is it an earthquake?" It was the only thing that made sense, and if that's what was happening here, shouldn't they get out of this decrepit cabin? This wasn't exactly earthquake country, but then again, hadn't there been a large one in Seattle a few years back? If it could happen there, it could surely happen here. She didn't like the feeling of the earth shifting beneath her feet, not one tiny bit. This cabin was such a pile of decaying wood she'd been surprised they didn't all end up beneath a heap of it. No wonder Loba hadn't wanted to come inside. The dog had way more sense than the three of them put together.

"I don't know," he said close to her ear. "Something isn't quite right. Less like an earthquake and more like a banshee has found us."

A banshee? He was talking Greek to her now. She'd never heard of a banshee. "A what?"

"The screams," he said. "According to Granny, a banshee always screams when it shows up."

"That's crazy. This is nature, not the paranormal."

He pulled her closer. "No. It's not nature and it's bad. Nature doesn't screech like this."

Like the screams were the only things bad about this. What about the blackness and the shaking ground? "It's an earthquake," she insisted, her lips pressed close to his cheek. Just touching him gave her strength in this cavern of darkness. As long as they were touching, she could hold it together.

"Death," he said into her ear. "A banshee brings death."

He was an Irishman through and through. It was one of the things she so loved about him. That said, it also filled him with fanciful stories. She'd spent many an evening listening to him regale her with tales his grandmother had told him when he was just a little boy. Granted, this was the first she'd ever heard of a banshee, but he'd shared stories of fairies, demons, fire-spitters, and even witches. Not the Molly kind of cool, bright-light witches, but rather the evil, destructive types who eat small children who don't behave. They were great stories of a rich, colorful cultural folklore, but that's all they were. This wasn't folk legend; this was hard reality, and that meant something more earthly had to be behind what was happening. The ground gave a huge shift, throwing her harder against Angus. His arms tightened as she screamed. Such a girly thing to do. She couldn't help it. The reaction was knee-jerk. "Make it stop!"

And just as the word "stop" flew from her lips, it did just that. Silence dropped as quickly as the sudden rain that had sent them rushing into the cabin. The ground stilled, and light flowed into the room, making her blink against the unexpected glare. Dust mites danced in the light as though the room was feeling joy instead of dread.

"I knew it," Angus said a little loudly for the now-quiet room. "A banshee."

Winnie blinked and turned her head to look up at him. "What?" Her ears were still ringing.

"Granny was right-on. The banshees are still with us. She swore that they were not just folklore but actually shared our universe. This was most assuredly the work of one. How I wish she was still with us so I could tell her she was right."

She still wasn't buying in. Even with Molly's very real background in things beyond the regular person's ability to see, in this instance Winnie believed nature was playing its hand rather than something magical was happening. In Spokane, they experienced occasional tremors, and that's why she was sure this was a full-on quake. It had really felt like the tremors on speed. The screams she heard? Well, that had to have an explanation too.

Then again, she looked at her dear friend, whose face was particularly pale. Molly was, after all, a real-life, flesh-and-blood witch, so Winnie's argument against anything supernatural wasn't quite as strong as she might hope. All that fell by the wayside as she studied Molly. She wasn't simply pale; she was pasty and, for lack of a better description, stunned. For a second, she didn't get why. If she understood earthquakes correctly, they might produce some mild after-tremors. She could deal with mild shakes. After all, the cabin had made it through without falling on top of them, and no one was hurt. She felt almost giddy and not in the least as sick as Molly appeared to be.

Slowly she turned and gazed around the room. No wonder Angus was talking about banshees and Molly looked about ready to pass out. Something was seriously fucked up here. Yeah, they were still in the cabin in the little clearing, only it wasn't the cabin they'd walked into. This one wasn't crumbling and stinky, with a decrepit roof. Not at all. There was the window with the broken glass in the corner. That was the only thing that was the same.

This one was relatively new, with a table, a bed, a fire, and shelves against the wall with bowls and cups. More surprising than the condition and the furniture was the little fact that four people were now in the cabin.

Standing tall and beautiful, with long black hair and dark, intense eyes, was a Native American woman. She was holding one end of the book from under the floorboard and staring right at Molly. She nodded and said in perfect English, "I've been searching for you."

CHAPTER SIX

1837

Aquene felt whispers along her skin, as if someone were brushing an eagle feather across her bare arms. The air had shifted, and the shadows became something more. Again and again in her dreams, her visions, she had seen a woman's face, beautiful and haunted as if she were lost. As if the Great Spirit had failed to show her the way. It was the same face she now gazed upon as they stood close enough for her to feel breath upon her cheeks, each holding one end of the book that had lain hidden beneath the floor.

"You," she whispered. "It's you."

The other woman stared at her with an expression that spoke not of fear but of something much deeper. Surprise and shock were there, and that she would expect. At the same time, she did not appear in any way afraid. That did surprise Aquene. So many of the people who came here, particularly the women, were afraid of her, as if they believed she would harm them. Little did they know that she was a healer and would not consider taking a life, any life, whether that of her people or those who invaded her lands. Not unless someone she loved was in danger. That had not happened to her.

Yet.

Aquene let her hands fall away from the strange book. It felt odd against her flesh. Not in a bad manner, but only as if it was filled with something not of this world. The moment she let go, the strange sensation in her fingers vanished.

"Who are you?" the woman asked, her eyes still on Aquene's. She liked the sound of her voice. It was not high or screeching. It was not filled with fear or accusation, such as she had heard again and again in the speech of other women who came here. In this woman it was infused with only the simplicity of her question. It told Aquene much about her in such a few words of her language.

For a moment, she stared at her and thought how pretty she was, so oddly dressed in pants like none she had ever seen on anyone, man or woman, and some kind of brightly colored overcoat. Again, it was strange and not something she had seen before. She had been around many people who had traveled to her lands, and she had learned their language and their ways. Their clothing had a similar familiarity to her, at least until this moment. This woman, this beautiful woman, with the strange clothes and the eyes she had seen many times in her dreams, was like no other. Thanks to her dreams, she already felt close to her, but now that she gazed into her face, she felt as though an invisible bond tied them together.

"I am Aquene," she said solemnly. "Of the Liksiyu."

"Of the what?" Her dark eyes were the color of the beaver pelts they often traded for guns, knives, and axes. She hated the weapons, though she understood their importance to her people. Much had changed in the season just past, and her spirit told her that more was beyond the horizon.

"The Liksiyu." Those who traveled to her lands knew of her people. They had found an uneasy peace, which allowed Aquene to trade with them and to learn their language and their ways.

"The Cayuse." It was a man's voice, and until this moment Aquene had not noticed that she and the woman were not alone. She had been focused on the dark-eyed beauty that had haunted her dreams and her visions.

At the sound of his voice, she turned her head and studied him. Or, rather, she studied them, for he stood not alone but beside yet another woman. He was interesting, with long, thick hair that was wild about his head and a strong body that spoke of power. He was much like the warriors of her tribe, save for his eyes, the color of the forest moss. His words were unlike the others here, for he spoke in a strange voice, which told her that he came from another place. Where might that be? She had never been beyond the limits of the lands of her people, though she had come to understand that a vast world existed beyond the horizon.

The woman at his side was also quite different. She wore the same man-like clothes of the other one but did not possess the same beauty that Aquene was beginning to think of as a gift from the stars. Kindness peeked out from behind her stunned expression, and Aquene knew this traveler was true-hearted. She carried no magic, but she also carried no ill-will. They were strangers to each other, but Aquene knew she could trust her.

Aquene gave the man a slight nod, acknowledging the word for her people that she had heard pass the lips of others who came here. Her language, at least to her, was beautiful and simple, yet the wagonloads who traveled through the vast prairies and mountains could not make it cross their tongues. Instead, they made their own words for them.

"Yes. We are the Cayuse." She still did not like the way the word sounded. It was too rough, too unfamiliar. They did not need another name, for the one the Great Spirit had bestowed upon them was enough.

"How did you get in here? One minute it was just the three of us, and then, poof, you appeared." Her dream woman cradled the book they had held together close to her chest, as though afraid Aquene would take it from her.

The book was not of importance to her. Not at this time. "Poof?" She did not understand that word and did not know what she was being asked.

"It means you appeared from out of the air. One moment nothing was there, and the next, there you were."

"Oh." Aquene smiled. "Poof." Now the strange word felt fine when she said it. "Yes, I did poof. You do not know why you have been brought here?" It seemed so very clear to her, and she always believed it would for this woman as well.

Still holding the book tight to her body, the woman shook her head. "Ah, no. I have absolutely no clue."

Aquene did. "Why, it is simple…you are here to save my people."

❖

This was a godforsaken place. The wind blew without break, the water of the wide river so rough with whitecaps that it reminded him of those he had seen on the ocean voyage when he left his home and came to this country. The thick weeds that smelled faintly of herbs grew everywhere. Great distances separated any type of shelter, and thus he was forced to sleep on the ground, where the faint scent of sage made him sick to his stomach night after night. At least it had not rained since he left the warmth of the fire in the home Tobias had shared with him. Despite the crudity of the accommodations, he missed the comforts it provided. He did not miss the evil taint that Prudence had left.

His path was taking him nearer and nearer to the witch's tiny cabin, and for that he was grateful. The thought of sleeping under her roof repelled him, though the thought of sleeping on a bed—any bed—did not. He would endure the indignity of taking shelter in her dwelling, knowing that he had destroyed her ability to perform evil deeds. He would say a prayer and cleanse it, as he also searched it again for the grimoire. She had been destroyed, and now he had to make certain her knowledge was as well.

He should have done a more thorough job at the time. The quick search he had undertaken on the night of her destruction while surrounded by the men who had come to help him stop the witch had been inadequate. He had not wanted them to witness the discovery of the book and had been pleased to believe it was not there. He could not trust regular men to resist the lure of something that powerful. It would not be the first time he had seen it happen. In this place of wilderness and violence, he did not wish to expose it to willing eyes and minds. After what he had witnessed with Prudence, he felt a particular urgency to return to the cabin and find it, now realizing with certainty that it was within the four walls. No hands beyond his should ever touch something that evil. He alone possessed the knowledge to destroy it.

"Ho, there."

Matthew shifted in his saddle, surprised by the sound of another man's voice. His gaze fell upon a trapper, his horse laden with furs. He was a slight man, wearing dirty buckskin and a hat that drooped low on his head. His beard was long and thick and, Matthew feared, home to any number of small creatures. His stomach rolled.

"Fellow pilgrim, how do you today?"

His hearty laughter revealed several missing teeth, the ones still in his mouth of a color he had not seen in many years. This man had been out here for some time, and the elements had not been kind to him. Matthew resolved to stay upwind. Continuing as if Matthew had not backed his horse up, the stranger said, "It's a pleasant day, yes indeed. Where are you off to, my fine fellow?"

He thought fast, for he did not want this man to know of his true mission. "The Hudson Bay Company at Les Bois." He had passed through the area east of his current location when he first made his journey out here. Given all the fur hanging from the trapper's horse, he was taking a risk by suggesting Les Bois. He just hoped it was a distance too great for this creature's business.

"Ah, my man. You should follow me to Fort Colville, up north. It is an easier route and a good place to trade. If you grow weary riding there, the old Spokane House provides a fine night's shelter. I have stayed there many times."

Matthew had not traveled that far north yet and did not know of either Fort Coville or the Spokane House. It pleased him that this trapper would not hamper his mission by suggesting they travel together. That would put him in a position he did not relish, for he could not have him at his side. At times, help was necessary, but this mission required solitude, and he would do whatever he must to make it so. Sometimes innocents perished to accomplish a greater good.

"I must continue on to Les Bois. Others await me there." It was a necessary lie, so God would not reproach him.

The rough man laughed again. "I hope for coin in my pocket and a return to Kanesville."

"Kanesville?" The question was out of his mouth before he thought. He did not want to engage this man in conversation, and yet he did just that.

"Iowa, my good man. Kanesville, Iowa, where I intend to find a pretty girl to settle down with. This has been my life for five years, and it is time to go home."

Five years? Matthew studied the man more closely. He would have guessed ten or twenty. If he had, indeed, been here for a mere five years, they had been rough ones. The sun had hardened his face, and his hair hung matted and dirty. There was no way to tell just what color it might be. It would take much coin in his pocket to make him presentable for any woman, if it was even possible. This time Matthew managed to keep his thoughts to himself. Instead, he rode beside the man until the sun began to dip in the sky, hoping with each passing minute that he would leave Matthew be. When he did not, he decided he must take the matter into his own hands.

"Here is where I must leave you." Matthew turned his horse toward one of the random grouping of trees that sprang up some distance away from the river. He hoped his chattering companion would continue to where he would turn and head north. God was watching over him, for mercifully his plan worked.

"Travel well, my friend." The man tipped his hat and spurred his horse on. He rode along the river, growing ever smaller.

Matthew smiled once he was alone and brought his horse to a standstill in order to gaze into the distance. In his bones, he felt a vibration and instinctively knew he was closing the miles between him and the witch's cabin. He might have left it behind a year ago, but soon he would find what he sought, and the world would be safer for it. Giving the man long enough to be out of sight, Matthew waited and then trotted back down to the river. He watered his horse before mounting once more and continuing. They had gone only a short distance when the clouds covered the setting sun and thunder crashed through the sky.

CHAPTER SEVEN

Molly had no damn idea what had just happened. She might be a witch, but honest to God, something like this had never occurred to her before. Her throat was still raw from the scream that had burst out when she touched that book.

Given her family origins, she'd seen her share of grimoires, but she'd never come across anything like this. It had been old and dusty when she saw it, and obviously down beneath the floorboards for a good long time. At least that's what she'd thought when she first reached in and took ahold of it.

Now as she stood cradling the book, it seemed to be different. The cover was no longer cracked and dry, or coated with a deep layer of dust. It didn't feel brittle against her fingers. In fact, as she pulled it away from her body to study it, the grimoire appeared to be relatively new, as if someone was in the process of creating it. The leather was soft and supple, with only a light layer of dust across the cover.

Slowly, she brought her head up and stared at Aquene. As if the book wasn't weird enough, where had this woman come from, this vision in a fringed skirt, beaded dress, and decorated leggings? Her long black hair hung down in braids on either side of her head like silken cords. And while her dress was fascinating, her face captivated Molly. Her broad cheeks, expressive dark eyes, and thin lips suited her, as did her skin, the color of a warm latte. In short, she was gorgeous.

Molly finally found her voice. "Save your people?" What exactly was that supposed to mean? She was a witch by birth but a baker by trade, so not exactly a caped crusader for the people. Any people.

"Yes, you—" Aquene squinted. "I do not know your name, only your face."

"Molly," she said without thinking. Her mind was still swirling around the last part of her statement: only your face. Unless she'd seen one of Molly's promotional ads or logged onto her website, how could she possibly know what she looked like? On the other hand, if she really did recognize Molly, that meant her efforts at promotion were working and not that this was some moment of madness, right?

Aquene smiled again. "Molly. It is a fine name."

Noted, but really, what she thought about her name didn't matter. Other things were more important right now. "Explain what you mean about knowing my face." Was it because of her online presence or was it something else? The part about saving the people, she could sideline temporarily. She was more interested in finding out what Aquene meant by that statement.

Aquene tilted her head and peered at Molly intently. "Have you not seen my face in your dreams?"

"Ah, that would be a no."

Confusion clouded the dark eyes. "Of that I am surprised, for you have been in my dreams for many days now. I have been waiting for you to come to me. I was certain you were waiting for me too."

Okay, a little freaky. How did she know Molly had dreams that sometimes came to pass? Her dreams of late had been filled with fire and ashes, not faces of beautiful women. "The only thing I've been waiting for is an insurance adjuster to write his report and close my claim." She hugged the book again. For some reason, it gave her comfort. Most likely for no other reason than it gave her something to hold on to.

The confusion deepened in her eyes. "The insurance adjuster?" The words sounded clumsy coming out of her mouth, as if she'd never said them before.

Molly waved her hand. "Never mind. You've seen me in your dreams?" She was still more interested in that than anything else.

The smile returned to Aquene's face. "Yes." That single word sounded so confident.

"Hey, Moll?" Molly turned to look at Winnie, who was wide-eyed and shaking her head. "I'm not a hundred percent on this, but I think we just stepped into a wormhole or something wonky like that. You might want to put on your witch hat and figure out what's going on here."

Wormhole? Not likely. To do something like that would take more magic than she possessed. "Winnie. What are you talking about?"

"We're in a different place."

Molly took a quick glance around. They were in the same place, and the only change was the plus one. "No, we're not. We're still in the cabin."

"Yeah, in the cabin, but look closer. It's in a different time. Wormhole, Molly. As in Jules Verne kind of stuff. You know, time travel." Winnie sounded like she was trying patiently to explain something to someone particularly dim.

"I don't think so." She knew she didn't sound all that convincing. Truth was, she'd heard stories of people being able to walk through time, but they were just stories, right? Even though she knew magic was real, even her beliefs went only so far. Except... She glanced back down at the transformed grimoire in her hands.

"I have to agree with my woman, here, Molly. We're not in the twenty-first century anymore. I mean, look around. Old and creaky it ain't. Doesn't even smell the same, if you catch my drift? Where's the dust and the mold?"

She looked around and her heart began to pound. Maybe Angus and Winnie had a point. The cabin did look different, and yeah, it smelled a whole lot better than when they'd first come through the door. She just couldn't get past knowing how much magic it would take to make a leap like that and also sure she didn't possess it. She took a deep breath and returned her attention to Aquene. This woman spoke perfect English, and if they had traveled in time, that wouldn't be the case. Right? Made sense to her. "Tell me, Aquene. What year is it?" She intended to put the time-travel question to bed once and for all.

Tilting her head, Aquene said matter-of-factly, "1837."

❖

"I knew it, I knew it, I knew it!" Winnie should be scared, but it hit her with sudden clarity that she wasn't, not even a little. In fact, this would make an awesome episode on one of those ghost-busting reality shows. They were going to be TV stars. How fun would that be?

Her enthusiasm took a sudden dip when she gave it a little more thought. They would be stars if they weren't currently in the nineteenth century. No television and nobody who would believe they had just gone back in time nearly two hundred years. Shoot, she wouldn't believe it either if she wasn't seeing and feeling it for herself. Everything had changed in the blink of an eye, along with a lot of earth shaking and screaming.

They were in the same cabin, only it wasn't old and dusty anymore, and it was warm and lighted by flames of a fire in the fireplace. Outside the window, the tree they'd noticed on the way in still stood there, only now it showed signs of burning in the not-too-distant past. The biggest change was the landscape. One glance outside and the difference was clear. The trees were thicker, the ground rougher, and most important, the trails that had brought them to this place were gone.

They were in the year 1837. It was a crazy notion, yet she believed it. A feeling deep in her heart told it was true, and darn it, she was going with it. Winnie would be the first to admit she adored those ghost-hunter reality shows. It was probably one reason she'd been attracted to Angus. She loved hearing his stories rich in the Irish culture of paranormal beings, especially with his alluring accent. The fact that he was screaming hot didn't hurt either.

Grabbing Angus by the arm, she stared into his eyes. "It's true, isn't it? It wasn't your granny's banshee causing havoc. We just took the express train to the past."

Angus studied her for a moment and then turned his gaze to the window. He was shaking his head. "I don't know, darlin', but things aren't the same as they were a couple of minutes ago. Sure sounded like the scream of a banshee. Don't recall Granny ever saying they could bend time."

"Oh, come on," Molly protested. "It's impossible. We can't just pop into another century. Things like that don't happen, especially not to people like us. I don't have that kind of magic."

Winnie looked around and disagreed. Not only did she believe it was possible, but she was sure it was true. They were in the same cabin, in the same location, but the differences were glaring enough to give weight to the time-change idea. Molly wasn't looking close enough. Denial wasn't going to change a thing.

"Me thinks thou dost protest too much."

Molly rolled her eyes at Winnie's badly quoted Shakespeare. "Really?"

Winnie wasn't giving up. She pointed to the left. "Does that table look a little newer to you?"

Molly dropped her gaze to the table and ran her fingers over the top. "A little," she said grudgingly.

"About her?" She nodded her head toward Aquene. "Did you see her when we came inside to get out of the rain? Did you see anyone who looked like her anywhere nearby during our hike or when we hauled ass here?"

"No…"

"I think my lady has a point." Angus was smiling at Winnie. "I believe, my dearests, that we have the makings of a great paranormal movie."

"A movie?" Molly sounded incredulous. "Seriously? Everything is going wonky around us, and that's what you think of first? You're as bad as Winnie and her Shakespeare."

Winnie laughed. First and foremost, her man was an artist, and she wasn't in the least surprised that's where his thoughts had jumped to first. His hobby might be historical research, but his bread and butter was performing art. "Actually, my initial thought was a reality show. Shakespeare was an afterthought, though I gotta say I like the movie idea better. It would be awesome."

"What is a movie?" Aquene asked, looking from one face to the other. She wouldn't have a clue, would she? If they were in the 1800s, it would be quite a while before anyone came to close to working out that little bit of technology.

"It's not important," Winnie said. "What is important is figuring out how we got here and why. Then we can see what we'll need to do to get back. This is interesting and all but don't think I want to spend very much time here. I'll bet there's not an indoor bathroom to be found."

Molly wasn't getting sidetracked by the talk of a movie in the making or the search for a bathroom. "I want to know why we ended up here in the first place."

Aquene spoke up. "I have already told you why you are here. You—she—will save my people." She pointed to Molly.

That part wasn't very clear to Winnie. A baker saving people? "How exactly is she going to do that? And save them from what?"

A frown crossed Aquene's face as she shook her head. "When the time is right, we will know."

"Well, isn't that just dandy," Molly muttered.

At the distant sound of pounding horse hooves, Winnie spun

toward the window. "Someone's coming. Obviously, this must be the party house." The expression on Aquene's face didn't exactly scream frivolity. Or on Molly's, for that matter, not that Molly could possibly have a clue who was riding into town, so to speak. Regardless of whether Molly believed Aquene's declaration that they had gone back in time a couple hundred years, Winnie did, and they were most certainly not in Kansas anymore.

"We must go." Aquene sounded grave.

"Why don't we wait and see who's coming? Maybe they'll have an idea as to what's going on here." It was a long shot, given where they were and when they were. Whoever was trotting their way was surely a frontiersman hunting, tracking, or searching for a new place to call home. Time travel was most likely not on their agenda.

"Darlin', I don't think so." Even Angus sounded worried, which didn't make sense either.

"What's going on?" Obviously, she was the only one not in the loop, because the rest of them were as jumpy as feral cats. She heard only the sound of a single horse, which meant one, possibly two, were heading their way. They couldn't possibly be in much danger from a couple of people. There were four of them, and they had the cover of the cabin on their side.

"We must go," Aquene repeated, and when none of them moved, she said harshly, "Now!"

CHAPTER EIGHT

They could not stay here any longer. The vibrations that came through the ground and up through the floor of Hannah's cabin brought the whisper of danger with them. It was less of a whisper and more a scream, or at least that was how it felt to Aquene. Without needing to peer out the window, she realized who rode in their direction, and she also knew he brought death with him.

She glanced at the scorched tree outside, and the truth of her conviction gained much weight. He had burned the woman there, taking her life as though he were a god. His face too had been in her visions, a haunting specter of the evil that walked her lands. As much as the visions of Molly had filled her with hope, his visage had radiated cruelty and despair. Now as she felt his presence growing ever closer, an urgency to flee filled her. They must leave, and though she wished for the speed of the wind a good horse could provide, they must do so on foot. Tilla could not carry them all, and she would not leave a single one behind. It was not her way.

The thought of her beautiful horse running free across the fields brought her joy rather than sorrow. Tilla would never truly leave her and would find her way back to Alumpum. The knowledge of that truth made her heart glad. Her friend would care for her horse as if she were her own. That was what sisters of the heart did for each other.

"Let us hurry," she said to the three who stared at her. "We must leave this place before he comes."

"Go where?" Molly asked as she held on to the book. "I barely knew where we were in the twenty-first century. I'm completely lost here."

Aquene wished she had the knowledge to understand everything her visions had shown her thus far. She did not. She knew only that they must get out of the path of the man who rode toward them as they stood here doing nothing. He brought death and violence. Her visions ran red with the blood he would spill if they could not stop him. First, they must conceal themselves from his sight. Then they would find a way to end the path of terror he brought wherever he walked, to dam the river of blood that had been his life.

Her gaze strayed to Molly, and a whisper of power flowed over her. She was not wrong about this woman; she was special, just as promised. The journey they must take together was to begin this moment, and where it would end, she did not know. But they must start in this breath. She stretched out her hand to Molly. "Come."

At first, she thought Molly would resist again, but she did not. She placed her hand in Aquene's, and the shock it sent through her was as unexpected as it was powerful. They both felt their connection, for she could see it in Molly's eyes. She did not want to let go. Rather, she wished to hold tighter.

"What's out there?" Molly's words were soft. In her eyes, Aquene could see the knowledge. As she felt his ominous presence, so too did Molly. That gave her great comfort, for they would work well together.

"Death." She had no choice but to speak true.

Angus was staring out the window, his eyes narrowed. "I don't know what or who it is, but I'm with her." He inclined his head toward Aquene. "I have a bad feeling about whoever's on that horse, and if my vote counts for anything, I vote we haul ass."

"Please." Aquene did not like to beg. It was necessary, and so she did, for they must not stay here a moment longer. Their lives depended upon taking flight as powerful as the eagles that soared across the mighty river.

"All right," Molly said. "Let's grab our packs and get out of here."

"Ah, Moll, we have a little problem." Winnie was turning a full circle. "No packs."

"Well, I'll be damned," Angus muttered. "We dropped them right there." He pointed to the spot by the door where they'd shrugged them off after coming in from the rain.

"Screw the packs," Molly cried. "Where's Loba?"

Aquene stared at them. Were these strangers soft in the head? Did they not understand the danger they were in? They had to get out of this place right now. Packs did not matter. Nor did this Loba, whoever she might be. The pounding outside grew louder and her feeling of dread deeper. "We must run, now!"

She could not wait any longer. Pulling on Molly's hand, she dragged her toward the door. The wind pushed it open and brought in leaves and pine needles, along with the odor of the charred tree. The scent of death filled the cabin so thickly it seemed to push out the air. With Molly holding her hand, Aquene ran out into the storm that had once again begun to rage, the wind whipping her braids around her head. Overhead, the sound of thunder filled the sky, and when lightning flashed, she let go and her vision went black.

She always appeared wearing white with her black hair free and flowing. She was the most beautiful woman Aquene had ever seen. She was the mother.

"You must hurry, child. He comes, and he brings darkness and death."

"I am trying, Mother, but I do not know what to do."

"Save her, my daughter. Save the book."

"Tell me how."

Her smile reminded Aquene of the sun in a blue, cloudless sky. "You will know. You will know."

Once Matthew was riding in the direction of the witch's cabin again, he felt more at ease. Purpose always did that for him. Though he was satisfied he'd done a good deed by putting Prudence down, the loose end here was like a rock in his boot that he couldn't get rid of. It poked at him with every step, bringing red-hot pain.

Overhead, thunder roared once again, and he pulled up on the reins. Tilting his head to the sky, Matthew stared up at it. It wasn't right. Not that thunder and lightning were unusual here. Quite the opposite. This, however, was different. He could swear he heard the sound of a woman's scream on the wind, though he wasn't sure that was possible so far away from the outposts that served to make up what passed for civilization.

Well, that and the bands of natives he encountered now and again.

He found their ways repellant, and perhaps when he completed his task by destroying the last of the witches, he would carry on his mission by eliminating those who refused to acknowledge the greatness of God. But that was for another day. Now he must continue to work toward concluding this mission cleanly and completely.

A brush of fingertips across the back of his neck made him start. Goose bumps that had nothing to do with the cool rain rose on his arms. Once before he had felt just such a touch. It had been the beginning. The first one. On that day he had believed it to be a blessing from God. He believed the same now. He sat taller on his horse, the slap of rain against his cheeks unable to dampen his spirit.

The wind kicked up, trying with all its might to pull the hat from his head and whipping the tails of his coat into a frenzy. This time he was certain screams carried through the air, and it made him smile. He stared up and let the rain pelt his face.

"Bring your worst," he said to the sky. "I cannot be stopped. I will not fail."

The storm for others might portend a bad omen. Not for Matthew. Through a break in the black clouds overhead, a ray of light shone through. He knew what that meant. Who it was meant for. As he prodded his horse into a gallop, he began to whistle a cheerful tune from his youth. He was glad to be on his way. He had no time to waste.

CHAPTER NINE

For at least a full minute, Aquene seemed to zone out as they rushed into the stormy gloom. Her eyes were blank, and she wore an expression that told Molly she was somewhere else. She was standing completely still, which was odd for the woman who'd insisted they leave right this damn minute. All the fire that had dragged them out the door was suddenly gone until Aquene's eyes focused again. She stared at Molly, her eyes filled with a storm that echoed nature's. "We must go. He comes for you." There it was again, and this time the warning sent whispers of alarm through Molly.

Aquene didn't need to tell her again. Suddenly, she was picking up on something so disturbing and elemental that it scared her. "Let's haul ass," she shouted to Winnie and Angus, who had both followed them out the cabin door and into the clearing.

"Our packs are gone." Winnie glanced back at the open cabin door. She seemed stuck on that detail, and while it bothered Molly, it didn't bother her enough to stop her forward momentum. A sense of dread draped over her like a blanket, yet she pushed on.

"Don't worry about it." The packs would surely come in handy, but she didn't want to take the time to figure out where they went. They were gone, and they'd just have to deal with it.

"But—"

"Let's go." Angus grabbed Winnie's hand. "We don't need them."

"The packs...Loba..." Winnie wasn't giving up without a fight.

That thought stopped Molly momentarily. Where was Loba? Not once since the whole paradigm shift occurred had she seen her dog. Why? The single word echoed in her head, demanding an answer that she simply didn't have. Loba hadn't wanted to come into the cabin to begin with. Her dog probably had better sense than the rest of them. If they'd stayed at that door or, better yet, outside, maybe they'd still be in the twenty-first century and not running away from some shadowy horse rider intent on hurting them. Or would that be one of the four horsemen of the apocalypse?

"Loba will be fine." Angus tapped her on the shoulder as he pulled Winnie past her and into the cover of the trees.

"Who is Loba?" Aquene looked around as if searching for another person.

"My dog." That sounded so inconsequential, given Loba's place in her heart. She was more than just her dog, but that was a conversation for another time.

"I do not see a dog."

That was the big problem, now wasn't it? Since the moment she'd encountered Aquene, nothing was as it had been only seconds before. Whether she liked it or not, things had changed, and she didn't have time to figure out what it was right now. She had to follow Aquene's lead and run. She had to believe that wherever Loba was, she'd be fine.

"No," Molly sighed. "Neither do I."

Without saying anything else, she followed Angus and Winnie into the trees, attempting to put as much distance as she could between herself and the cabin. The wind was picking up in intensity, and raindrops were falling faster and faster.

With several long strides, Aquene passed her, and together they traveled quickly away from the cabin. Her eyes were on Aquene as she moved like a gazelle through the trees and over jutting rocks. Her black braids trailed behind her as the wind blew against them as if it was trying to push them back. That wasn't going to happen. Storm or no, they were going to cover some ground and put as much distance as they could between themselves and the mystery rider.

Twice she tripped, and twice Aquene was immediately at her side to help her up. It was like she had a sixth sense about Molly. It was nice to have help. It was strange to have someone she'd just met be so in tune with her.

The storm suddenly vanished like someone had turned off a gushing faucet. One minute rain was pelting them, and the next it was eerily calm. She wondered if Aquene thought it strange. Hard to tell because she was ahead of her moving with purpose.

She wasn't sure when she lost Angus and Winnie. They'd taken off first, and Molly had been so focused on Aquene she didn't realize their paths had diverged. It made her uneasy. That and the unsettling sensation of someone at her back. It didn't make any difference that they had covered enough distance to make the sound of the approaching horseman disappear. She still couldn't shake the feeling of a dark cloud following her. While her family was in the business of white magic, she knew black magic when she felt it. Or in this case, when she was being beaten up by it.

❖

At first Winnie thought the whole time-travel scenario was kind of cool. It was getting less cool by the second. In fact, she'd shifted into believing this was majorly messed up. Yeah, she got the whole witch thing with Molly and most of the time thought it was sweet. But not right at the moment. She'd just wanted to spend a couple of leisurely days with the love of her life, her best friend, and an awesome dog, hiking along the Columbia River. It had sounded great when Angus came up with the plan.

Now...not so much. Her earlier suggestion that it would be an excellent reality show was kind of dumb. Even if there had been reality TV in 1837, the show they found themselves in wasn't a very groovy rehash of history. No, this was more like being dumped in the outback and left to their own devices to survive. Not her idea of fun at all.

So here they were running into the woods like they'd just robbed a bank and trying to get away from what? Molly and Aquene both said someone was coming and that someone was real bad. She didn't hear anything, making it a little harder to work up enthusiasm for running around in the wilds like the flocks of turkeys that were everywhere these days back at home. Then again, she'd been with Molly before when she'd had premonitions, and damned if they weren't dead on.

Even though the landscape here was nothing like the thick forests that surrounded the Spokane area, running through the trees wasn't exactly easy. Lots of low bushes with prickly leaves. Way too many fallen branches and rocks sticking up from the ground had her stumbling many times over. Without Angus, she'd have done a face plant more than once.

"Stop," she gasped when the exertion finally got to her. She could swear a three-hundred-pound man was sitting on her chest. This was totally messed up.

Angus stopped and helped her sit on a fallen tree. "Are you all right?" His expression made her think he was afraid she was about to have the big one. She had to believe she looked awful.

She'd make some witty remark but was too busy gasping for air. He didn't look as though he was even breathing hard. In fact, he looked downright hot. She loved him, but right now she kinda hated him too.

Finally she took in a deep breath and let it out slowly. "I am now."

He laid his palm against her cheek. "You should think about trail running. You're not too bad at it." Apparently he didn't think she was ready to have the big one. Her moment of hating him was fading away.

"Are you kidding me? That just about killed me. This ass was not made for leaping over fallen trees and skipping over rocks."

"Oh, darlin', I hate to break it to you, but you were pretty impressive. And that arse is most fine. You don't give yourself enough credit."

Okay, hating him was totally out. This man was a keeper. She was not under any delusions about herself. She was no striking beauty, and her figure, at best, would be defined as curvy. Even so, he had a way of making her feel as though she was the most beautiful woman he'd ever seen. He might be lying, but she'd take it.

"You're just trying to get lucky." She gave him a small smile. Her breathing was evening out, but despite her taunting words, sex was most definitely off the table.

He leaned down and kissed her. It wasn't a sweet peck. The passion of it rocked her and once more robbed her breath. "I'm already lucky," he said against her lips. "And don't you ever doubt it."

She wasn't sure she could make him that promise, but her resistance was fading. When she got her breath back, she glanced around. "What happened to Molly and Aquene?"

Angus looked in the direction they'd come from and frowned. "I don't get it. I thought they were right behind us."

"I don't hear anything." It had struck her how quiet their surroundings were once her labored breathing had calmed enough to hear something besides her own gasps. But there was nothing to hear. If Molly and Aquene were, indeed, running behind them, they should be able to catch the sounds of their feet against the earth and the snaps of fallen branches. Lord knows they'd made enough noise as they'd dashed across the unfamiliar ground. Well, if she was being honest, she'd made all the noise.

His frown deepened. "Neither do I."

Fear began a slow creep up her spine. Being with Angus always made her feel safe, and she still felt that way now…sort of. The thought of being separated from Molly filled her with an icy chill. Whatever was going on was so outside normal that it defied any kind of understanding. She wanted, no, needed, for the three of them to stay together.

She tilted her head up and looked at Angus. "We have to find her." She didn't know if he'd get it. Angus had always said he liked Molly, and she believed him. It was just that he might not truly understand the close bond the two women shared and why it was critical that she find Molly now.

Her fears were unfounded. He nodded as he agreed. "We do."

Tears pooled in her eyes, and she silently berated herself for being weak. This was not the time to be soft. She couldn't help it. Her worries about being separated from Molly were strong and soul-shaking. "How do we do that?"

Angus sat next to her on the tree and took her hands. He was warm and solid, and reassuring. "We'll go back the way we came and see if we can pick up their tracks."

She protested. "We're not trackers." She was sure she'd fail miserably at even trying to make out a track. Lord, she'd barely made their run intact.

"Oh, but I must argue that fine point, my dear. I am a trained tracker."

She turned and stared at him. "What? No way." How could she not know something like that?

His smile was a little wry. "All right, trained tracker might be stretching it a wee bit, but a few years back, I was a cameraman on that series where they dropped people in the wilderness and gave them seven days to find their way back to civilization. I learned a ton following those folks about."

She actually remembered the show, though his time as a cameraman on it had occurred before they became a couple. "I didn't know you worked on that one."

He shrugged. "It was my last gig before I went into business for myself. Decided it was time to settle down and give stability a shot." He kissed the side of her head. "Quite glad I did too."

Couldn't argue the point because she was glad he'd decided to choose Spokane when he could have gone anywhere. But how could his revelation regarding the show be helpful? "Those people didn't track anybody." From what she remembered, it was more about navigation and survival. Besides, he'd been following them, not trying to find anyone.

"True enough, but one guy on the second season specialized in man-tracking. He did search-and-rescue kind of stuff back where he lived, and after his episode we became friends. He actually gave me a wee bit of instruction, and it was fun. I still remember a few of the basics and am sure I can dig up enough of it to help us now."

Angus was full of surprises, and honestly, they gave her some hope. She kissed him on the cheek, which flooded her with warmth, and once again she thought of how much comfort his presence brought her. "Is there anything you can't do?"

His smile was broad and his eyes bright, even in the growing darkness. "No. I don't think there is."

"And so modest too."

"That I am."

Feeling more positive than she had since they'd found themselves in this altered reality, she stood. Even though she had no clue how they were going to do it, she held out her hand and said, "Come on, handsome. Let's put your so-called skills to work and go find Molly."

CHAPTER TEN

Power rolled off Molly, and Aquene was glad of it. Before their journey was done, they would need her wisdom and strength. The path they were to travel was troubled, and it would take all their strength combined to survive it. That they would was not certain.

Molly—how she liked the way her name felt on her tongue—was as fierce as she had seen in her visions. What she had not seen as clearly was how beautiful she had turned out to be in the flesh. Gazing upon her face now made the wings of butterflies flutter in her stomach. It was a new feeling for Aquene, and she wondered if this was how Alumpum felt when she was with Ouray. She thought that it was. Why she would feel the same thing when she looked upon a stranger was something only the Great Spirit could explain.

Aquene gazed up into the sky as she navigated between the trees. She was grateful for years of doing the same with her friends as they played. It made her swift and sure on her feet. Soon darkness would take hold, and she wanted to find a safe place to hide before the moon rose high above them. It was worrisome that the man and woman who had appeared with Molly had run into the woods without direction, for they could easily lose their way. At this moment she could not stop and use precious time to try to rejoin them. They would have to take care of themselves, for she must guide Molly to safety.

"We must go in this direction." Though she would like to stay closer to the water, Aquene had a strong sense that they must remain where they were assured of cover while still having a good view if others approached. The danger she had sensed back at the cabin had lessened somewhat as they put distance between them. But it was not gone. Their lives were still balanced between this world and the next. Safety was not a given.

Molly was following silently, her gaze moving, her body tense. Suddenly she stopped and spun in a circle. Her eyes searched and Aquene knew what she sought. "We have to find Winnie and Angus."

The panic in her voice made Aquene stop too. How well she understood, for if Alumpum were lost she would feel the same such anguish. She glanced back up at the sky and to where the sun had nearly fallen completely behind the mountains. The day would soon leave them.

"We will find them when the sun comes up."

"No." The one word was filled with fear that came from somewhere deep inside her. "We have to find them right now."

Aquene took hold of Molly's hand. In her heart she was certain the man and the woman were safe—for now. "We do not have time. Not now. Please. We must not stay here. It is not safe."

"We have to find the time," Molly insisted. "I'm not leaving my friends out here. If it's not safe for you and me, it's doubly dangerous for them."

Aquene shook her head, even though she understood the desire to protect friends. "I beg you to trust me. They will not come to harm on this night. When the sun comes up, we will look for them again and reunite. It shall be so. Of this you have my word."

In the rapidly dimming light she could see the sheen of tears that glistened in Molly's eyes. "I can't leave them." Her voice wavered.

Aquene had to make her understand. "You are not leaving them. You are but separated by distance for the rise and set of the moon." Molly's hand in hers trembled. It was as cold as if they stood in a winter wind. She wished she could bring her warmth and solace.

For a breath, Molly said nothing, and then she brought her gaze up to meet Aquene's. Tears were still glistening but did not fall down her cheeks. "You swear they will be okay tonight?"

"Okay?" Aquene did not know this word.

"That they will be safe? You're sure?" Her eyes didn't move from Aquene's.

She nodded, for this she understood. "I give you my word."

The trembling of Molly's hand seemed to lessen. "I will hold you to it."

"As you should." Aquene never gave her word lightly, and she did not do so now. If she did not believe the truth of what she said with her whole being, she would not promise it to be so. "We must go. Please."

She thought Molly might turn back, still trying to find her friends. Thankfully she did not. Instead, she told Aquene, "Lead the way."

Those three words were like sunshine on her face. Aquene had feared Molly might disappear into the night in search for her friends, and she could not have allowed that. Danger lurked hidden in the shadows, waiting for its turn to harm them.

For tonight Aquene felt it best to take shelter in the rocks. They would protect them from the cold air sure to come on the heels of the sunset, and they also would provide them a lookout spot in case the stranger was closer than she believed. She and Molly would need to be on alert as well for the snakes that also sought the warmth the stones provided. If one did not take good care, the bite of the snake would bring sickness and sometimes death.

"Here," she told Molly when they had climbed to a depression in a grouping of rocks big enough for the two of them to lie down. "This will protect us through the night."

Molly looked around in the dim light and, from the expression on her face, did not seem as sure of the spot as Aquene. It was a good place to take shelter, and Molly would understand once they settled in. It gave them protection from the wind and had an overhang that would cover them should the frequent rains come.

The air was cooling quickly, and for the first time Aquene took a close look at Molly's odd clothing. While she had never seen such garments before, it appeared they were keeping her warm. She was not shivering, which was good. On any other night Aquene would build a fire to chase away the cold. But not this night, for she feared the one who hunted them would be on the lookout for just such a signal. The flames would light the night, the smoke would rise, and the scent of burning wood would float across the air as if to beckon him to their den.

"I will prepare a place for us to sleep," she said as she dropped her deerskin bag on the ground. "Wait for me. I will return."

"I'm not waiting alone." Molly looked determined to follow Aquene.

"Please," she pleaded. "I ask you to trust me. Stay here, and I will be back very soon."

"I…"

"Please." This would be much faster if she did not have to keep watch on Molly.

Molly sighed and sank to the ground next to Aquene's bag. "Fine."

Aquene did not wait. She ran back to the trees with her knife in hand. It did not take her long to cut an armload of tree boughs and carry them back to their temporary camp. Soon she had them arranged on the ground into makeshift mats that would allow them to rest in a bit of comfort.

"Come," she said, and held her hand out. "These will keep you off the cold earth and give you a little softness. We will need our rest."

Molly had watched her work in silence as she had arranged the boughs. Now she studied the mats with an expression Aquene did not understand. Surely the woman had slept on a mat before this night.

"I'm not tired," Molly finally said, the book held close to her chest. She had not parted with it since the moment they had faced each other in the cabin, each holding one end of it. Her protective gestures toward it did not escape Aquene. It was the manner of a mother protecting her child.

"You must rest." How she could make her understand they must sleep so they would be ready for the coming battle was unknown to her. She had to just keep trying to earn her trust and persuade her that she only had their safety at the heart of her words.

Molly was shaking her head. "Seriously, I'm not tired."

Aquene did not feel weary either. "It is time for our bodies to rest if we are to travel tomorrow." Just as she told Molly she must rest, Aquene must as well. They were together in this, beginning to end.

"We have to find my friends tomorrow."

Aquene laid a hand on Molly's arm. She did not blame her for her determination. "We have much to do, and you will be reunited with them. Of that I am most certain. It is not to be tonight, for now we must sleep. When the sun rises, all will change. Our journey will begin, and we will find those who traveled with you."

Molly's eyes met hers, and Aquene could feel the emotion behind her gaze. Molly understood even as she resisted. And Aquene shared her feelings. Slumber would be hard to embrace if she did not know where Alumpum laid her head.

Slowly Molly sank to the makeshift bed and her shoulders relaxed. "Tomorrow?"

Aquene nodded. "Tomorrow."

Molly bounced a little on the mat, and a slight smile brightened her pale face. "You know, this isn't so bad."

Aquene had been well taught to make camp whenever and wherever it was necessary. All the women of her people were given the skills that allowed them to live off the land that had been their home for many generations. Her people had been here since the beginning of time, and she felt a kinship with the land, the air, and the trees every day. It filled her with pride and peace.

"No. It is not bad." She frowned, knowing that she had done well with the tree branches. If she had more trees to work with she could have made it better, but still, it was far better than the bare ground.

Molly laughed. "I didn't mean it was bad. I meant it's pretty comfortable, all things considered. You did a great job, Aquene."

Her words of praise brought a warmth to her cheeks she was unaccustomed to feeling. She liked it, or rather she liked Molly's words of admiration. "We will sleep well here, and then we can complete our journey."

"You keep talking about a journey. I don't have a clue what you're talking about. This whole thing is pretty crazy, if you ask me. We were out for a hike, I found this book, and here we are. Even given my family history, things like this don't happen to people like me. I've never heard of a single person in my family, or any other family, taking a little trip through time."

"Crazy?" It was the word she locked on. Aquene believed her understanding of the settlers' language was broad, yet Molly kept speaking words she did not know.

Molly made strange noises, waved her hands around, and rolled her eyes. "Crazy," she said.

The surprise of her actions made Aquene lean away. What was she doing? Suddenly she understood, and as she did, the memory of the young man who had one day walked into the river and let the water carry him away came to her. From the time he was a child he had been like no other. He often screamed at nothing, would crouch behind the rocks and talk as though someone was with him, and once he jumped from the cliffs when he had no reason to flee. After that day, he had never walked the same again. She believed he was this crazy that Molly spoke of.

What was not as clear was why she used it to describe what was happening between them now. No, she did not believe any of it was crazy. They were embarking on something important, and moving through time did not worry her as it seemed to do for Molly. All things were possible. "I have seen you in visions, and I knew you would come."

Molly inclined her head. "You got one on me if you knew I'd take a trip back a couple hundred years. It was pretty much news to me."

That detail she had not seen in her dreams and visions. Since the first vision, she had known she would come and they would take this journey together. That the one she waited for did not exist in her own time was as much a surprise to her as it was to Molly. She had believed she would come from the east, as all the others had. That she came through the shadows from another time was unexpected. "No. I did not know where you would come from, only that you would appear."

"To do what?" Molly was still studying her face. "I still gotta say, none of this makes much sense to me."

"To save my people." It was so simple to Aquene. She did not know why it was so difficult for Molly to see.

Molly was shaking her head "You're wrong about that, sister. You can make that declaration as many times as you want, and it won't change a thing. I'm a baker, so unless you need me to bake you a cake, you've got the wrong girl. I'm not a caped superhero. Oh, sorry. You probably don't have superheroes, so just suffice it to say I'm a baker, not the savior of people."

"You cook?"

Molly frowned a little. "No. I'm a baker. Oh, I can cook all right, but I leave the chef stuff to Winnie. I like to create art with my baked goods"

This time it was Aquene who shook her head. All she really gleaned from what Molly tried to explain was that she worked with food. The difference between cooking and baking was of little importance. What was important was Molly's presence here. "You may well be, as you say, a baker, but you are much more, and you will save my people."

❖

The instant Matthew stepped foot inside the cabin, the difference hit him full in the face. The air had an emptiness that had not been here before. It told him everything he needed to know in a second. The grimoire was gone. The fury that surged through him at the realization was red hot. That he had been foolish enough to leave here without fully searching the cabin for her grimoire was unforgiveable.

Yet the failure was not his fault, for it was the men who assisted him who had carried the night, and it was those men who prevented him from completing his task in a thorough manner. They had been full of joy at their success in destroying the witch before she had time to cause harm in this beautiful land. Man's land. She had brought her wicked ways into this glorious wilderness, believing that she would hone her craft at the throats of honest men. She had been wrong. For over a year he had tracked her, knowing that he would one day catch her, just as he had done with every other evil soul throughout the years, including many from her own family. His prey always put great effort into eluding him. Each and every one of them underestimated his skill. By the time he was a mere year into his first career, he had become a great master. Now he had no equal, not in this life or in any that came before. No other hunter had ever matched him in skill, and each of the hunted failed in their attempts to outwit him. The same was true for the one who called this pitiful cabin home, as she had learned on the night he put the rope around her neck and stoked the fire at her feet.

But here, though he had stopped the witch he had hunted for those long months, the tragedy created by his workmen's joy had given another the chance to find the book. It was dangerous in ways he dared not think about. If it were to fall into the hands of one with even a touch of the evil that had lived within the burned witch... That was something he could not allow to happen. Letting those buffoons who had accompanied him prevent him from doing his job was criminal. They were to blame for what had happened here now. If they were still with him, like the witch, they too would pay with their lives.

As he stepped farther into the cabin, frustration accompanied him. The darkness falling outside was deeper in here. His eyes adjusted, and he could make out the fireplace, which still held the embers of a glowing fire. He was not surprised someone had been here, for it was the lone shelter for miles. When the rain fell, the coolness it brought with it could chill a man down to his bones. After walking over to the fireplace, he put several small pieces of wood on the embers, feeling satisfied when they caught. It served to bring a bit of light into the dull room. That was when he noticed the missing floorboard. He walked over to it, knowing full well what he would find even without looking.

But he did look anyway. He stared down at the darkness inside the hole revealed by the missing floorboard. Fury returned and rolled through him again like the waves of the ocean that had carried him across the waters to this new land. This time, he did more than just let it rush through his body. This time he picked up a stool that sat next to his feet and hurled it at the wall. It struck with a resounding crash, breaking into several pieces that flew in different directions. The destruction gave him only a touch of satisfaction. Next, he grabbed the edge of the lone table. He pulled up on it and pushed with all his might. It turned easily on its side, tipping onto the floor with an even louder and more gratifying boom. Now he felt better.

His hands clenched at his sides, his breath coming hard, he stood and stilled with his eyes closed. It was important to control himself, for that was what a great hunter did. Such men did not ever, under difficult circumstances, let their emotions show. In this isolated place, he had allowed himself this one moment of indulgence. Only a moment, and then he gained control once more. When calm and rational thought returned, he understood what he must do next. The solution was simple. He had to find the grimoire. Truly, it was that simple.

He walked to the fireplace and held his hands over the small fire, pressed his lips together in a hard line, and straightened. More than a feeling of warmth crept over him. At first he had believed a random traveler had built a fire here, but now he knew that was not the case. God was showing him the truth and the way. *She* had been here to build this fire and take the book from beneath the floor. His certainty that it was a she was absolute, and now he knew what he hunted. She was no different from the others, for he knew their smell, their secrets, and their tricks.

Striding out the door, he breathed in the still-lingering scent from the burned tree, and it turned up the corners of his mouth in a smile that chased away his melancholy. Things would be fine. He would fix this, as he did everything. He paused long enough to study the outline of the tree. It was still sufficiently sturdy to handle the burning of yet another evil soul. Yes, it would be the right thing to do, and to do it here would be perfect.

Clouds once more began to gather high above his head, helping the darkness take full purchase. Wind kicked up pine needles and fallen leaves, sending them to dance without music. The trees began to sway as if they were trying to keep time. A storm was again beginning to collect strength, or perhaps his heavenly father was giving him a sign that he was on the proper path but needed to be on his way. He smiled more brightly, and peace flowed over him.

He would be on his way soon, following her trail and bringing justice to bear. First, he put his hands together, lowered his head, and began to silently pray. When he was done, he looked toward the tree and nodded. All was right with his world, for he was confident he knew exactly where to go.

Chapter Eleven

The first raindrop hit Molly right smack in the middle of the forehead as she lay back against the pine boughs, staring at the sky and contemplating Aquene's declaration that she'd been hurtled back in time to save Native Americans. "Oh, no," she said as she wiped away the moisture and sat up. When she did, she pulled the grimoire close in a protective embrace. She didn't want it to get wet if rain really was on its way. The slight overhang of rock that they'd set up camp beneath wasn't nearly wide enough to protect them from rain.

Aquene jumped up and began to gather the tree boughs that made up their mats. "We must hurry. A storm is on the way, and it comes like an eagle chasing prey."

"Hurry where?" Molly looked around and couldn't see any place that would afford them any better cover than they had right here. Not that she could see much in the darkness. She did know they were actually a fair distance away from a refuge with enough trees to protect them from the rain. All they had were the boughs Aquene had gathered and brought back for their beds. At least her jacket was rain-resistant, so it would keep her dry for a while. Too bad she hadn't opened her wallet a little wider and bought the rain-proof jacket. Live and learn, she guessed. Then again, how exactly was she to anticipate finding herself here?

"We will stay here."

"And do what?"

"Use what we have," Aquene explained to her as she began to arrange the boughs in a different configuration. "We have all that is needed to keep our bodies dry." Was there anything this woman couldn't figure out? Molly was amazed at how fast and efficiently Aquene was able to take the makeshift bedding and turn it into a decent overhead shelter, albeit a tight one. Before the rain had a chance to gather strength, they huddled together beneath a canopy of branches. Definitely the person she would want to take with her on a backwoods expedition.

By all rights she should be terribly uncomfortable sitting here on the cold ground, leaning against a woman she didn't know, and not just hundreds of miles from home but hundreds of years away from home as well. Holding the grimoire and with her knees pressed to her chest, oddly, Molly felt exactly the opposite: snug and comfortable, warm and almost relaxed. The air was clear and clean, and their tiny home away from home, cozy.

Now what was that about? How could she possibly be this relaxed? In this insane situation she found herself in? She must be losing it, but that wasn't anywhere she wanted to go. She had to buck up and figure out how to get back home. She wasn't anyone's savior. She couldn't even save herself from that stupid fire that had set this whole bizarre situation into motion. If that fire hadn't shut her down, she'd be back home baking away and not worrying about being a witch or needing her powers to finally manifest so she could return to her own time and place.

Though the rain was beginning to fall in earnest and the sky was filled with clouds, overhead the moon still managed to cast a milky glow. Even the clouds and rain couldn't shut it down entirely. Under different circumstances, this moment would be romantic. Figures it would be here: wrong time, wrong place. She almost sighed out loud. Instead, she leaned back against the rock, keeping her shoulder firmly against Aquene's. Maybe she could shift the other way and give Aquene a bit of space. She didn't want to. Closing her eyes, she willed herself to rest. If she was able to go to sleep, she'd be surprised.

It was hard to judge the passage of time. She just knew it was passing and she wasn't any closer to sleep. A thought occurred to her and she patted her pocket. Surprise, surprise. While her pack might not have made the journey to the wilds, her pocket flashlight did. At least something was going right. She pulled it out and twisted the end. A beam of light filled their little shelter with illumination. Not quite a floodlight, but it would do.

The sudden appearance of light seemed to shock Aquene, who bolted up. "No!"

The single word uttered with such fear shocked Molly. "What?"

"The light. He will see us."

Oh, she hadn't thought of that. Molly twisted the end again, and they were once more plunged into darkness.

"What kind of magic is that?" Aquene's question was filled with shock.

Molly smiled. "We call them flashlights and not as much magic as technology." She could almost imagine what it would be like to see something like this for the first time. It even seemed like magic to her right at the moment.

"Tech…"

This time she laughed. "I'm sorry. I keep forgetting a lot of this is brand-new to you. This—" She twisted the light on again, holding the beam low between them so that its illumination was confined to their small space. She moved the flashlight back and forth. "This is another thing that will come to pass many years from now. Everyone has them, and they're awfully handy."

Aquene gingerly touched a finger to the flashlight and drew her hand back quickly. "It is hard and cold, like the metal of the knives we trade for."

Molly supposed that would be surprising. If she was from this place, she guessed she'd expect it to feel warm like an oil lamp or a torch. It might be confusing to see light and feel the cool touch of metal. "It has a metal case, and inside are what we call batteries. They make the light. A wonderful thing, and tonight it's light and that's good."

"It is good. You have some very strange things that are wonderful." Aquene leaned back and relaxed. "I like your light."

Molly pressed herself close to the rocks before she played the beam across the grimoire. She didn't want to upset Aquene any more by brandishing the little sliver of light into the night. Aquene probably did have a point about it being seen by others. If any others were out there besides Winnie and Angus. Come to think of it, wouldn't it be a good thing if her friends were able to see the light? Probably, but no sense in tempting fate.

"I do too." What she didn't say was that the flashlight was a tiny connection to home and that gave her solace. The feeling of being out of sync was almost overwhelming, and something as little as the penlight gave her something to grab on to.

She had yet to open the thick leather cover so like many of the grimoires she'd seen through the years. The ones of the witches of her family that came before her. Each had one, and each shared the hard-won knowledge of time and experience. Her own was slim, at least right now, but she had hope that it would someday hold important knowledge.

"It is important to our journey." Aquene's words were very light on the night air as they broke into the web of thoughts and emotions weaving through her. It put Molly off a little that Aquene seemed to be able to draw her very thoughts from inside her head. But it also excited her a little. She'd never been that in tune with anyone before.

She nodded. "Yes, I think it is." Touching it brought them together. Perhaps reading it would show the way. Slowly she opened the cover, surprised that it began not as a typical grimoire but more like a journal. She trained the light on the page, making sure to keep it confined within their small shelter, and began to read.

August 28, 1836

Dearest granddaughter. I know not when you will come, only that you will, and this is for you. I must tell you my story so you will understand what you have to do. I left New York City many months ago, hoping to hide in the wilds of the West. So much land and so many places where I hoped to find peace. It seemed like the perfect place, and for a time it was. Alas, I fear my time here is coming to an end, for as he pursued our ancestors across Europe, he follows me in his unholy war against our family, against our kind. His darkness is a sickness that cannot be healed, and he seeks to destroy us all. He will not succeed, for I have made certain our family will survive even if I do not. He will never win.

Forgive me for what I do from here forward. Your journey will not be easy. Your path will be filled with danger and death. My book granted you passage here, and it will also take you home. Of that you have my promise, my precious child of my blood. The key will reveal itself when

the universe is ready to take you back to your time. Be brave, my granddaughter, and know that I am and always will be with you.
    Hannah

❖

"Did you see that?" Winnie crouched behind the grouping of trees, her eyes glued to the man who was mounting his horse.

"Yeah, a psycho out here in the Wild, Wild West. Who would've guessed?"

"Sarcasm becomes you. You know that, right?"

"I do what I can."

"I wonder what he did inside. There was so much crashing around, he had to have trashed it. You think he was looking for us?" The thought somehow made her fear level notch up a whole bunch. After seeing that guy, she had an awful feeling in the pit of her stomach. Something about him screamed bad. Here they were in the middle of nowhere, and they ran into a guy who wrapped himself tight in an inner-city, gang-banger vibe.

"That was a motherfucker if I've ever seen one. He just looked like an asshole, but to answer your question," he kissed the side of her head, "no, I'm certain he wasn't looking for us. No way the bloke could even know we're here."

Angus had a valid point. They were more interlopers than residents, and in some ways that gave them a measure of safety. No one would expect them. No one would be looking for them. She stood and glanced down at her cargo pants. On the other hand, if people did see them, they'd wonder what in the world they were. Women in this time did not traipse around the woods in pants like these. They most likely didn't even know what cargo pants were.

Oh, who cared right at the moment? It was getting dark, it was cold, and even though the storm had stopped for a while, it was back and starting to rain harder by the minute. No pack meant nothing to make a shelter out of, and these trees weren't all that thick, so their shelter capacity wasn't that great. They'd have better luck with the thick pines back home. Now those were forests.

They weren't home. They didn't have their forests for cover, and so the next best thing was to get inside that cabin again, get warm, and try to figure out how to find their way back to where they started. Yeah, it had been all fun and games until the crazy showed up. What she wouldn't give to be in the kitchen of one of her restaurants creating a beautiful dinner she could share with Angus by candlelight.

"Come." Angus held out his hand. "Let's get inside before we get soaked."

Winnie hesitated. Was the guy gone? Like really gone? The sound of his horse's hooves had faded away. All she could make out was the sound of their own breathing and the rain as it fell on the trees and the rocks. It was a pretty comforting sign that he'd left, and in her mind that was code for getting out of the rain.

She ran with Angus to the cabin and sighed when they were inside. The warmth of the fire that had earlier burned in the big fireplace still lingered in the air and felt like heaven. It was hard to see much, since no light shone in from outside and only a few embers glowed in the fireplace. At the same time the storm had rolled in, night had fallen like a curtain dropping on the first act of a play. She wasn't accustomed to this kind of darkness. No lights from a nearby city glowed in the distance. No switch inside the door turned on an overhead. No, it was deep and dark and very strange. She changed her mind. She still wanted to be in her kitchen whipping up a world-class dinner for Angus, but there'd be no candlelight. No, indeed, they would be eating by the light of a bright, overhead, electric fixture.

Ever dependable, Angus made sure she didn't dissolve into a puddle of panic. The headlamp he pulled from his pocket shone like a beacon in the dark room. She couldn't help but smile. It amazed her how something so minor could mean so much. The light enabled them to survey the room, which was not as they had left it. The remains of a broken stool lay on the floor near one wall, while the table rested on its side in the center. They walked around the wreckage to the fireplace.

Warmth still emanated from it, and she loved the feeling. Angus kneeled and began to assemble a complicated web of kindling and small logs to reignite the fire. It worked, and soon he had a blaze going that chased away the chill that had been her companion for at least the last hour. As wonderful as it was, they didn't have enough wood inside to keep the small fire ablaze for long. That was disappointing. She'd like nothing better than a blazing fire all night to keep the shadows at bay.

"What now?" Winnie held her hands in front of the blaze, appreciating the warmth and trying not to let the panic take hold again.

He hugged her as if sensing her mood. "Not to worry. We'll keep this going. I'll find us more wood."

She didn't feel her normal optimism at his plan. "It's dark and raining. Not to mention there really isn't much of a forest out there to even find wood." Fear wrapped around her heart.

"Not to worry. I'll find enough to keep us warm."

She doubted it. "I'll go with you."

"No," he snapped. It was the first time she'd ever heard that tone in his voice. "I don't want you out there. I can find it easier by myself."

"I don't want you out there alone." It wasn't like she could do much. She just didn't want to be alone. Didn't want Angus out there alone. She'd silently hoped that just as they'd circled back to the cabin after their race away earlier, Molly and Aquene would have done the same thing. When they didn't emerge from the trees, she'd been disappointed.

A tiny smile curved up the corner of his mouth. "Aye, but I'm a tough Irishman, my love. We've been dealing with the creatures of the night for more centuries than you can imagine. I'll be fine, and I'll bring back wood for my woman. I'll find enough to keep us cozy."

"I'm scared, Angus." She hated the way her voice quivered. Being weak was new to her. She ran several successful restaurants and was the go-to woman in all of them. Handling a crisis was nothing new for her, yet the idea of being alone in this cabin without Angus terrified her.

He put his arms around her and pulled her close. "I'll be back before you know it, and we'll be safe and warm here. I promise. Trust me."

She nodded and managed not to cry. There was no one in the world she trusted more. Besides, maybe Molly and Aquene would show up while he was gone. "Okay."

Angus kissed her cheek. "Soon enough, love. We'll be sitting together by the fire very soon."

After he walked out the door, the fire no longer gave her any warmth. The light it provided didn't provide her comfort. With her knees pressed to her chest and her arms wrapped around her legs, she tried and failed to ignore the darkness that crept near, like a predator closing in for the kill. The wind blew outside and the rain continued to fall. The door didn't open. No Angus. No Molly. No Aquene. She'd never felt so alone.

She continued to stare at the fire, stirring it every so often with a stick and wondering if each sound she heard was Angus returning with an armload of wood. A shadow fell across her small circle of light, and her heart leapt even as she was certain she'd not heard the door open. Thank God, he was back. Breathing a huge sigh of relief, she stood and turned toward the door, smiling.

Her smile faded. It wasn't Molly or Aquene. It wasn't Angus either.

CHAPTER TWELVE

Aquene found the feeling of Molly's body next to hers nice. Despite the companionship, the trouble she sensed on the wind did not lessen. They were at the beginning of what she recognized would be a dangerous journey, yet she felt comfort and almost joy.

Though she understood that the happiness her friends enjoyed in the unions they had with their warriors was something they also wished for her, what they did not understand was that her life was happy enough. She was powerful and learned. She was respected. Most importantly, she was gifted with the visions revered by all. Her place with her people was solid without the need to join with a man. She had spent her life trying to make them understand this.

Despite the serenity she found in her world, at times she allowed the loneliness to touch her heart. She longed for the same closeness of her friends, to believe that she too might share her life with another. Not a warrior who could give her children and work by her side as they moved across their lands. No, she wished for the touch of another...like the one who sat next to her now.

Exactly like the one who sat next to her now.

Perhaps it was another test, and Molly had been sent to her now to see if she had the strength of will to set aside her longing and focus on the journey. She did, and she would show her determination to the universe so that there would be no doubt. She must move her thoughts away from the sweet feel of Molly's closeness and to the words she read from the book. She must focus on the battle ahead of them and what they would need to do to be victorious.

"What do her words mean?" She understood the coming of people like Hannah. Slowly they appeared, traveling through the lands that had sustained her people for more generations than she could count. She would like to believe they would all pass through to other places, but she knew better. They built their outposts, their forts. They brought their English, their unsuitable clothing. They prayed to their strange God. As Hannah had lived in the cabin up from the river, so too would others come. Their world was changing day by day, year by year.

Molly was running her fingers over the page she had just read in the same way Aquene would do as she smoothed Tilla's mane. There was care in her touch, as though it was more than a book. "I don't know what it all means, but it does seem clear enough that she's the one who brought us here. We have to figure out why."

"She could not be the one who brought you here, for the men killed her." Besides, Aquene felt certain something far more powerful had brought them together.

"How do you know?" Molly's eyes met hers.

Sadness filled Aquene as she remembered. Through her life she had witnessed cruelty and violence, and she understood the lengths men could go to in order to destroy another. Tears pricked at the back of her eyes as she thought about the particular cruelty visited upon a woman who never harmed another.

She and Tilla had ridden by the lonely cabin where the woman lived one sunny day, and, unlikely as it might have been, they had become friends. Many times they sat near the river and learned from each other. She had often wished that those who came could all be like Hannah. Not knowing it would be the last time she and Tilla would journey to the cabin to visit her friend, she had been filled with happiness as they had ridden into the clearing. Great shock and despair had washed over her as Aquene came upon the blackened body of her friend lying on the ground. Hannah had been left there lifeless and nearly unrecognizable. Why would someone do this to a woman who did no harm? She respected the land and the people who lived on it. Unlike so many others, she carried peace and harmony in her heart.

Her body told another story. The rage that took her life had still lingered in the air around her, in the smell of the fire that had charred her skin, and in the insult to the tree used as a tool in her destruction. Someone had stolen her life and offended all that was good and right.

The men, and there was no doubt in her heart the travesty was done by men, who had done that to her cared not for her passage beyond this world. They had left her body for the scavengers that would have come to ravage had Aquene not gotten there first. Their disrespect hurt Aquene's spirit. Even now, she could walk to the spot where she had buried Hannah. It had been the only thing she had been able to do in order to restore what she could of her honor.

She did not know how to explain to Molly the knowledge she possessed. Many did not believe in the grant of sight bestowed upon her. While her own people knew of her gifts, she shared her truth with those who came to her lands only when she was certain they could be trusted to believe. Hannah was the first one. Would Molly be the second?

In the darkness, she smiled. Here she sat next to a woman who came from many years hence, and all she wanted to do was share her whole life with her—all that she was and all that she wished to be, including her secrets. If any was to believe her, surely this one person would do so. "I am the one who gave her what dignity I could restore after they took her life. I put her in her final resting place and said a prayer to help her as she made her way to the beyond."

"She was murdered." The words Molly spoke did not appear to be for her, and so she said nothing. Instead, she simply waited until Molly said, "They knew she was a witch, and so they took her life. Bastards."

Before she lost her life, Hannah had warned her of the man who was like a dark shadow at her back. Aquene did not truly understand his threat until the day she found Hannah's body. Only then did she know of the depths of his evil and his terror of those who had been blessed as Hannah had been. A bad feeling flowed through her each time she remembered, for she, of all people, should have taken heed of Hannah's warnings. "He believed she brought harm to them, and he made others believe as he did."

"Why?"

"You understand why. You do not need me to tell you."

Aquene's visions had been clear about Molly's coming to keep her people safe, even if they had not explained how it was to happen. What she had not seen but understood now was the connection between Hannah and the woman of her visions. The ties that bound them were deep, and Aquene sensed they were important. Only time would show them how, and she was willing to wait until it was time for her to know.

"Because I am like her."

"Yes."

She could feel the resistance in Molly despite her words. Again, Aquene waited. There were times when a woman had to make peace with destiny in her own way and her own time. Better than most, Aquene understood that fact. If Molly did not yet possess that knowledge, she would soon.

Molly switched off the small light, and it plunged them once again into complete darkness. Aquene could no longer see her face, though she could feel the way Molly's body grew soft. She was no longer fighting against the truth. "I am," she admitted softly. "I am like her. They call us hereditary witches because our families go back for hundreds of years. We have had magic in our souls for centuries."

"They hunt you. It matters not where you go in the world. Peace is never yours." That was the truth Hannah had shared with her. Aquene had not truly understood what that meant until the night she returned Hannah's burned body to the earth. Her people revered those with the powers of sight. Not so with those who were now invading her lands. They dreaded what they could not see or understand. How soon, she wondered, would it be before a dark rider came for her?

"Not me so much. Not anymore anyway. My ancestors were tracked down and destroyed for many, many years. I'm surprised any of my family line survived the so-called flames of the righteous. I'm living proof that at least a few of us survived being burned at the stake."

"Burned?" Aquene had believed only Hannah had suffered such a fate. To hear that many had been destroyed in the same way made her sad.

Beside her she could feel Molly nod. "Burned. Alive."

❖

Matthew tried hard not to let the rage overtake his good sense. As the hours passed he had an unsettling feeling he had taken the wrong path, and instead of getting closer to her, he was putting more and more distance between them. He should have started earlier so that he could have tracked her better during daylight. This was when he appreciated the rough men that called this wilderness home. They would have put him on the right path.

Between the darkness and the rain, he had no choice but to stop for the night. If the disgusting man had not delayed his travels earlier, he would have arrived at the cabin much earlier, and he might very well have met her face-to-face. Instead, the one who had what he needed had quite simply had enough time to get too far ahead of him. He would not be able to close the distance this night.

It was not right. He had killed the witch, and it should have been finished when her charred body dropped to the earth. Despite all his fine work, there were times when more was needed. This was one of those times. The good Lord had shown him the way and assured him that vengeance was still his. All he had to do was be patient. He needed time, and rest. As frustrated as he was, he must follow the path he was being shown. God did not make mistakes, though it felt like he tested Matthew daily. It was fine. He would pass each and every one.

Sitting astride his horse, he studied the dark hills looming in the night. This weather was not the best in which to navigate in the dark. Surely the one who held his prize would also be forced to stop and camp, and that gave him an idea. He nudged his horse, and they began to climb the nearest hill, the darkness forcing them to move very slowly. He did not want to risk injury to himself or his horse. He believed the ones he pursued were on foot, and his horse gave him an advantage.

When they reached the ridgeline, he straightened and swept his gaze across the scenery below, or as much as he could see given the lack of daylight. In theory, this was what he hoped for, a broad view of the land below. His instinct to come here had been exactly right. Except for one small detail, it did not provide him with what he needed. He threw his head back and howled. Just as he was being forced to do, they would have to stop and make camp, and his vantage point should have been a perfect place to spot them. The rain made the night cool, and that meant a necessity to build a fire, giving him a glowing beacon to follow. Below him spread out nothing but darkness. No flames, no flickering lights, no campfires. How could that be? Where was the damn fire?

The thief had nowhere else to go. The witch's cabin was the only shelter for many miles, as she had chosen her solitude well. Not skillfully enough to hide from him, but none could hide from him.

Except for this one. Or two. He was not certain how many he hunted at the moment. Not that it mattered. One or twenty, he had faced it all before and come out victorious. Only one was a witch, and his sights were on her. The friends who might accompany her, well, it would be their bad luck, for those who befriended evil were just as guilty as she, even if they knew not what she was. Witches were very skilled at hiding their true nature from everyone except him.

For a while longer he sat on his horse and scanned the land fanning out below, hoping a light would appear and guide him to his prey. As the time passed and the night grew deeper and darker, it became increasingly clear that he would have to wait. His prey was either very smart or very lucky. He was hoping for the latter. Luck ultimately failed.

Dismounting, he loosened his saddle and took it from the horse's back. It was not necessary to tie him up, for the animal was true and loyal despite his own dislike of him. He would wander in search of fresh grass to eat, but he would not leave Matthew. His bedroll was tied to the back of his saddle. Once he had untied it, he spread it out inside a depression in the rocks and lay back against the hard earth. The thin blanket provided some warmth against the cool air, though very little in the way of softness against the rocky ground or protection from the rain that still fell upon him despite the bit of cover from the rocks.

This was not his idea of relaxation, not at all, and as was often the case, he resented this part of his job. It was necessary and he would endure it. It did not mean he had to like it. After all he had done for the world, he deserved better not part of the time. All of the time. Soft beds and soft women. Good food and fine wine.

Soon enough he would be done here and, in a few weeks, would be back in the civilized world, where he could indulge in the pleasures he was due. His mind drifted to the magnificent Astor House, its comfortable rooms and delicious meals. As soon as his business was done in this no-man's-land, he would go directly to New York City and to the front desk of the lovely new hotel. He smiled as he thought about the additional comforts nearby, everything he needed and desired within blocks of Broadway and Vesey.

With that warm, uplifting thought, he closed his eyes and settled into a dreamless sleep.

CHAPTER THIRTEEN

The letter to Hannah's granddaughter intrigued Molly. What had it all meant? How long had it had been beneath the floorboards? Had the granddaughter ever even seen it? Given the apparent newness of the book, she suspected not. It was an intriguing mystery.

Aquene was right when she said that Molly and Hannah were alike. They were. That then led her to a different line of thought. Perhaps they shouldn't have taken the grimoire with them. If the person it was intended for came looking, it wouldn't be there. Earlier she'd felt like it was Hannah's magic that had brought them here and that the book would take them home. Now she was having second thoughts. She was thinking more about the granddaughter.

Molly would be devastated if her ancestor left something like that for her and someone picked it up and took off with it. Even though she'd read only the first few pages, whatever was between the covers was vitally important for the unnamed granddaughter. Bottom line: they had to get it back to the cabin. She refused to be the one to upset history. She'd read about the theories on disrupting time continuums. Who knew if any of it was true? She didn't plan to be the one to find out. Aquene might or might not agree with her, given she seemed to have a pretty set agenda. Rigid agenda or not, Molly's mind was made up. When daylight made its appearance, they would return it to the cabin and put it right back where they found it.

She put a hand on Aquene's arm. "We have to take this back." She felt her stiffen.

"No. We cannot return."

"We have to. It's important."

"There is too much danger in that place. It is not safe for us to be there."

She got it, and honestly she felt as though a spiderweb stretched across the place just waiting to catch them. At the same time, she knew that they had to do this. "I know, and we'll need to be careful, but it doesn't change anything. This has to go back." She patted the grimoire.

"I do not like this."

Molly squeezed her arm gently. "It's not my first choice either."

"You are sure?"

"I'm sure." She could feel Aquene's shoulders slump and knew she would go with her in the morning.

To decide something gave her a feeling of being back in control, at least a little bit. She relaxed and let her gaze drop to the book. Since they wouldn't be able to return it tonight, what the hell? She might as well read it through first. The odds of her falling asleep out here were pretty slim, and she figured she could finish it by the time the sun came up again. Besides, what could it hurt if she read it as long as she put it back where she found it tomorrow? No harm, no foul.

Shifting, she put the book in her lap and opened the cover.

"I have to read this," she told Aquene as she pulled her flashlight back out of her pocket.

"Can you read it all with your magic light?"

Molly smiled at the amazement in Aquene's voice. She wondered how she'd see things if, instead of going back in time, they'd been propelled forward a few hundred years. If technology advanced as much in that time as it had since the early 1900s, it would be a world she'd find as astonishing as Aquene found her small flashlight.

"I think we need to."

"Her words contain much truth."

Probably, and if nothing else, the book would give Molly some perspective. It would be hard to put it in context, not being all that familiar with the time or Hannah's family. Some things, however, were timeless, and that's what she was looking for. "Perhaps for the person this is meant for, though I'm not tracking where she's going with her diary-type entries. It's unusual for a grimoire to have letters included. I'm curious what passage the book secures for her granddaughter. A ship? Except if the granddaughter is coming to the cabin, we're inland a fair distance for it to be a ship. A wagon perhaps. Or I guess it could be a barge on the river."

Aquene was shaking her head. "I do not believe that is the passage she speaks of."

"It would have to be. How else could this mysterious granddaughter show up out here? I'm thinking a group of travelers in wagons would be the most logical, though she might have to make the last bit of the journey on horseback." History hadn't been her best subject, and she was searching for the tidbits she could remember about the area.

Aquene studied her face. "I believe you must read what she has written, for only then will we understand all that she writes of."

Molly didn't know what there was to understand. Well, that wasn't exactly true. Despite those second thoughts, she still sensed that the book somehow had a hand in their arrival here, even if it was written for someone else. After all, they'd both touched it at the same time and ended up together. So Aquene wasn't wrong in saying they needed to read it through to figure it out. It had brought them here, and hopefully it would take them home. This was a beautiful place in Molly's century, and it was even more so in this one, but still, she wanted to go back. She had a bakery to get up and running again, and a dog to find. She had to hope that, just as Hannah promised her granddaughter passage, she too would find it for her and her friends.

"Agreed. Let's see what else she can tell us." She twisted the light on and turned the beam of the light to the pages of the grimoire, careful to make certain the illumination stayed inside their tiny shelter. A thread of excitement trilled through her as her fingers touched the pages. She had grown up with magic, even if she hadn't been the enthusiastic student her mother hoped for. Truthfully, she'd been less than thrilled about having to train. She'd spent her whole life constantly barraged by her *duty*, and frankly, she resented it. All she really wanted was to be like her friends, a regular girl. What was so important about being a hereditary witch anyway? She'd often thought the craft was an art no longer needed in the world. Science and progress had made it obsolete, so what was the point?

Of course, she kept her opinions to herself. She loved her family and wasn't willing to purposely hurt her mother and grandmother or any other of the women of her blood. Their heritage was incredibly important to them, even if she believed it good history and was more than content to leave it at that. In the interest of family harmony, she tried to be a student of the craft and thus keep everyone happy. The fact that she still hadn't come into her full powers was further proof, in her mind, that she wasn't really witch material.

Her heart lay in the kitchen. The true magic she was able to create was her food. As much as she failed to understand her mother's embrace of the craft, her mother still struggled with Molly's decision to be a baker. Time and time again they'd argued over what her mother saw as Molly's destiny. She just couldn't understand that, for Molly, genuine happiness was in every cake she baked, every muffin she created, and every cookie she handed to a child at her counter. Most were healers through and through. Doctors, nurses, therapists. They all looked at her as if she'd lost her mind when she'd announced she planned to go to culinary school. In short, her family simply didn't get her.

And if she was being honest, she didn't really get her family. Not that she tried very hard, and that was on her.

Now, however, she called upon the lessons of her mother and opened her mind. Time and time again, Mom had admonished her to stop thinking so hard and simply be. If she'd rolled her eyes at that suggestion a hundred times, that was probably a low estimate. Funny how things change when seen in a different perspective. She liked to make sense of things, to put them in order, like perfecting the best cake recipe possible and lining up a perfect row of cupcakes in the display case. Order made her happy. This grimoire was important, if not to her, then at the very least to the granddaughter Hannah wrote it for. She wouldn't analyze it or try to read between the lines. She wouldn't try to make it fit into what she perceived as the perfect grimoire. She slid her fingers across the page with the old-fashioned script handwriting. "Tell me your secrets, Hannah. Tell me how to get home."

"Hello…" What else should she say to someone who appeared out of the air in the doorway? After all, they were in the middle of nowhere. She'd hoped Molly and Aquene would find their way back here, but no. It wasn't them. By all rights, Angus should have been standing there looking at her. Not Angus by any stretch of the imagination. At least it wasn't the frightening guy who rode out on his horse.

That guy was definitely a scary bastard, and she didn't want to find herself alone with him. Come to think of it, she didn't want to face him even with Angus here. Something about him, even from a distance away, gave her the full-on creeps. It was beginning to dawn on her that she wasn't a frontierswoman out to settle the new world. Nope, she was just an ordinary city girl who loved civilization and all its comforts.

"You must find her."

Hmm, no hello? No saying my name is Jane Doe? Just "You must find her?" Nothing too weird about that, lady. Then again, everything that was happening right now was weird, so why not the woman standing the doorway? No sense changing things up now. This little time shift they found themselves in was consistent if nothing else.

Thin, almost anorexic thin, with long, black hair and dark, haunting eyes, the woman who stood in the open doorway struck Winnie as somehow familiar, though, for the life of her, she didn't know why. Her threadbare dress and dirt-streaked face were from another era, this one where Winnie knew she personally didn't belong, though the woman speaking to her obviously did. Not surprising there either. She wasn't really expecting any additional time travelers to come waltzing through the door to say "Hey." On the other hand, it was hard to figure where she'd come from, given this wasn't exactly a suburban neighborhood. Maybe there was another cabin nearby but she sure hadn't seen it when they were stumbling about outside. Of course, she wasn't looking either, so what did she know?

Returning to the odd question, she asked, "Who must I find?" Let's narrow down the list of suspects.

"My granddaughter."

That declaration didn't narrow down a single thing. "Your granddaughter? Lady, I wouldn't know your granddaughter if she was sitting right next to me. I'm not exactly from around here, if you know what I mean."

She didn't blink and continued to stand rock still, her hands at her sides. The wind from outside caught her hair and blew it around her face. She didn't try to push it out of her eyes. "You know her well."

Not likely. What part of the I'm-not-from-around-here was she not getting? All she had to do was take one look at Winnie to drive home that point. "Look, I've never been here before and haven't met anyone from this place." Winnie waved her hands toward her body. "I would think my clothes would be a dead giveaway that I'm a stranger." In a strange land, she thought silently but didn't add.

"This I know well."

Rolling her eyes, Winnie repeated herself. "We don't seem to be making any ground, ma'am. I can't help you find your granddaughter. I can't even figure out how to get home, let alone track down some stranger."

"You must listen to me, for I do not have much time." She glanced over her shoulder as if looking for someone. "Soon I must leave, so listen carefully."

Winnie shrugged. "It appears I have all the time in the world." Given she didn't have the first clue how to get back home, all she could do was hang out here. All this woo-woo stuff sounded so much easier on TV. When it was happening, it was as confusing as all get-out, especially considering that the only one of them with any juju was MIA at the moment. If they'd ever needed Molly and her witchcraft, it was now. But no, was she here? Nope, she was off somewhere in the Wild, Wild West with a cute Native American woman, and who knew when or if she'd be back? Top it off with Angus out there stumbling around in the dark looking for wood, and things were most definitely messed up in her world.

"No," the woman said. "You do not have all the time in the world. He will be back, and he will kill you. I cannot help you if you do not listen."

"How do you know that?" She didn't need any clarification on what guy she was talking about. What had she or Angus done to him anyway? Sure, from the temper tantrum they'd seen him throw earlier, he was a brick short of a load, but that didn't mean he was the killing kind of crazy. Even as the thought flew through her head, she knew the woman was right. He actually was the killing kind of crazy. There was only one running around with the hit-man vibe, and he was it.

"You must trust me, for I know of what I speak."

Where was Angus? The longer Ms. Strange stood in the doorway prophesying doom and gloom, the more Winnie was buying in. Not in any detail, just in that pit-of-the-stomach, twitchy kind of way. That and something about this woman still bugged her. Maybe it was her eyes or the shape of her mouth. Maybe it was all in what she was saying. While Winnie couldn't pinpoint what it was, something tickled her subconscious, and damn it, she didn't like it. Things were so much easier in her time.

"I don't know what you want from me. Details, you gotta give me details if you want me to help."

"You must find her, and you must stop him. He is dangerous, and he cannot be allowed to continue. Too many years and too many lives. He is the devil."

Apparently, her request for details went right over the top of her head. Telling her somebody was dangerous and the devil didn't mean jack if she didn't tell her why she was supposed to be afraid. And what did she mean by too many years and too many lives? Since she wasn't giving her much, Winnie tried for something a little more basic. "Who is he?"

"You know." Her words were a whisper.

No, actually she didn't. She fielded a wild guess. "The guy?" She had to mean the man who trashed the cabin, because he was the only one besides Angus they'd even seen, and no way was she referring to Angus. This was going to be a really long conversation if she had to pull every single detail out of her.

Her nod was barely perceptible. "Find her, for she is the only one who can stop him."

"Your granddaughter?"

"Your friend."

Seriously, this was like talking to a room full of first-graders "Make up your mind. You want me to find Molly or your granddaughter?"

"They are the same."

"What?" Craziness had just cranked up to another level. "Not likely. Trust me, there's no way they can be the same person. My girl is way too young to be your granddaughter."

"It is true."

Winnie opened her mouth to explain to her in detail exactly how it could absolutely not be true, but she didn't have a chance: the woman was gone. Angus had walked through the door and through the woman.

Yeah, right through the woman, who vanished as if she'd never been there at all.

"You talkin' to yourself?" Angus dumped a load of wood at her feet.

CHAPTER FOURTEEN

Aquene loved the whispers in the air. They comforted her. All that she had seen and all that she knew was to come waited just beyond the voices of the night. The future did not frighten her. No, she felt a lightness that told her all was right and as it should be, despite the danger that lurked in the shadows.

It was much more difficult for Molly, for she had traveled a great distance only to be surprised by the journey that awaited her. Aquene was prepared. Molly was not.

That did not mean Molly was weak.

That she was moving forward with grace made Aquene's heart swell. She had awaited the coming of this woman with much anticipation, and when she appeared at last, she was much more than she had hoped. Her destiny was to be great.

"She speaks to us. Let us listen to her words."

"You want me to read more?"

Aquene nodded. She could read, write, and speak the language of the settlers very well. Though it had been hard, she had found herself in the company of the strangers that came from beyond from the time she was quite young. She had easily learned their language and their ways. Her knowledge became important as the years marched on and more and more invaded her homeland. It had also been difficult, for they had little respect for the ways of her people. While she had tried to learn their strange language and customs, they had tried to make her forget her own. She had not.

"Yes." The woman who wrote this book was not like the others. She respected Aquene, her family, and friends. Aquene had trusted her in life and still did. The book Molly cradled like a small child held only truth and wisdom.

Molly moved her hand so that the small magic light shone back on the words written on the pages. Aquene was quite taken by the tiny light and wished she had that kind of magic in her bag. Perhaps when it was time for Molly to go, she would gift Aquene with the treasure. It was a selfish wish that her mother would scold her for, but she still wanted to slip that light into her pouch. For the moment, she was grateful for the way it illuminated the words without the need to build a fire and thus give away the location of their small camp. She settled with her back against the rock and her shoulder touching Molly's. Listening to her was quite pleasing.

"Okay. Let's see what else Hannah has for us." She began to speak, her voice soft and melodious on the night air. It was more enjoyable than listening to Alumpum sing.

August 29, 1836

I have traveled a long and winding path to find this place. Upon my arrival at Fort Vancouver, the kind people there offered me safe haven within their walls, and Dr. John McLoughlin personally extended that invitation. I knew I could not stay, for he would find me far too easily. The good doctor with his strong faith would be swayed without difficulty if my truth was to come to light. Though he has a kind heart, he is no match for the hunter.

The peril of staying was too high, even if outside the walls of the fort many other dangers awaited me. I feared not the people of the land, for they would understand my heart if they had occasion to look past my skin. I felt certain we would find a way to join in the worship of our cultures and the praise of the spirits that make the world so wonderful.

And thus I left the safety of the walls of Fort Vancouver and the warm sustenance Dr. McLoughlin and his wife, Marguerite, shared with me. I ate their meal and drank their tea and then disappeared into the night. Not before I cast protection over them. I know they believe their God will protect them, but I know better. The hunter comes, and he brings hell with him. It will take all of their prayers and all the protection I can leave for them to repel his evil.

I traveled for many days, through forests, across vast grass fields, and along the river. In my heart I believed that I would find the place where I was destined to be, and my faith was rewarded. The cabin sat amongst the trees and far enough away from the water so as to provide it shelter from the casual look. Those who traveled this path moved as quickly as possible from trading post to trading post. They did not stop, as I must. It took work to finish what someone else had begun, but soon enough I had a home. For a little time I enjoyed peace.

My destiny will come to pass within these walls. I do not know the day, only that it is to be soon. My hours are dwindling, and thus I hurry and write down all that you must know, for it will be your destiny, my dearest granddaughter, to stop this madman.

My candle grows weak and my hand tires. I have many more words to share with you that will have to wait for the sun to rise once more. Only then will this story continue. The wind sings gently now, and the stars sparkle like thousands of candles. For what remains of this night I may rest in peace, for he has not yet found his way here. You too must sleep, sweet girl. Sleep, and gather the energy that you will soon need to draw upon.

Before I go, I leave you this. May it help to keep you safe as the universe unfolds for you.

The spell that followed the entry was interesting and detailed enough that Molly would be able to cast it, or so she told Aquene. She closed the book and put both of her hands on top of it. Her gaze was fixed somewhere in the darkness, and Aquene believed she was thinking over the words Hannah had written. She finally turned and looked at her. "Well, she was certainly expecting some kind of trouble."

Aquene felt the desperation as much as she heard it in the words Molly had read. As much as she heard it in Molly's own voice. She understood, for just as Aquene was blessed by the visions that guided her life, so too was Hannah. They were, or had been, in many ways the same. It was often hard to know or sense what awaited beyond the clouds, yet that was the truth of Aquene's life. It had been, she understood, the same for Hannah. The words she had left in the book told her she was correct.

"She knew what she was to battle, and she readied herself."

Molly nodded. "I agree, and she wanted her granddaughter to be ready too. The spell she left for her was detailed enough that even a less-than-stellar student like me could follow it. She wasn't taking any chances."

They sounded like simple words to Aquene, yet in her heart she knew they were not. Yes, Hannah had written her words for the granddaughter she awaited; she was very clear about that. Still, the manner of the words as they passed Molly's lips made her wonder. Aquene turned and studied Molly. Who was the granddaughter, and did she come from very far away…very far indeed?

Matthew kneeled on his blanket and put his hands together. "Father in heaven, hear my prayers. As you have guided me throughout the ages, guide me now. Show me the way. Show me the path that will take me to this book of blasphemy. Show me the way and thy will be done."

The familiar whoosh of emotion that followed every successful prayer assailed him now. God had heard him, as he always did, and sent him precisely the answer he knew Matthew would understand. It had been that way for him right from the beginning. His earthly father had seen the special nature of his relationship with God and had nurtured it. As a child, neither of them knew the full measure of what his destiny was to be, but as the years passed and the threat against the good and pious people of his village became clearer and clearer, his life's work became just as clear. His pride in his work was obvious to all, and his father had approved.

He used his arms to cushion his head as he lay prone on the ground. The rocks gave him a small measure of cover. The best he could hope for was to not get soaked all the way to his skin. It would not be the first time, and it would not kill him. Nothing did. He would find what little comfort he could and wait for the night to pass.

Tiny pebbles rained down upon him, and he brushed them away. It would be an animal of some kind looking, as he had, for shelter from the storm. He heard the light step of its feet as it scurried away. Danger lurked here in the wilds, and for those not blessed, it could be fatal. It was not so for him. Not now, not ever. He had been freed from the troubles of the common man. God spared him the indignities rained upon others. Nothing, and no one, harmed him.

Staring up at the sky, he let his mind turn back once more to his home and the beginning of his life as the Witch-Finder. He still remembered his first mission. Oh, she had been a devious one, hiding her true nature behind a mask that made her look as though she were a simpleton. Her tangled, long hair had been streaked with gray, while twigs and hay poked from beneath her filthy cap. Her face was always smudged with grime and her clothing torn and dirty. If one spared her but a glance, they would only have thought she was a most unfortunate peasant.

In fact, that was his first thought, as it was Father's. They were walking past her on the village road when a sweep of emotion took him in its grasp. It was more than her appalling appearance and horrid stench. He remembered turning and studying the creature with new eyes. It was then the sight came to him, and it had been with him ever since.

Beyond the dirt and the smell, beyond the gray hair and the dull eyes, he glimpsed the monster and had discovered his calling, for deep down in his soul he was being commanded to destroy it. He had known without question that had he laid hands on her that day he would have seen her black heart.

The satisfaction he had felt upon her destruction was the beginning of something magnificent. It was still that way today. Every dark soul he sentenced to hell filled him with joy. Soon he would watch as another burned. He smiled as he closed his eyes.

CHAPTER FIFTEEN

Molly leaned back against the rock in their cozy shelter and closed her eyes. In her mind she could see the words Hannah had written. More than the diary portion of the grimoire, what she had written after that had stayed with her. She thought about the spell Hannah had included, with its attention to detail as if she sensed the person who would need to use it was not a skilled student of the Old Ways. Kind of like her. Just like her.

The craft her family practiced had always been nurturing and healing. It was their way and was a big deal to her mom and the rest of the women who came before her. It's also what had struck Molly about what she had read tonight. It had the same feel to it as the lessons she'd learned from her family.

In fact, it rang way too familiar. Not surprising, because much of what she'd learned had been passed down for many generations. She might not be the enthusiastic witch her mother hoped for, but that didn't mean she hadn't paid attention along the way. How could she not? It didn't really matter whether she bought in, because the power was there and had been since her birth. She was a hereditary witch, and that was pretty much self-explanatory. Despite her efforts to be just a baker, she couldn't escape her family, and in the back of her mind she wondered if she really ever wanted to.

As she'd read Hannah's grimoire, she'd felt a tingle of familiarity when she found the protection spell for those who faced forces they were unprepared to repel, such as the indigenous peoples of the land fighting against the waves of settlers. Hannah was perhaps trying to help those who had helped her. Her own mother would absolutely do something just like that.

It might have been left for someone else to use, but Molly saw it differently. An opportunity. She saw with sudden clarity how the spell could also protect her friends. Despite the comfort she felt snug here in their makeshift shelter beside a woman whom she felt at ease with, she was worried about Winnie and Angus. She'd hoped that, as they waited out both the storm and the night, she would hear them coming. Angus walked with a light step. Winnie not so much. They'd have been able to hear her trudging along a quarter mile away. Thus far that hadn't happened. Yes, Angus knew his way around the wilderness. Though Winnie had told her about his skills, she'd also seen them in the way he handled himself from the time they left their vehicle. He was an artist and also a survivalist. He would keep Winnie safe. Still, he wasn't accustomed to this particular brand of wilderness. He didn't have his pack with all his high-tech, cool gear, and while the topography might be pretty much the same, it was still different from the land they traversed two hundred years in the future. Things change, simple as that. He would have to rely on basic skills, and she really hoped they weren't perishable.

It was time to put the serenity prayer into practice because she had no power to change anything right now. Letting go of her worry about Angus and Winnie, she returned her attention to the book. There was at least one thing she could do. She tapped her fingers against the cover. "I need to try the spell."

"The spell?"

"Hannah's protection. She obviously felt it was important, and I think we need to follow her guidance." As comfortable as she was sitting next to Aquene, she also wondered what was out there that they couldn't see. If there was ever a time to call on the family heritage, this was it.

"Protection," Aquene said softly as she nodded. "Yes, he is coming, and I believe that would be good. You can send out this protection from her words?"

There was that *he* again, and she didn't get what about this man had frightened both Hannah and now Aquene enough to want to flee. While it was true she caught the uneasy vibes triggered by him, truth was, he was just a guy and they outnumbered him, especially if they could hook up with Angus and Winnie again. Then they would really have the advantage. Four against one? No problem. And it would be even better if Loba was with them right now. Regardless of where they were or what they were doing, she always felt safer with her dog at her side.

"All right. Let's do this." She didn't need to open the book because the spell, though slightly different, was well-known to her. She'd learned it from her mother, who'd learned it from her mother, and so on and so on. Mom would be proud that she remembered it well enough to recite from memory. Instead of opening the grimoire, she took Aquene's hand. She expected her to pull away, but she didn't. She liked that.

After taking a deep breath, she slowly blew it out. She was ready. "We come to you on this night and acknowledge the grace of the Earth Mother and the Sky Father, of the Great God and Goddess. We give thanks for all that is good in this world and in our lives. We call out to you and pray that you receive our pleas as they rise up to you on the night air. May you grant our request and bring to all who deserve it your protection from the forces of darkness that seek to destroy goodness and kindness. Blessed be the mysteries of your divine protections. In your names, so be it done."

In the midst of the rain storm that pounded down upon their makeshift shelter, a warm wind blew across their faces.

"Oh my god, did you feel that?" Winnie stiffened and stared around the shadow-filled room. The hair on her arms raised, and she could swear little ghost fingers passed across the back of her neck. Talk about scaring the bejesus out of her. It was almost worse than the ghost in the doorway.

Angus had just dumped the pile of wood he'd brought back from the fire and straightened up. "Feel what?"

"A hot wind. You had to feel it." He couldn't possibly have missed it. He didn't see the woman. He didn't feel the wind. Maybe she was losing it.

Angus raised an eyebrow and looked into her eyes. "Did you find some hooch in this place or something? First you tell me you're seeing phantom people that I actually walk right through, and now a tropical breeze is flowing around the place. You do realize you're sitting right in front of a fire? You know, as in warm breeze?"

He wasn't totally off base, even though she found his words a little insulting. To begin with, she wasn't seeing things. Damn straight she'd seen and talked to someone, or something, while he was gone. And now, not just a little heat was wafting off the fire. It was a gale-force wind warm enough to heat the whole room that brought with it tendrils of something indefinable. Surely he had to notice the difference.

"Angus, I'm not going off the deep end despite the bizarre situation we're in. Some serious weirdness is going on here, and I think it's all tied together." She pointed to the doorway. "A woman was standing there when you came in, and whether you believe me or not, I felt a wind, not a warm draft from the fire, blow through this room."

He ran a hand over her hair, the sort of comforting gesture one gave a child. "Okay, my beauty. I believe you."

She did not care for his patronizing tone of voice and had the urge to shake off his hand. "I know what I saw and felt." She sounded snippy, and she didn't care.

This time his hand cupped her cheek, and he stared into her eyes. "I believe you," he repeated.

She tilted her head and studied him. Was he simply pacifying her because they were in such a peculiar situation? Keep the skittish woman calm? As she gazed back at him, she decided he wasn't. Bless his Irish heart. All the fight went out of her. "You do believe me."

He sank down next to her in front of the fire, pulled her into his arms, and kissed the top of her head. "Darlin', we are up shit creek here, as my granny was prone to say. If we can jump a few hundred years backward, anything can happen, and that includes ghosts and tropical winds. If you say you saw a ghost in the doorway, I believe you. If you say you felt a strange hot wind, I believe you."

Seriously, was it possible to love someone more than she did this man, right this minute? She didn't think so. Tears pooled in her eyes and she hugged him tight. "God, I love you."

"Ah, I know, and I love you right back."

She pulled back and stared at him. "You know?"

He actually looked a little confused. "Of course I do. Don't tell me you didn't know."

"I didn't."

His brow furrowed. "How could you not?"

The answer to that one was pretty easy. "You've never said it. I never said it." Her heart was pounding, and this time it wasn't because of fear.

"Words aren't everything."

Winnie laughed. "For you? Are you kidding me? You make your living with words."

He joined in her laughter. "That, my sweet woman, is quite true. I suppose I need to remember to say what's in my heart and not just assume you know."

Putting her head on his shoulder, she took a moment to absorb this new twist. "It makes me happy that you feel the same way I do. I was worried."

"What in the world is there for you to worry about? Why would you do that?"

"A better question is, why wouldn't I? You could have anyone. You're smart and successful, and that accent of yours is sexy as all get-out. I'm chunky, I have a career that sucks up a million hours, and I'm not even a tenth as interesting as you are. I always think you'll see the real me and take off running."

He pushed her out at arm's length and stared at her. "Are you serious? Winifred Marie, you are a thrilling ball of dynamite. You're beautiful, successful, funny, and always game for any of my crazy ideas. I couldn't have found a better woman if I'd searched the whole world, which, if you think about it, I kinda did. I think I knew ten minutes after I met you that you were the one granny always told me I'd find if I just kept my eyes open."

Maybe she could love him even more. "You always know what to say to make me feel better."

"It's because I tell you the truth, and when we get home—and we will get home—I'm going to make good on my words."

"And how exactly are you going to do that?" Honestly, she didn't know how he could improve on anything he'd just said.

His smile glowed in the firelight as he pulled her even closer. "I'm going to take you home to meet my mum, and then I'm going to marry you."

CHAPTER SIXTEEN

Aquene's faith in Molly had not been displaced. She was everything her visions had promised and more. But those visions had not shown her how beautiful Molly was, both in body and spirit, and how her simple touch could make Aquene's heart race.

She should not be shocked, for her lessons had taught her that all was revealed in its own way and in its own time. She had learned of the coming of their savior, and here she was. Her lessons had also taught her that, though much was revealed to her, not everything was to be shown. She had to discover some things without aid. That was the very thing happening as they sat beneath the shelter listening to the sounds of the storm-filled night, and the lesson was all the sweeter for it.

Molly's words had trailed off, and warmth had swirled around them as though they were sitting out in a summer night rather than in a harsh storm. She had felt Molly's magic in her soul, and the peace that came with it was unlike anything Aquene had experienced before. This the visions definitely had not showed her. The surprise was exciting, the discovery thrilling.

Even more amazing was her absolute belief in Molly's prayer. It would protect them. She could feel it, and it filled her with peace. The touch of Molly's hand against hers made it even more so. She closed her eyes and rested her head against the rock. It was hard, though not uncomfortable. She had slept on far worse and without the comfort of the hand she still held. The night could go on forever, if it felt like this. Yes, she was certain this was exactly how Alumpum felt about her warrior. No wonder she was always trying to find a life mate for Aquene.

"We will be safe here," she said.

Molly squeezed her hand gently. "I feel it too. Hannah's magic is much like that of my heritage. I read it in her words and felt its power as I used it just now. She might not have written it for you and me, but darned if it didn't work for us just the same. It would have been nice to meet her. I have a feeling I would have liked her."

"She was a good woman. She was my friend." It was true. She missed Hannah.

"I'm glad the spell worked."

Aquene knew that it did. "He will not touch us this night."

"I agree. We're in good shape for a while. Aquene? Who is this man you keep talking about? Is it the same one Hannah writes of in her grimoire? Who is he?"

Aquene had to pause and consider Molly's question. While she did not know his face, she had felt his presence for some time. The blackness that surrounded her each time she thought of him scared her. Whether it was same man who had come for Hannah was unknown to her.

"I do not know the answer to your question. It is possible, but I am not certain if it is likely. She ran from someone who came from far beyond the sunset. The one I fear is close. They might be the same man. They might not."

"Could be the same creep. Maybe he simply followed her out here, and you picked him up on your radar."

"Radar?"

Molly laughed lightly, and Aquene liked the sound. It was like the bells she had heard in the house of worship she had attended with the newcomers. "Once again, something from my time. It means that someone has become known to you."

"Ah." This she understood. A man was out there, one who carried darkness in his heart, and she had been feeling his presence for some time now. He was, as she said, known to her.

"I'm kind of leaning toward it being the same guy."

"Why is it you believe he is the one?" Aquene did not carry the same conviction in her soul, even as she could hear it in Molly's words.

"I don't know. Have you ever felt something to be true and yet not had anything to base your belief on? You just know it deep down to be a truth?"

Aquene did not have to think long to be able to answer either of Molly's questions. What had come to her as they sat beneath their shelter, side by side, was that she had two new truths in her life on this night. Molly was the one the visions foretold to be the savior of her people. And she loved the woman whose shoulder touched her and whose hand she held in hers.

She did not hesitate as she answered Molly. "Yes."

❖

Matthew jumped to his feet and made a complete circle. His heart was pounding and his pulse racing. She was close. Oh, by God, she was close. He smiled and tipped his head to the sky.

Raindrops hit his face, and above him the sky was dark, the stars hidden by the clouds that brought the storm. It did not matter, and the blackness did not dampen his delight. How many signs did he need to prove to not just himself but everyone around him that he walked a divine path? Except he was alone at the moment, with no one nearby to share the proof of his glory. It was a shame. Everyone should know and appreciate the righteousness of his quest, to bow to him in respect.

"But you know, do you not, my God," he said to the dark sky. "You blessed me with greatness, and I have taken it to even higher glories."

Earlier he had believed the night was for resting. Now he changed his mind. This sign told him the hunt was on, night or day. He moved back to beneath the overhang of rocks, where he'd spread out his bedroll. The driest place he could find when he stopped for the night, it was still a bit damp as rain dripped from the lip of the rocks to soak into his blanket, but he rolled it up anyway and tied it to his saddle. When the sun came back out, he would dry it properly.

After mounting his horse, he adjusted his hat and stared out where all blended together into impenetrable gloom. The draw he felt told him to head west. In the black of the night, it was difficult to gauge direction. He was not worried. Just as God had given him this sign, so too would his heavenly father show him the way to go. He urged his horse forward, happy to be on the hunt.

They had only gone a short distance when his horse reared up and then stepped backward. A snake perhaps? He peered down and saw nothing so he urged him forward. He would not move. No matter what he tried, it refused to continue in the direction he pushed him. He dismounted, took the reins in his hand, and walked forward. Still nothing. The horse neighed, shook his massive head, and backed up, dragging Matthew, still holding the reins, with him.

"You stupid animal," he bit out. "We must go this way." His horse acted as though Matthew was asking him to step into a giant fire. He stared ahead, trying to determine what was spooking the usually compliant animal, but could see nothing. He could hear nothing.

His continued efforts to get the horse to move failed. He was stuck for the night, for he could not do this on foot. He was too far out into the wilds of this land and too far away from any settlement to walk. He must have this horse for transport.

When he tried one last time to get him to venture into the darkness, the horse once more refused to budge. His anger rose and he wished for a whip. If the animal would not move willingly, he would go at the end of a whip. Unfortunately, he did not carry one with him.

Then a chilling thought flashed through his mind, and as it did, the truth of it flooded his body. It wasn't the horse's fault. No, the horse was innocent, his resistance to move forward beyond his control.

"You," he snapped to the sky. "You demon witch." She had done this. She had bewitched his horse. "Enjoy your fleeting power this night. It will be your final one." His blood ran cold, his determination to put an end to the witch's black magic stronger than ever.

He snatched the bedroll back off his saddle and returned to his shelter beneath the rock overhang. She had stopped him this night, but it would be the last time she would ever cast an evil spell. On the morrow, she would die at his hand.

CHAPTER SEVENTEEN

Aquene's answer didn't surprise Molly. She'd known the truth of her words the moment they'd passed her lips. Something was happening here that went far beyond the very real time-traveling event that had brought three people from the twenty-first century to this wilderness landscape along the Columbia River. How amazing that it looked so familiar to her in many ways yet foreign at the same time. She was accustomed to the sight of the massive river as it flowed strong and beautiful between Washington and Oregon. But the river she had followed many times was bordered on each shore by highways, railroad tracks, small towns, dams, and even a concrete replica of Stonehenge. She particularly liked the replica, and every time she drove to Portland she smiled when she reached the familiar sight that was commissioned in the early twentieth century by wealthy businessman Sam Hill.

None of the familiar sights existed in this time and place. As far as she could see stretched wilderness, unspoiled nature, and riverbanks free of rail lines. If they were to travel west, the hillside where the replica had stood for nearly a hundred years would be bare. This massive expanse of unspoiled nature humbled her. The only thing that hinted at the impending encroachment of settlers was the primitive—very primitive—road she could see, if she looked closely, near what would one day be the Oregon side of the river. To see a faint trail instead of a highway she had so many times traveled on at sixty-five miles an hour in her car was an experience sure to stay with her the rest of her life.

It gave her a whole new perspective on what the native peoples of America had been through. Once she'd been in Fort Smith, Arkansas, standing along a portion of the Trail of Tears. Her heart ached as she'd thought about what had happened on that beautiful stretch of nature. But that was nothing compared to what she felt as she sat next to a woman she knew would soon lose everything she held dear. It wasn't right. Not now, and not in Molly's time. The helplessness that consumed her was nearly crippling.

"What makes you sad?"

Aquene's voice came through the darkness, a whisper on the night air. That she could sense Molly's distress amazed her. Then again, this was a woman who not only wasn't surprised to see three time travelers, but who also claimed to be expecting them. The fact that she could sense Molly's deep-felt emotion really shouldn't be much of a shock. In a sense, Aquene was a psychic who had the ability to see the future, though she suspected Aquene would argue she was not psychic but a vessel chosen by the Great Spirit. She could be right.

At the same time, Molly hesitated to reveal any of her thoughts. How could she explain that not just an individual, but entire native cultures across the land, would be pushed to near extinction? She couldn't, so instead, she opted for the easy and the vague. "Changes are coming to your life and that of your people."

"Yes."

Aquene's quick and simple answer surprised her. "I don't think you understand. It's going to be terrible. Wars. Death. Loss."

She could feel Aquene's nod. "I understand. It is why you are here."

Oh, fuck, no, she wanted to say. For some reason Aquene mistakenly believed she was Christ incarnate. That was so far from the truth it was ridiculous. She was a damned baker, and bakers didn't save the world. "I can't stop any of it." That was the cold truth. It didn't matter what any of them did while they were here. It didn't matter that she came from a family filled with magic. Even with all the theories floating around about the dangers of time travel changing the course of history, Molly understood another simple truth: the waves of people coming would not be stopped. Wars. Death. Loss.

Aquene pulled Molly's hand to her chest. "Do not worry. You will be shown the way when it is time. You have power in your spirit, and it is exactly what my people need. It will all be as it should."

She made it sound so simple, and it was anything but. "I'm not very powerful, and I'm certain you're mistaken about my coming to save the world."

"The Great Spirit does not make mistakes. You are the chosen one, and you will bring salvation. Of this, I am certain."

She wanted to argue more with her and try to make Aquene see the reality. She couldn't. For some unexplained reason, she wanted to be the person Aquene believed she was. But how? Aquene had no way of understanding the massive subjugation of not just her people, but all the native cultures in this land, and Molly could do nothing to stop it. Nobody could. So it was impossible to wrap her head around how she was to *save her people*.

Then again, her family had always told her that one day she'd understand her place in the universe and that her strengths would show themselves. Time travel was an impossibility, wasn't it? Yet here she was. Here they all were. So, maybe, just maybe, this was that day.

❖

"What?" The single word came out more like a squeak, but Winnie didn't care if she sounded like an injured mouse. She was still trying to grasp what Angus had just declared as if it were the most ordinary comment in the world.

His laughter was full and rich. Pulling her close he kissed her. "I said, I'm going to marry you."

"Why?" Okay, now that did sound stupid, but this was pretty surreal. Here they were in a rustic cabin in the middle of nowhere in the middle of a time that didn't belong to them, and he was talking about taking her to Ireland to meet his mother. Talking about getting married. Sure, she'd been dreaming about it and hoped someday down the road it might actually happen. She simply hadn't seen any of it coming down quite like this.

He tilted his head and studied her face in the firelight. "It's pretty obvious to me."

"Humor me."

"All right, humor you, I shall. I want to marry you first and foremost because I love you. My granny always told me that one day I'd meet a woman who would make me want to drop my mates so I could be with her, whose smile I would think about when we weren't together, and who could cook a meal that warmed me for days. She was right, you know. I did meet that woman."

Winnie wanted to believe him. God, how she wanted to believe him, but self-doubt had been her companion for so long that she had trouble shaking it now even in this heart-stopping, beautiful moment. "That doesn't sound like me."

This time his laughter filled the room. "Of course it does. Trust me. Now shut up, kiss me, and tell me you'll marry me."

Warmth flowed through her, and Winnie brought her hand up to cup Angus's cheek. "You know what, you're right. I don't know why I'm fighting this. I love you. I think I've loved you from the first time I saw you. Of course I'll marry you, and I can't wait to meet your mother."

Angus kissed her. It wasn't a passion-filled kiss but gentle and sweet and full of promise. "Mum is going to love you."

"You think she will?" Insecurity was her fallback.

"Yes, I do, especially if you make her dinner. Once she finds out what a wicked chef you are, she'll convince you to stay in Ireland and move in with her."

Winnie thought about that possibility. "I could probably learn some new things across the pond." She'd done all her training in the U.S., and it would be exciting to expand her skills in Europe. Moving in with his mother might not be so bad. "Your mother and I could cook together."

Angus grimaced. "Not to bad-mouth my mum, but trust me, you don't want to follow her lead. If there's any cooking to be done, I suggest you do it."

She laughed and hugged him. "It's a deal. Oh, Angus, I do love you."

His expression turned serious. "And I you. Now, let's try to get some sleep. As soon as it gets light, we've got to find Molly, and then we'll all figure out how to get home. Somewhere in this place," his gaze traveled around the darkened room, "is the key to finding our way back. I know it, and we're going to find it."

She followed his gaze and saw nothing different from when they first arrived. Well, nothing different save the mess the angry man had made when he tipped over the furniture. "God, I hope you're right."

CHAPTER EIGHTEEN

If only Aquene could do more to assure Molly that all was as it should be. True, they were in danger. It was Aquene's way of life. The waters that helped give them life could also take it away quickly. The rocks that provided shelter could also hide dangerous creatures that struck without warning. Strangers could prove to be deadly as often as they could come in friendship.

She, and all her people, had to be aware and alert at all times. Especially now with the newcomers, who brought strange customs and beliefs. Though familiar with their language and their ways, she did not truly understand them. She could be in their company, speak with them, and trade with them. She did not want to live with them, not for any length of time.

Already she had spent much of her life with these strangers. It was only when she was out here in the wild, the sky full of the light of a blanket of stars, that she felt at home. Here she took in the true power of nature and the purpose of the path she was set on. She was much more certain of the rightness of it all because she had been living with this for much time. Molly had not.

"You are more powerful than you know." It amazed her that Molly did not know how special she was. Aquene had known it long before she had gazed into her beautiful eyes.

Molly shook her head. "I don't think so. You believe I am because you want to. I came out of seemingly nowhere, and that appears to be the magic you're hoping for. The reality of who and what I am is quite different. I think you'll be very disappointed in the real me."

In turn, Aquene shook her head. "You believe I am a simple

woman because I live here in what I am sure you see as a primitive way. The savage way, as I have heard others describe it."

"No!" The force of Molly's single word startled Aquene. "You're wrong. It has nothing to do with the way you live. I respect it more than you can possibly know."

Aquene had to find a way to get through to her, to make her understand. Soon he would come, and Molly must be fearless. Courage lived in her heart, Aquene was most certain of that, but somehow she must make Molly trust her own fearlessness.

"I do not believe these things because you appeared out of the air, that I imagine magic brought you here." She laughed lightly. "That is not all true. I do believe a little magic did bring you here, but it is the same magic I know exists in our world. Destiny and the will of the Great Spirit delivered you here."

Molly pushed her hands through her hair. "Each person in my family holds a special power, a special talent. I'm no kid, yet I've never really known what I can do, what the universe has seen fit to gift me with. I know the Old Ways, I understand the craft, and even so I've never understood my place. I became a baker because there I feel like I belong. I always felt like an outsider in my own family, until now."

Aquene sensed that at last Molly was beginning to believe, and her heart grew lighter. "This is your place. This is your personal power. The universe brought us together for something much greater than either one of us can know."

Molly turned to look at Aquene, and even in the darkness she could make out her features. Their eyes were intent on one another. "As much as I hate to admit it, you might just be right."

Dawn broke slowly, very slowly, in Matthew's opinion. He had little doubt about the power of the magic that had impeded his progress last night. She had not just chained him to this place; she had kept away the light so that his movements were halted far longer than they should have been. The witch had thwarted him once. It would not happen again. That was a promise that would be kept.

He had managed a little sleep once the storm passed, not much, but he had never needed sleep like others. He could go for several days and still be alert and powerful, which also revealed to him the divinity of his life and his mission. If he were a mere mortal, he would have required a full night's sleep in order to be effective. He counted his constitution as another blessing from God.

Compared to yesterday, this day had a glorious beginning. It might have taken much longer to arrive than it should have, though now that it was here, the sun was out, the sky was clear, and the air held a hint of warmth. Another sign. He would succeed in his mission today and stop the evil one as she tried to carry forth the witch's ill intent. She should enjoy this morning because, before the sun set again, he would destroy her and any who would try to help her.

In the days long past, he had set his eyes solely on the witches themselves. How well he remembered the year he began. East Anglia had been teeming with those of evil intent in 1644. He knew it firsthand, for he had heard the disciples of the devil speak of their plans in Manningtree on that fateful spring day. It was at that moment his destiny became clear, and he did not hesitate to act. Many were grateful for his work, and they paid him handsomely for doing it well.

Years later, he had read some of the accounts of his work and understood what was suggested, though perhaps not written in so many words. Some, those ignorant of its importance, suggested that he made false accusations in the name of his own personal gain. They went so far as to send reports to Parliament with stories of how he and his team employed questionable means to extract confessions. Torture. Knives. Near drowning. They were wrong, of course, and that Parliament took no action spoke tomes. While they did not condone his work, neither did they condemn it. He did use torture, knives, and water in his work. His methods were justified then, and now. They were far from questionable. They were effective.

He was right. His detractors were wrong.

How else would one explain his long existence in the world? He had died before he attained the age of thirty. In his home in Manningtree, he had lain in his bed wasting away and coughing up blood. One of the witches had put upon him a curse; of that he was absolutely certain. His body had weakened, and far earlier than it should have, death had come to him. Temporarily, of course. After the mourners had left and the sun had set, he had risen from the ground in the graveyard of St. Mary's and ever since walked the earth doing his important work.

He was not one of the devil's minions, for they too often received immortality. He was from God's army, and though he had never seen or heard of another like himself, he spoke the truth.

This witch, this elusive practitioner of the black arts, would change his life. His wait had been long, and once he stopped her, his reward would make it all worthwhile.

This morning his horse was as calm and focused as he was. Whatever the witch had done last night to spook the horse had faded away, along with the dark of the night. This morning they were free and the hunt was on. He stood on the bluff and looked out. In the distance, the massive river stretched calm and glassy. He mounted the horse and scanned the land below, hoping to glimpse her. Just as last night, he saw nothing, and again anger burned in him. That she had not built a fire to chase away the chill was a smart choice for her, a frustrating one for him. That she still managed to hide herself from view was troubling. It was not right. He should be able to see her. His hands began to twitch, and his breathing grew more rapid. His horse neighed, shaking its head and pounding the ground with his hoofs.

Closing his eyes, he silently prayed for guidance. The prayer helped, and his sense of calm returned. The twitching stopped, and his breathing evened out. The tension that moments before had made his body feel like glass flowed out of him. As he calmed, so too did his horse. Matthew tilted his head toward the sky and felt the warmth of the rising sun on his face. Yes, his heavenly Father would show him the way. He smiled and patted the length of rope attached to his saddle.

CHAPTER NINETEEN

Molly woke up, disoriented for a few seconds. She felt stiff yet oddly at ease. Happy, as if all in her world was perfect. Had to be the lingering result of a good dream, except her eyes were open and she was staring up at a canopy of tree branches. Then she remembered where she was and figured out her ease had a lot to do with the hand she still held: Aquene's.

Aquene hadn't awakened yet, the gentle rise and fall of her chest rhythmic. The grimoire still lay right next to Molly, exactly where it had been when she'd finally drifted off to sleep last night. It would have been nice to have read more, but she'd decided not to tax her small light or risk it being seen by whoever, or whatever, awaited them out in the darkness. Besides risking their safety, who knew how long they'd be stuck here, and the batteries, while the good lithium variety, wouldn't last if she kept the light on all night. There could very well be other nights in the coming days when she might really, really want her little flashlight.

Now she had plenty of light and used her free hand to open the book to where they'd left off last night. Instead of reading aloud, she silently scanned what was now becoming the familiar script.

August 30, 1836
    I have found a sanctuary in this wilderness, far from anything that rings familiar. By its very foreignness, it gives me a feeling of safety. He too has traveled his many lifetimes in the places populated by cities and people he is accustomed to. Here, it is a new world with strange people and strange customs. The comforts of the cities we each know so well do

not exist here, and survival depends upon ingenuity and the charity of those few who pass by.

The people who have always called this land home are very different from any I have met before. Their customs are not of those I know, yet I do not find them strange. Quite the opposite. I find a certain amount of comfort in the different yet familiar way they speak and live and worship. Perhaps that is why we have become friends. In a sense, I understand them and they me. I do not feel all alone out here, knowing that I have allies nearby.

It does not mean I am safe. Nor are my new friends. During the long journey that brought me here, I heard much of the fear and revulsion the settlers carry with them. That brings me sadness, for those who seek out this new land do not even try to understand the people who lived here first. They want only what they know and do not try to see the beauty that is already in this glorious land.

Then again, why should I be surprised? Is it not the reason I run now? Have not our people been misunderstood for centuries? And the one who pursues me now has been on a crusade to destroy our family for generations. He has almost succeeded. The hate he carries in his heart is as deep as an ocean.

Only the two of us remain now, and soon I fear it will only be one. I hope that I have kept her safe and assured for her a life that will keep our blood flowing through the generations to come. I feel much hope that I have, or what would be the point of leaving this for you?

So heed these words, my dear granddaughter, for much is to be laid at your feet. I believe in the visions that the universe has gifted to me, and those visions show me you will come. I see your face, the eyes, the mouth, the hair that are much like my own. In your face I see a promise that he will not succeed in destroying us. For everything, there is a time and a season. Alas, it is not for me to be that time or season. For you it shall come to pass.

Look into your heart and find the magic that will fulfill the destiny that comes your way. You, Molly, are the chosen one, and through you, the gates of hell will open for him. The wisdom of our family will come to you in the moment you need it most. Seek the knowledge, accept it when it comes, and do what you must. Molly, you are my only hope. You are our family's only hope.

Molly gasped and jerked her hand, releasing Aquene's as the book fell from her lap. Startled, Aquene jumped to her feet, on instant alert.

"Who approaches?"

It took a second for that question to sink in. "No one," Molly told her. At least no one that she knew of.

"Then what has happened?"

It was hard to explain what she'd just read and why it had smacked her in the face like a painful slap. Though her name appeared in the grimoire, its message surely wasn't personally directed at her, yet it hit Molly deep in her heart. This woman from two centuries past had left this for her, and even as she tried to argue otherwise, the truth lay right there in front of her eyes. Everything Aquene had been pushing to make her understand was now as clear as if she'd just seen it on a television investigative report. And truth was a bitch.

"You're right." That was all she could think of to say.

"I do not understand."

"You were right about everything. I'm supposed to be here."

"Yes."

Aquene made everything sound so matter-of-fact. None of it felt that way to her, except suddenly she understood why she was supposed to jump through time and that it all had happened for a reason. Winnie and Angus, well, she still wasn't sure why they ended up down the proverbial rabbit hole with her. If this grimoire had been left for her, it made sense that she would find herself at Aquene's side. Her two friends were most likely in the wrong place at the wrong time.

"Hannah is a relative. A great, great, or more grandmother, I believe."

Nodding, Aquene said, "That is as it should be."

"Maybe to you, but it's pretty damned weird to me. I always figured I'd come into my powers someday but thought it would actually be in my century. Who time-jumps anyway? What kind of power is that? Then to find a book written two hundred years earlier and written specifically to me—well, that's just mind-blowing. Maybe this kind of stuff happens to you all the time, but not to me."

"As I said last night, the universe does as it sees fit. We do not decide these things on our own."

"Yeah," she murmured. "Ain't it a bitch?" Of course, even if Mom or anyone else in her family had told her some great-great-grandmother would write to her so that when she time-jumped she'd have a guide, she'd have never believed them. Her mind was far more open than most, but that would have been a bit much even for her.

Aquene looked at her oddly, and she realized the saying so common in her century made no sense whatsoever to this woman in this time and place. It was amazing they were able to communicate at all, given how many times Molly said something she couldn't relate to. "It's another saying from my time," she explained.

"It is strange. You have many odd sayings from your time, do you not?"

"I suppose we do." She laughed and then turned serious "You were right about some guy coming for us. He's a killer."

Nodding, Aquene stood. "It is true, and we must not stay here longer. We must find a way to stop him. Now that daylight is upon us, it is important that we go in search of him."

How she wished for the tools of her century, especially a cell phone—a working one, anyway. A GPS wouldn't be unwelcome either. Oh, and a Starbucks would be awesome. She'd give her left arm for a venti latte right about now.

Not likely to see any of those things in the near future, so, like Aquene, she stood. Unlike Aquene, she put her arms over her head and stretched. Wow, it was amazing how stiff she was after sleeping sitting up against a rock on hard ground. Not quite like a night on her queen-sized memory-foam mattress. Didn't seem to bother her companion at all. Go figure.

"What do you suggest?" Frankly, she didn't have a clue where to go from here, beyond trying to track down Winnie and Angus. She was afraid they'd gotten lost in the trees and rocks or, God forbid, slipped into the water. Out there it all looked alike to her, and it would be a simple matter to get turned around. Get too close to the river and how easy would it be for the bank to collapse? They would be swept away before they had a chance to do anything. The most she could hope for was that they'd circled back to the cabin. Angus was a smart guy and might just figure their best bet for reconciliation was to return to the only familiar place they had. Not to mention he had a far better sense of direction than Molly and Winnie put together.

"We must eat and drink before we journey forward."

Aquene tossed out a lot of must-dos, and while that all sounded good, what exactly were they going to eat and drink? Molly didn't even have a protein bar in her coat pocket. All her snacks, along with her trusty water bottle, were in her pack, wherever it had ended up. "I don't have anything to eat or drink." Now that she thought about it, she was actually pretty hungry and would love a bottle of water. Like the latte, a cold bottle of water was another dream guaranteed not to come true.

"Come." Aquene held out one hand to her. In the other was her bag tied with the leather cord. All of a sudden, Molly was really interested in that bag. What exactly did Aquene carry in it? Bacon? A granola bar? Wait. They probably hadn't even heard of a granola bar yet. Okay. Bacon would work.

She didn't ask. Instead, she followed her from their overnight shelter. It wasn't far to the river, where they used their hands to scoop out cold water. In her day, she'd never in a million years consider drinking straight from the river, despite how beautiful the water always appeared. She figured a couple of centuries without pollution meant she had a good shot at getting untainted water, so why not give it a try? When in Rome and all that. It was cold and clear and wonderful. She still might pay later for drinking it, but given how parched she'd been, she was willing to risk it. She rocked back on her heels and tipped her head to the sky. There was a lot to be said about warm sunshine and a drink of cool water.

Behind her, Aquene sat on a rock and opened her bag. She left the riverbank and sat on the rock next to Aquene. Out of her pouch she pulled dried meat and handed Molly a piece. She wasn't exactly sure what she was looking at, not that it mattered. She was hungry enough not to care. After taking a bite, she smiled. "Salmon." She was relieved to discover it wasn't something like dried rattlesnake. Even as hungry as she was, Molly wasn't sure she'd get that past her lips.

Aquene smiled back. The sunshine made her face bright and her black hair shine. A natural beauty that made Molly's pulse quicken. "Yes." As quick as her smile crossed her face, it disappeared. Molly watched in confusion as her face paled and her eyes rolled back in her head. When she realized what was happening, she got to Aquene with just enough time to keep her from hitting her head on another rock as she tumbled backward toward the ground.

Winnie woke up smiling. What an insane world this was. She'd known of Molly's family history for years and always thought it was pretty cool. She hadn't realized the depth of the belief in things beyond the rational world that Angus subscribed to until now and found it equally cool. Last night they'd talked for a long time, and he'd shared with her how he so easily took this quantum leap in stride. His family had a long history of embracing the world unseen and had many of those with powers similar to Molly's. He kept telling her he didn't possess any magic. She wasn't convinced. She was pretty sure there was most definitely something special about him.

His background explained a lot, not the least of which why he saw their current situation as unique rather than dire. He kept telling her they would find their way back, and she believed him. If she hadn't already been deeply in love with him, this would have put her over the top.

What amazed her the most had nothing to do with all the history he shared with her. No, it was that he wanted to marry her. She'd hoped. Oh, God, how she had hoped for just this feeling, but deep in her soul she'd believed it was a secret dream she'd hold silently in her heart forever. She'd have never admitted it to him for fear of rejection. She'd had enough of that to last her a couple of lifetimes. It was easy to backslide if she let herself. Growing up had been tough. She was the girl who was always a little plump and just outside the circle of cool kids. Everyone liked her, and no one bullied or ignored her, but no one took her seriously as a girlfriend. She was everyone's best friend. Even Josh Contrares's. How she'd loved him and dreamed of what it would be like to go on a date. It had never happened because she was always his good friend, good buddy, the girl he could talk to about other girls. Oh, how she'd listened and offered him advice, never once summoning the courage to tell him how she really felt. Things with Josh hadn't changed over the years either. Who did he call to cater his wedding to the beautiful Olympic-hopeful runner? His good pal, Winnie.

Later, when she went away to college, she'd had some boyfriends, and as she thought about it now she realized that the demise of those relationships probably had more to do with her feelings than theirs. She had been—probably still was—so scared of being left behind as that "good friend" that she always pulled away before she could get hurt. Not letting anyone get too close was her standard operating procedure. On the surface, it had worked very well.

Until she met Angus. This beautiful, smart Irishman had burst into her restaurant like a Tasmanian devil and since that day had turned her world upside down. The fact that he kept coming back to her restaurant over and over hadn't registered. She'd figured he just liked her food. When he'd asked her out, she'd been floored and scared and thrilled. The ride had been like that ever since. Even as terrified as she was about feeling so in love with him, she couldn't run. Not this time. Now maybe she understood why.

So here they were, a couple hundred years away from home, engaged and trying to figure out how to get back to their own century. She'd never been happier.

"Whatcha thinking about, beautiful?"

She put her hand on his cheek. He still lay stretched out in front of the fire that had burned down until it was all but a pile of embers. "That I'm a really lucky woman."

He propped his head up on one hand and studied her. "You know we're stuck somewhere in the nineteenth century."

"Why, yes, I do."

"And you still feel lucky?"

She smiled broadly. "I do, because I'm stuck here with you."

CHAPTER TWENTY

Aquene felt it coming as the air rushed from her lungs and her body flowed away from her. Vaguely she heard Molly's voice and felt her arms around her. It felt really nice. Then it was all gone. The sunshine. The warm rock she sat on. Molly.

Aquene turned in a full circle. She knew where she stood and yet it looked different. It was no longer open fields with summer shelters, horses grazing, and children playing. She saw houses and people and things she had no words for. Even the houses were different from those she had witnessed at the outposts and forts. They were bigger and like nothing she had ever seen before.

When the warmth came to the land, they often traveled here to fish. The Umatilla River was a fine place to bask in the sunshine and fill their stores with salmon and the plentiful small trout. As a child, she had run along its banks, and in the summer, she had played with her friends in the warm waters.

On this day, though it was warm and filled with sunshine, no one was in the water, and only a few walked along its banks. One young boy ran to the edge and, with a cupped hand, started to drink. A woman screamed, her face filled with fear, "No. Don't drink that. It'll make you sick." The boy let the water flow through his fingers.

Aquene did not understand. The river had always been an important part of the cycle of life. They fished there, they drank from it, and they traveled on it. It was a blessing that she gave thanks for every day, yet now it scared her to hear the terror in the woman's voice. Though she could not say why, she was truly frightened about what would happen if the boy drank from its depths. Never had she been afraid to let the river waters take away her thirst.

In the tongue of her people, Aquene said, "Help me. I know not where I am."

No one turned or acknowledged her. They went about their lives, oblivious to her distress. Not one face resembled hers, and she longed to see just one she could call her own. Where were her people?

"They hear you not, my child." She had heard the Great Spirit's voice only a few times, and each time, she had brought great knowledge.

Aquene's heart raced and tears pooled in her eyes. "What has happened?"

"Time has changed this world."

"Would they answer if they could hear me?"

"No."

"What has happened?" she asked again. Dread pooled in her center, and the tears in her eyes threatened to fall.

But she did not receive an answer, for once more she stood alone.

Matthew was right. The sunlight had taken whatever magic she had cast and made it disappear like dying fog. Their descent from the rocky cliffs was slow and without incident. Once they reached flat ground, he guided the horse to the river, where they refreshed themselves. He did not tarry there, for he wanted to be on his way, to make up for the time lost last night.

His comfort on the back of the horse was nothing new, for he had always had been good on horseback, except that with this animal, it was a struggle. For some reason, the beast did not seem to like him, which was no big loss as he did not care for it either. He was a beautiful horse but had no loyalty. Beauty did not count for much when an animal was horrible, and he did not tolerate disloyalty in people or animals.

The reason this beast was difficult did not escape him. The horse had belonged to another—a native man, indigenous to this area. The man had underestimated Matthew, not long after he had arrived in this godforsaken place, close on the trail of his quarry. His horse at the time was thin and losing strength with each step. Matthew had used him hard and lost patience with the stupid, weak beast. He had needed to be free of the failing animal the moment he found a suitable replacement. So, when the native had tried to sneak into Matthew's camp and steal his supplies, he had been ready. For him, it had turned out quite well. He was relieved of the presence of an inferior mode of transportation. The thief had made a poor choice. In the end he didn't succeed in his quest to relieve Matthew of his goods and, instead, lost both his horse and his life.

He suspected the scavengers of both land and air had picked clean the man's body, for he left it where it fell after he'd snapped his neck. It did not concern him. All that mattered to him was the strong, massive horse the man had tethered to a tree some distance away. Matthew had been quite pleased to see it and had quickly transferred his saddle, roll, and rope from his fading mount to the new, stronger version. He did not look back as he rode away and did not know what happened to the other horse. It died, he supposed. He did not care. As far as dependability, this horse was far superior. As far as temperament and loyalty, Matthew was looking forward to the day he put a bullet in its head.

On this sun-filled morning, he rode tall in his saddle and studied the landscape spread out in front of him. His skills tracking the practitioners of the dark arts told him that she was near. Not more than a day's ride away. He also felt certain that she was on foot. Horses, though many were wild in this area, were difficult to come by. Only the very skilled could even begin to hope to restrain one from the untamed herds that roamed the plains. His instincts whispered that she was not that person. Yes, he was quite certain his prey was on foot. With time and persistence he would have her hanging from a tree limb and fully engulfed in flames before the moon was high in the night sky.

While he had taken to high ground overnight, now he wanted to move back toward the river. It made sense to him that anyone on foot would stay near the water. It would provide both drink and food, if she possessed enough basic skills to catch a fish. Of course, given she was a witch, more than likely she would simply cast a spell that would bring the fish to her. It was this kind of unnatural act that he was compelled to destroy.

The sun had come out, and it warmed him. His broad-brimmed hat kept the morning rays out of his eyes, and he gazed around as he guided his horse toward the river. It was quiet, the only sound the huffing of his horse and the clop of its hooves against the occasional rock. A few hours of warming sunlight would banish the remnants of last night's rain from the ground covered with damp green grass. As much as he detested the weather here, it did bring with it a renewal that reminded him of God's grand plan.

Once again at the shoreline, he slipped from the saddle and helped himself to the fresh, cold river water that satisfied his thirst. With his hands in the pockets of his coat, he stared around. He was close but unclear which direction he should travel now. Had she continued west toward the coast and the occasional ship that could give her passage, or was she moving east, intent on hiding within the wilds of the interior?

Closing his eyes, Matthew turned, as he always did, to silent prayer. It had never failed him, and he did not believe it would do so now. As he mouthed the words, overhead he heard the screech of a bird so loud it startled him. His eyes snapped open, and he turned his face to the sky. Above him, the bird soared, his wings wide.

The river was broad and the water a deep blue. Unlike the waters of his homeland, though it was nice, it did not speak to him. He missed his home and the world that had passed by long ago. In his first life he had felt most powerful and at peace. He had been important and respected. Now he had to do his work in quiet, stealthy ways. Granted, everywhere he traveled, through every age, he found help, for some always appeared who shared his vision and his quest. Still, too many did not truly understand the importance of his work.

They were pious fools who, believing that witchcraft was not an evil or destructive force, wished to convert both the savages and the witches. Most of them made him sick. Like that holier-than-thou couple Marcus and Narcissa Whitman. Matthew had met them more than a year earlier as he was trailing the witch. His encounter with the good doctor and his wife had been brief because it became clear very quickly that their paths diverged. The Whitmans came to save. He came to destroy.

CHAPTER TWENTY-ONE

"Oh, good God," Molly uttered as she cradled Aquene in her arms. What had just happened? Did she have a seizure? Was she epileptic? And if she was, what the heck should she do? Her mind whirled as she tried to remember what she'd learned in basic first aid for something like this. In her life, burns from the ovens had most often required opening the first-aid kit. Not once had anyone dropped like this. Everything went blank, and she didn't have a clue how to help. The woman was going to die right here while she did absolutely nothing.

As she held Aquene, the stiffness she'd first felt when she'd gathered her into her arms eased. In fact, her own body began to buzz as if an electrical shock was running through them both. Kind of like sitting on the ground where a downed power line was pouring electricity into the earth. Except that wasn't possible in these wilds. Nothing existed out here. All she had was a small pocket knife, a flashlight that would probably help out one more night, and a tube of lip balm. Oh, yeah, she was up for a survival challenge, all right. No doubt she'd be voted off the island in the first round. Once more, she thought longingly of her pack with the big water bottle, power bars, first-aid kit, and extra clothes.

With one hand, she smoothed the tendrils of hair that stuck to Aquene's damp forehead. Even in the throes of the attack, or whatever it was, she was a beautiful woman. Her skin was a gorgeous shade of pale brown, her face smooth and unlined, with lips that seemed to beckon to be kissed. Odd that she would think about kissable lips in a moment like this, when she should be focused on helping, but damned if that wasn't what she was doing. Screw first aid. Without giving it another thought, she leaned down and gently pressed her lips against Aquene's.

"What in the world just happened?" Molly looked around in astonishment. Everything was gone. The river, the grass, the rocks. Aquene. Instead of sitting on the ground holding Aquene in her arms, she was standing somewhere else. She didn't quite know where, but she was definitely back in the twenty-first century. Around her were houses and cars and pickups. People wore blue jeans, hoodies, and ball caps. Yes, indeed, she was home, in a manner of speaking.

It wasn't exactly home, though. As she swept her gaze around she found that she recognized the area, having driven through it many times on her way to Portland. Standing in a field, she looked down where the small community of Umatilla, Oregon, spread out before her. A quick drive across the bridge from the State of Washington, Umatilla was the entrance to Oregon from southeast Washington. It always made her smile when she crossed the river because she loved the unique, interesting drive that took her from the Umatilla River to the mighty Columbia.

Except now she wasn't driving, and she wasn't quite here. She was somewhere in between, like one foot was still in the nineteenth century and one foot was touching its toes back into the twenty-first. Try to understand that one. When she looked up and saw Aquene standing on a rise and gazing down at the town and the highway, she was even more confused.

Molly made her way over to Aquene. "Do you know what's happening to us?" Since the moment she first saw Aquene she seemed to have an expectation about everything that happened. This shouldn't be any different, right?

Aquene slowly shook her head. "I do not. We are being shown something. I do not know what it is." Her voice cracked, and Molly turned her head to study her. There was a deep emotion in her voice that, up until now, she'd not heard even a trace of.

Molly was finding this alternate dimension strange, but the note in Aquene's voice troubled her more than her own disorientation. In fact, it downright frightened her. "What is it, Aquene?"

She waved her hands toward the landscape below. "Is this what my land becomes? Where are my people? Why will they not drink the water? How can the Great Spirit allow this to be?"

Molly followed her gaze down and saw what she always did. A small town. Family farms being worked by the people who called the town home, cattle, and, of course, the Umatilla River. She opened her mouth to reply and then shut it. A thought occurred to her, and for a moment, she studied the area with not her own eyes but instead tried to imagine what she would be seeing if she were Aquene. Suddenly, everything she was seeing morphed into something completely different.

What was there didn't change. Only her perception of it did. She still saw the town, the farms, the cattle, and the river, but it was the people that caught her attention now. Each one she saw looked like her. Not one in her field of vision was a Native American. No wonder Aquene was upset.

"Things have changed over the years." Her words were lame, and she wished more than anything that she could say something more comforting. The harsh reality of what had come to pass left her with no words of reassurance.

"Where are my people?" Aquene asked again, and this time her words were tinged with anger. Or perhaps it was bitterness.

How could she explain? She couldn't. The truth was harsh and very real. Nothing she could say to Aquene would make it better. "On a reservation many miles from here."

Aquene tipped her head back and yelled into the air something that Molly didn't understand. At first anyway. Then it hit her that Aquene was most likely calling out in her native language, which had disappeared quite a long time ago. She still had no idea what she said, though she thought she could understand the emotion behind the words.

"No one can hear us." Molly had already figured out that they weren't really standing here, not in a physical way.

"They will hear my words even if they are far away. My voice is on the wind and they will hear." Aquene sounded almost defiant. Not that she blamed her. It was strange for her to go back in time and experience the natural state of areas she was accustomed to seeing as fully inhabited. Aquene was experiencing the flip side of that. She was witnessing what she probably considered destruction, and that had to be hurtful.

Molly closed her eyes and sighed. She couldn't avoid the reality of what would happen several hundred years after Aquene's birth. She couldn't make it better, and what she had to say now was sure to make it worse. When she opened her eyes again, she told Aquene the brutal truth. "Even if they hear you, they won't understand. Your language died many, many years ago."

❖

Winnie stretched and looked around. "I don't know about you, but I'm hungry." The room had a little chill to it, but only a little. The fire Angus had built last night had kept away the cold. Though it had burned down now to little more than a pile of embers, the cabin seemed to retain much of the heat. Of course the fact that the storm finally ran its course didn't hurt either. She hoped the day would turn out to be sunny and warm. Easier to figure out a way home if they weren't soaked and hungry.

Angus also stood, his smile big. "Never leave home without it," he announced as he pulled a bag of trail mix from an interior coat pocket.

"Oh, my dear man, I have never loved you as much as I do right this minute. The only thing that would make me love you more is if you pulled a cup of coffee out of that jacket. Come on. Dazzle me. Please!"

He shook his head. "Afraid I'll have to do with superficial love. The trail mix is the extent of my magical skills this morning. No dazzle today."

She honestly wasn't so sure about that. Yes, it was true that Molly was a real witch. That didn't mean Angus didn't have magic too. Honestly, she'd been feeling it since they found themselves in this strange world. He seemed to have an aura of power that engulfed them both. It made her feel protected, safe.

Off and on since this whole thing began, she'd find herself flooded with the fear they would end up stuck in this alternate world and never see home again. Not that this wasn't home in a skewed way. She just wanted the home that had highways, electricity, running water, and indoor plumbing. Oh, and the coffee shops that were on just about every corner in town wouldn't be so bad either. First thing she'd do was take a hot shower and then go grab a nice, big mocha.

After actually being able to catch a little sleep overnight, she felt different today, calmer and more confident. Talking with Angus and knowing they were on the same page emotionally had made a huge impact. Beyond that, though, the more she rolled it over in her mind, the more she had a hunch they were here for a reason. Didn't things always happen for a reason? She liked to believe that anyway.

She'd already been treated to at least one of those: Angus had made clear his intention to build a life with her. They might have eventually reached this point back in their own time. Probably much further down the road. For whatever reason, being here brought everything to the forefront. Emotions were deeper, connections tighter, and words seemed compelled to come out into the open. In a lot of ways that was good. Odd but good.

It was more than their coming together, though. Regardless of how she came at it, she felt safer in Angus's arms than anywhere else. His strength and power filled her, and together they were stronger.

For her and Angus, it was all good and positive. Not so for Molly. Something dangerous existed outside the cabin's door, and it was gunning for her. At least that was the conclusion she'd come to. She doubted anyone out there gave a hoot about her and Angus, but Molly? Danger seemed to echo in the silence, and that scared her a lot. It was entirely possible the two of them were here by sheer accident. It was also possible they were not. Maybe they followed her through the wormhole to keep her safe, and she sure didn't want to let her friend down. Perhaps it was that touch of magic she glimpsed in Angus that would be the one thing that made a difference.

Taking a handful of the trail mix, Winnie picked at the nuts and dried fruit. She was hungry yet couldn't shake the tumultuous feeling in the pit of her stomach. The mixture of hunger and terror made her feel as though acid were swirling inside her. "We have to find Molly."

Angus was moving around the embers in the fireplace, working, it appeared to her, to try to put out the last of the fire. Not much was left, and the job wouldn't take long. It meant he planned to leave the cabin that had provided them shelter overnight. He still wasn't looking at her as he said, "Agreed, and I had a thought on what might help."

"She'll come back here, don't you think?" She didn't know what he was pondering. She really believed Molly would find her way back to the cabin. Staying here doing nothing might be counterproductive. Leaving might also be a mistake. Talk about being between a rock and a hard place.

He nodded as he dropped the stick he was using to move the embers and put an arm around her shoulders, planting a kiss on the top of her head. "Yes, I do, but I want to hike to higher ground. We'll have a good view of the surrounding area from the cliffs. Once we're up there, we'll be able to see for miles. I doubt she and her new friend will have gotten too far on foot last night. If they were smart, they'd have found shelter to ride out the storm just as we did. Hopefully, we'll be able to spot them heading back this way." He left her side to bound out the door. Obviously a little sleep had done wonders for his energy level.

Winnie followed him outside and turned to look in the direction he was pointing. Her first thought was: not happening. "You want us to go up there?" Did he not know her at all? She was not a nimble mountain climber in any universe. No, indeed, not even close. Waddle was more her style. "No way on God's green earth you're going to get my big butt up there. Not in this lifetime anyway. You do know who you're with, right?"

His laughter was like silver bells on the morning air. Reaching over, he pulled her close and hugged her. "You always underestimate yourself. You've really never paid attention to how you move, have you?"

His question sounded sincere, but for the life of her she didn't know where he was going with this. Yes, she knew how she moved. Kind of like a Clydesdale. "What do you mean?"

"Honey, you're like a tornado when you're in chef mode in the kitchen."

"Yes, but that's a kitchen with a nice, flat, tiled floor, and that's a far cry from mountain-goat status. I was lucky enough just to make that run yesterday without killing myself. I do not climb mountains or rock cliffs." She didn't want to either. It was way too far out of her comfort zone, not to mention her legs were sore from yesterday's exertion.

"That's where you're missing the point. You have the strength and the stamina to do all sorts of amazing things. I can help you with the rest. You'll be on top of that ridge before you know it."

Love made people do stupid things, and this situation was no exception. She loved this man with all her heart, and if he wanted her to crawl up that blasted basalt rock, well, then, by golly, that's exactly what she would do. Disappointing him wasn't an option. Her comfort zone was going to have to expand. Besides, what else did they have to do in this familiar yet totally foreign place? Might as well get a really good look at their altered reality. Had to admit, despite her hesitation about climbing, his plan was a good one. It would be interesting to see if she felt the same way once she made it to the top.

"Okay, team leader, show me the way."

His smile was broad. "That's the woman I love." He held out his hand and she took it. "Let's go climb a mountain."

The warmth she felt when her hand touched his was so lovely. She studied the long, flat apex in the distance, where soon enough they'd stand side by side searching for Molly. Despite its imposing height, the basalt rock was beautiful. It was hard not to appreciate what Mother Nature had created thousands of years before. Embarking on yet another adventure with Angus should make her feel like she was in heaven. Instead, the feeling in the pit of her stomach seemed to warn her that, on the top of that ridge, hell was waiting.

CHAPTER TWENTY-TWO

Aquene returned to her body and, for the first time in her life, understood her full destiny. At the same time, she wanted to fall to the earth and sob. She wished to believe that what she had just witnessed was a dream and nothing more, that perhaps it foreshadowed what might be rather than what was to come.

Her soul told her the truth. Molly told her the truth. Her people, her proud, fierce people, would be all but wiped from their lands. As they had stood in that field and surveyed what should have been familiar to her, her heart had ached, and tears had come to her eyes. Gone were the wide-open spaces, the animals that roamed without threat along the banks of the river, the women of her childhood working as the men trapped and hunted. Instead, she had seen buildings and land marred with ribbons of blackness. Roads, Molly had explained to her, though they were roads like no others she had seen. Things—she did not know what they were—moved across the black roads as though they were wagons that could travel without horses. Everything was foreign and frightening, but worst of all were the people. Not one single face looked like hers. Not one single face. Rather, it was a sea of the same people who lived in the outposts. Where once they were few in the vision, they had spread across the land as far as she could see.

Molly told her that her language was gone, and she was not surprised, for so too were her people. How could a language survive slaughter when no one was there to save it? The tears falling from her eyes were too strong to stop. For just a breath she thought that she should end her life, for what was the point of going forward? All that they believed in, all that she held dear, would one day be gone. How could this happen?

And then she looked up into Molly's face and knew that she could not stop. She did not understand any of what she had seen. But she did understand that she had been sent on this journey for a reason. When she had started out all those days ago, she had believed she was to find this woman and stop the man who carried darkness in his soul. What she had just witnessed showed her that her journey was far bigger than the one evil man. Yes, she and Molly still had to stop him, but once they did that, her true work would begin.

"I'm so, so sorry," Molly was saying as she cradled Aquene in her arms.

Aquene felt safe with Molly's arms wrapped around her. It would be nice if she could stay here until the sun fell behind the mountains. She could not, for they must travel on. The man was near; she could feel his presence on the wind. Molly must too, for Aquene knew that she carried true magic inside her. It was in her eyes and the way the light seemed to circle her like a cloud. She was special, and not just because Aquene felt an intense kinship for her.

She could not deny how she felt, even though she knew she had to. In less than a full day, she felt Molly's touch on her heart as if they had known each other for a lifetime. It was as strong as her connection to Alumpum. No, that was not right. She felt closer to Molly than to Alumpum, and she knew why. It was the kind of closeness that came between two who shared a lifetime together.

She left behind the thoughts of lifelong partnership and gazed into Molly's face. Though she did not feel joy, she smiled. "It is not for you to be sorry."

"But I am." Molly's arms tightened around Aquene. "My heart broke when you saw what this place had become. It's so beautiful here, and it all changes in ways that are shattering to see."

Freeing herself, Aquene pushed to her feet and shook out the grass from her hair. Then she extended a hand to Molly, who took it without hesitation. The connection they had been sharing all along was still there, although no sparks sent them into another place this time.

"Did you send my people away?"

"Well, no, but—"

"Our actions belong to each of us and no one else. You did not do this to my people, and I do not put the fault onto your shoulders."

"It's just that it's so wrong and many of us feel bad."

"And that is good, for it means that we can work together to change what is wrong."

Molly looked sad. "So many years have passed, and it's never been made right."

"Have others tried?"

This time she nodded. "Yes, but the damage was too great."

"Change takes time. Healing takes time. What has taken many years to destroy will take many years to rebuild."

Molly reached out a hand and touched her cheek. "You amaze me. If I'd seen what you did, I would have flipped out. You see the good in everything."

Aquene did not understand. Again. "I do not know flipped out."

Molly laughed. "It means I would have been very, very angry."

That she understood, and at first, anger had tried to cloud her vision. Thanks to many good teachers, she had kept it at bay. "It makes me sad, but it gives me purpose. We all do what we can to make this earth better. I will try to do what I can."

"You are the most amazing woman I've ever met."

Aquene thought the same thing about Molly.

Matthew was sitting tall in the saddle, feeling the strength of his righteousness fill him with pride. Everything this morning seemed and felt divine. Now that God had shown him the direction to follow, he was riding with purpose.

Something flickered to the right, catching his attention. He turned his head to see what it was. At first he thought his eyes were playing tricks on him. Pulling up on the reins, he brought his horse to a stop. Something about the woman standing in the tall grass felt familiar, although he could not quite determine what it was. She was pitifully thin, as though she was starving, and dirty to the point of pure filth. Her dress hung in tatters, and from beneath her bonnet that was as grimy as the rest of her clothing, her hair lay limp on her shoulders. Even from this distance he could swear her putrid stench was thick on the air.

Yet again, as he sat aloft and looked at her, something about her made him continue to stare. Then it struck him why. This woman was the exact image of the first witch he sentenced to death. In his hometown, he had overheard her and three friends speaking of their meetings with the devil. He had used her own words to convict her. Unlike most of his cases, she had not been hanged. Rather, she had been imprisoned, and there she had died. Though he would have been much happier had he been given the opportunity to hang her or, as he later determined to be more effective, burn her, the fact that she had died demonstrated that God had approved of his righteous accusations against her.

Except right at this moment he wondered why that same woman was standing out here. He wanted to believe she was someone who simply looked like the witch. He could not convince himself of that. His heart told him this was her, despite the improbability of that being the case.

It was impossible for her to be here. The thought almost made him laugh out loud. It was about as impossible for her to be standing in this field as himself. Dead men do not crawl out of their caskets. Yet here he was, in the living and breathing flesh. Impossibility had nothing to do with anything.

As he had done with each witch he sentenced to death, he had seen her lifeless body and had witnessed her burial in the pit behind the prison. She had been destroyed in that prison, utterly and completely. That he believed he could see her now was a trick of his mind brought on by the quest to stop yet another witch. Most likely, the one he sought now was casting another of her spells, to which he was immune. There was no end to the tricks they would employ in their struggle to stop him. They all failed.

He started to turn away, intent on continuing his tracking of the witch while ignoring the harmless apparition that appeared to him now, and then stopped. In his town, the custom of ringing bells and lighting candles protected them from returning spirits. Around his grave, his brothers had brought candles and, once lit, rang bells to protect him, just as he would have done for them had they gone before him.

As his mind turned back to the day they had carried her shriveled body from the dark, dank corridors below the prison-keeper's quarters, he remembered every little detail. His memory was as clear as if her death had occurred yesterday. There had been no mourners, no bells, and no candles. She had been poor and wicked, and no one had seen fit to waste time or effort on her burial. It had been a miscalculation, he realized in this moment, for in doing nothing, he had failed to banish the witch, and now, all these years later, she had returned to show him how foolishly arrogant he had been at the time.

Well, not again. He had been new to his profession at the time of her death and perhaps not always as thorough as he should have been. Because he had not put basic protections in place, she had taken advantage of his inexperience. In the intervening years, he had learned much and improved his hunting skills to the point of becoming an expert with no equal anywhere in the world. Slipping from the back of his horse, Matthew unhooked the rope from his saddle and began to walk toward the woman. It would be easier to simply ride away and continue his current task. But he was never one to choose uncomplicated. He found no fun or satisfaction in easy.

He expected her to cringe as she had done all those years ago. She, like all others, was afraid of the power he wielded, as well they should be. Unlike the last time they were face-to-face, she did not cower or lower her gaze. Her back straightened, her stringy dark hair hanging on either side of her pale face like streaks of grease. Her dark eyes were huge in her face, but they showed no fear. This was not quite like the woman he had faced all those years ago. When she smiled, her rotted teeth gave him chills. "We all await ye, Witch-Finder. We have been waiting for ye a long, long time."

"Silence, witch!" His roar was loud in the still morning air. He was surprised when she remained erect and smiling, though he did not allow it to show. His voice normally put even the toughest onto their knees.

"Nay. I will be silent no more. Ye have made a blunder of this world, and judgment of ye crimes awaits."

Her display of bravado did not sway him. He laughed as he made a show of the rope, one end tied in a noose. "It is you who have blundered. And it is I who will send you back to hell."

Her dark eyes seemed to sparkle in the sunlight. "A long time I have waited, and this day 'tis judgment day. Be wary, Witch-Finder. We come for ye. We all come for ye."

No more, he thought silently, and began to run. As he did, she disappeared.

CHAPTER TWENTY-THREE

It was the absolute last thing that should be happening, yet there it was. Molly was falling hard for the woman who was staring into her eyes. It didn't make sense, given they'd known each other for, what? Twenty-four hours…maybe? People didn't fall in love after a single day. She'd dated women for months and never felt a flicker of anything remotely similar to love. Attraction and like, sure, but love, not even close. To feel this intense rush of emotion was, well, ridiculous, and that wasn't her. She didn't do ridiculous.

How did one fall in love with a stranger anyway? It went beyond the simple reality that they didn't know each other. The complications were numerous, like the little fact they were from vastly different cultures. Not to mention they were separated by a massive gulf called centuries of time. Everything between the worlds they were born into was poles apart. To even think they could find a way to bridge that gulf was mind-boggling. Or, in other words, impossible, and that meant she just needed to keep her blooming emotions to herself. No sense complicating an already complicated situation.

"What do you think we should do now?"

Aquene didn't even hesitate. "We must find him and stop him."

Damned if she wouldn't give a hundred bucks to know exactly who this *him* was. At this point, she completely bought in to the notion a man was out there hunting for them and not with the noble intent of rescue. Quite the opposite. If he was anything like the bad guys in the typical Western movie, he'd ride in on a big black horse wearing a big black hat and waving a gun. Unlike those old Westerns, they weren't damsels in distress who had to rely upon a man to protect them.

She leaned down and picked up the grimoire from where she'd dropped it when she caught Aquene. "Let's see what Hannah has to say." Might as well go straight to the source and see what Grandma would tell her next. Instead of picking up where she left off, Molly flipped to the back of the book.

September 28, 1836

My time here nears its end. I feel his hand on my back and his breath upon my neck. He is walking through the shadows, and he walks to me. I prayed for more days to complete this book. I fear it is not to be, and I must hurry and finish as much I am able before he comes. The words I put down will help you, and you must use them, for they will grant you power. They will help you take hold of the light. Most of all, you must stop him, for I cannot. His might is too great. The strength that the king of darkness has given him is too much for my wanting skills.

It is you, my dear granddaughter, who will send him back to the purgatory he crawled out of. My hopes, all of our hopes, are in your hands. Be brave and be strong. Do not fail.

"Well, that was clear as mud," Molly said as she closed the book. Cryptic as it was, it also frightened her because, just as Hannah had written about feeling his hand on her back and his breath on her neck, Molly felt the same thing. He was getting closer by the second.

"I sense a change in the air," Aquene told her as she looked up at the sky. "Do you feel it?"

Oh, yes, indeed. From head to toe. It worried her as much as it seemed to concern Aquene. Not so much because she felt like she and Aquene would be harmed. No, she believed Aquene was as tough as they came and that, between the two of them, they could protect themselves. She worried about Angus and Winnie. Both of them were capable, no doubt about that, but this wasn't their normal environment. Nothing about where they found themselves was even remotely routine for them.

Then again, maybe she was selling Angus and Winnie short. Both were smart and accustomed to taking care of themselves in unique situations. Molly was figuring this out as she went, and they probably were too. She was sure they were. Give them a few more hours, and hopefully they would all reunite.

Once they were all together again, she would be better able to concentrate on the prophesies in Hannah's grimoire. She hoped the spells Hannah had left her would work too because, if not, she didn't have a clue what they would do when they came face-to-face with the boogeyman on their tail. It wasn't like she really had a strong hold on her powers or could recite very many of the spells her mother could produce from memory. As her mother liked to tell her, she knew just enough to be dangerous, though now that she thought about, maybe that wasn't a bad thing.

"Yes," she finally said as she looked into Aquene's eyes. "I feel something, and I don't like it."

"Not to be vulgar, my handsome man, but this is fucked up." Winnie could already tell her shins were going to be black and blue, not to mention she'd scraped her hands clawing her way up the basalt rocks. Her modeling career was most certainly on hold. How she'd ever admired these damn hills, she didn't know, because right now, she hated them. She would never look at them the same again.

When Angus had the brilliant idea to climb up for a better view, and after his pep talk, it had seemed like a good idea. After all, it would give them a great panoramic view down toward the river. Surely that was the direction Molly and Aquene would take. In addition to anything else they did, they still needed to find Molly. It was most certainly Molly's magic that had got them here, and it was also certain they wouldn't get back home without it. Angus might have a twitch of something inside him, but it was a speck compared to what Molly could do.

Winnie wanted to go home. She appreciated history as much as the next woman. Once or twice she'd even attended living-history presentations out at the Spokane House and Riverside State Park. They'd been interesting, and she'd loved the walks back in time. Taking the trip intellectually was one thing. Doing it in the flesh was something quite different, and this wasn't nearly as interesting. When her only choice was to live in the past, it was kind of freaky. A little too up close and personal. She was a twenty-first-century woman, and living off the grid wasn't her style.

"Oh, sweetie, suck it up."

His endearment wasn't taking any of the sting out of his words or her body. She was meant to cook, not climb, and Angus had to know that better than anybody. To be fair, he was always looking out for her, protecting her, and loving her. Pep talk aside, if he didn't think she was capable of this, he wouldn't have brought her along. He wasn't the kind of man who put someone else in danger. That thought made her take a deep breath and stop worrying about how much her body screamed in protest as they moved higher and higher. She could do this. She had to do this.

Winnie managed a laugh. "Sucking it up."

He glanced over his shoulder and smiled. "That's my lady." He winked and her heart took a leap. Yes, she could climb this damn thing, even if it left her black and blue from head to foot.

For the next twenty minutes, she actually did manage to suck it up and escape grave bodily injury. She was silently patting herself on the back. They were almost there, and in about two minutes, she'd be standing at the top searching for Molly with only minor bumps, bruises, and scrapes. Yeah, she was feeling pretty good, at least until she heard Angus gasp and yell, "You manky bitch."

At first, she thought he was talking about her, and then before she could get pissed off, realized he'd pulled himself up to the ridge. Staring up at the spot where he'd been just a few second ago, she screamed when all of a sudden a snake went sailing past her head. It was a miracle she didn't let go of the rocks and fly backward to a very untimely death. Or a broken leg if she got lucky. Instead, she scrambled up the last five feet and was breathing heavily when she plopped down next to Angus. It took a whole lot of effort to pull her butt up and over that ledge, and she'd done it all by herself. She wouldn't have refused a little help, had it been offered.

As happy as she was to finally be on the ridge, she was dismayed to see him holding his hand down, his arm ramrod straight. His face was as white as a piece of copy paper. Now she knew why he hadn't offered her a hand as she'd pulled herself up and over.

"What happened?" she gasped.

"Fuckin' rattler."

Her heart dropped. "A rattlesnake?" She hated snakes—all snakes—but rattlers were poisonous, as in kill-people poisonous. With so much on her mind, she'd never imagined they might run into one, which was stupid. This was a prime habitat for the snakes. If she'd have remembered that before they started climbing, nothing he could have said would have gotten her up here. No way. No how. Now it was too late. "What do we do?"

With his uninjured hand, Angus dug in one of his pockets and pulled out a pocketknife. "I need to bleed it out."

"Bleed it out?" Just the thought of what he was thinking of doing with that knife made her stomach turn. She wasn't afraid of blood. Anyone who worked in a kitchen for a living had better have a strong stomach for the stuff. But just the thought of intentionally cutting into skin bothered her. Before she could say anything, he sliced the top of his hand where the two red puncture wounds marred his flesh. Blood began to spill onto the ground, deep and crimson.

"A little back-country first aid," he explained as he held his dripping hand close to the ground. "Not ideal but it will have to do."

"Should you hold it up?" It seemed to her that the bleeding would stop sooner if he held it up rather than down. In the kitchen, the first line of defense was to staunch the flow of blood.

He shook his head, and it troubled her that he was still so pale. No, that wasn't right. With each drop of blood he seemed to become paler. "Need to keep the venom from moving toward my heart."

She hated the sound of that. "Okay." The word came out as a breathy whisper instead of sounding confident, like she hoped. He was consistently strong for her, and she wanted to do the same for him. So far, it was pretty much a fail on her part.

He gave her a wan smile. "It will be all right. Very few people die from snake bites."

Very few people died from snake bites in the twenty-first century, but she didn't say what she was thinking. No need to throw salt on the wound.

"What do we do next?" She should be helping him somehow instead of sitting here asking dumb questions. He was the one hurt, and yet he was also the one doing everything. Not right. She had to step up.

He had ripped a piece of cloth off his shirt and was wrapping his bleeding hand with it. When he was done protecting the wound, he took his jacket and used it to tie his arm tight to his waist.

At her quizzical look, he explained. "I need to restrict movement, which limits blood flow. It's a protective measure." Once he finished, Angus slowly stood and, for a second, swayed on his feet. Winnie put her arm around his waist to steady him. In answer to her unasked question, he told her, "We're going back to the cabin."

It seemed like the smartest thing to do, even if she dreaded climbing back down the rocks. At least for her, going down had to be easier than climbing up. What would it do to Angus as he tried to make his way down with one arm? Staying up here felt more like a death sentence. They were in a damned-if-they-did-and-damned-if-they-didn't situation. They needed to work their way back down and return to the cabin to wait for Molly to not just join them but get them home ASAP.

"Okay. We go back." As she headed toward the same spot she'd come up and over, she gazed down and almost screamed. "There," she managed to say in a calm voice. "Look."

Molly and Aquene, it had to be, and it was the most beautiful thing she could ever remember seeing. They were near the river, walking through the tall grasses. One woman was tall and dressed in pants and a jacket, the other in her knee-high moccasins with long black braids down her back. The sight brought tears of joy to her eyes and hope to her heart. At least until she scanned the other direction. A man, mounted on a horse, was galloping straight toward the two women. While he was still quite a distance away from them, he was moving faster than they were.

Angus was leaning against her while following the direction of her gaze. "Even from this distance, I don't like the look of that bloke."

It was impossible to make out any details, yet the sight of the man gave her icy chills. "I don't either. We have to warn them."

"I have to stay calm." He kept his voice as steady as his words. "Running to Molly would..." He didn't have to finish the sentence for Winnie to understand.

Fear shot through her, and tears of a different kind threatened. Once more she took his earlier advice and sucked it up. She tightened her arms on Angus. Molly and Aquene were on their own. "Let's get back to the cabin."

"I think we should."

By the time they made it to the bottom of the basalt rocks, he was even paler than before. Winnie was very scared.

CHAPTER TWENTY-FOUR

The vision had shaken Aquene in a way none other had. Not simply the strangeness of the landscape, the odd things she saw, or even the settlements that had wiped away so much of the natural beauty of her land affected her so deeply. Nor did not even seeing a single face like hers. What filled her with sadness as big as the sky was what Molly had told her when she screamed out her call: no one would understand.

That the descendants of her friends and family could no longer speak their language made her want to drop to the earth and weep. She was proud of her people, their ways, and of the beauty of their native tongue. She wanted to believe that these things would carry on for all time, and if Molly spoke the truth, that would not come to pass. They would end much as her own life would one day pass into the great beyond.

Looking into Molly's beautiful eyes told her everything she needed to know. In that place where they had found themselves earlier, that piece of time, her way was gone, her people diminished, her way of life wiped away as if it had never been there at all. The tragedy of that knowledge was almost more than she could bear. She had started this journey with great anticipation, but now she was filled with great sorrow.

Rather than let the sadness take her heart, she turned her mind to the man who shadowed them. She moved her thoughts away from that which she could not control and to that which she had a chance to change. They had to banish the darkness he carried with him and had carried with him for longer than she could know.

"Any ideas on what we need to do?" Molly was looking around

at the endless stretch of nature, appearing confused. "I feel the urge to move. I'm just not sure where to."

From the time she had left her family and friends, Aquene had gone forward with a true sense of purpose, her faith in what she was to do unshakable. Until now. For the first time, she was unsure where to go and what to do. She did not know either the man's face or how to stop him. They had walked some distance from their temporary camp, though it seemed they had not made progress.

How she wished she were home for Alumpum to hold her hand and help her find her way. She suddenly felt lost, and her courage began to waver. Perhaps it had been a mistake sending her on this journey. The quest that had seemed so clear to her in the beginning was now so confusing she wondered if her mind had gone feeble. The crushing weight on her spirit was like a chant that told her she was doomed to fail over and over again.

Molly did not appear to notice her sudden change of heart. "We have to take this asshole down and keep him from hurting anyone else. If Hannah is right, we have to stop him from knocking me off in any event. Kind of sounds like my family's future depends on it."

"Knocking you off what?" The words brought Aquene out of her introspection. It was not like Tilla was here for them to ride and be knocked to the ground from her back. Perhaps the man came on horseback and Molly wanted to throw him from the horse's back to the ground.

Molly laughed. "God, I'm so sorry. I keep forgetting. It's another one of those things we say back in the twenty-first century. It means he plans to kill me."

She had heard of those who fell from their horse and did not ever rise again. Perhaps over time that was why Molly's people used those words. "Ah, I do understand. You talk so strangely. It will take me a very long time to understand you."

"In my world, yeah, I talk pretty strange. Around my place, I talk like everybody else."

It was hard for Aquene to imagine a place where everyone spoke so strangely yet no one could speak in her tongue any longer. It was interesting and sad. Mostly sad. It also helped her shed her indecision. At this time she did not want to focus on what would be lost in the future. It was more important to finish what she had started. "I believe we need to return to the cabin."

Molly gave her a puzzled look. "Wouldn't that be the first place this guy would come looking for us?"

"Yes." She hoped he would. While she had been content to take this journey as it came, that was no longer true. After what she had seen in her vision, she was ready to stop this creature before he could do any more harm to the world. It was only a tiny thing, but it was something, and that made her feel as though she had a little dominion.

"So why go back? Don't we want to track him and take him by surprise?"

Surprise was a very good hunting tactic, and Aquene would employ it if she thought it would end their journey without either of them being harmed. She did not believe it would happen in that way. As she stood here breathing in the fresh air and letting the sun warm her skin, she understood that they had to confront this evil spirit face-to-face. They must do battle looking into his eyes. If they did not, they would never be able to stop him. His power, his influence on the world, would go on and on, and that was something that could not be allowed to happen.

She did not know from where this knowledge sprang or why it appeared in this moment. She could only accept that it came to her for a reason, which was to end the years of domination by a demon that never should have walked the earth.

And it would help her save the life of the woman who stared at her with beautiful, soulful eyes. Aquene hoped that when this was over and Molly returned to her own time, she would be able to remember those eyes for the rest of her days.

❖

Matthew swore he could smell her. It was not the filthy, unwashed body of the witch who had appeared to him in the field and spewed her worthless dribble. On the air now an acrid scent floated to him, and it meant only one thing: he was closing the distance. That whom he sought was near. He patted the rope at the back of his saddle and smiled. The thing he had seen some distance back had shaken him, though he would never tell any of the way the sight of her had affected him. It had to be something dredged up from his memory only because he was weary. The night had been uncomfortable and sleep elusive. Sometimes lack of sleep could make a man believe things that were not there. He had seen it happen with others. Never before to him.

The witch was most definitely not there. Right before she had appeared, he had been recalling how successful his work was, how he was close to wiping every trace of their kind from the earth. Surely her appearance was nothing more than a vision from a tired mind. Or if not that, then evil forces trying to keep him from his just rewards. When every last witch was burned out of existence, the Father would surely bring him home for the glory he was due. He was certain of it.

Now he brought his horse to a standstill, threw back his head, and inhaled deeply. Yes, it was true. She was close. Excitement rushed through his veins, and he kicked his horse. He wanted to catch up with her soon and light the fire beneath her feet in order that the flames could consume her earthly body and destroy the darkness in her soul.

As he looked around, he realized he was backtracking, traveling on a path that would return him to the witch's cabin. Interesting that this one would revisit the site of his last pyre. Fitting, actually, and he liked the idea of circling back to where it all began. His initial inclination to rush faded, and he slowed his horse to an easy walk. He might as well savor the sunshine that was gracing the day. He would enjoy the flames more after the sun set. He would relish seeing the dancing firelight and listening to the screams as the blaze ate the witch's soul. Once she was a blackened husk, he would take her devil's book and burn it too. No other man or woman would ever see those wicked words.

The other one from the cabin had denied him the pleasure of hearing her screams, just as the one who had appeared to him in the field had done. That one had died while in jail, and the one here had dropped into death after the arrows of his scouts had pierced her. By the time they had dragged her out of the cabin and had her hanging by her neck, her eyes had dulled and her head lolled. It had been disappointing, though her death had not kept him from lighting the branches and logs they had piled beneath her feet. It had not kept him from standing in the darkness and watching until the flames died away and all that was left was a charred outline of a woman's body and a bit of rope, one end blackened, dangling from the tree. He did not walk away until he was certain he had done the job right.

Only then did he pay his companions for their work and send them on their way. Their hoots and hollers could be heard for a long time, even after they disappeared into the deepening night. He had left her remains for the scavengers and had also ridden away in the darkness, hoping to return at long last to his home across the sea.

But God had not allowed him to go home. For, he was to discover, another had come for the knowledge the burning witch had left behind.

However, as he pondered the events a year past, he came to see that it was less a failure and more a trap. The witch he sought now had come to this place lured by the promise of the book. Had he taken it before this day, she might have slipped away from him. He would now accomplish a dual goal: destroy the witch and destroy the book. He suddenly saw the verity. He had not failed before. This was as God decreed. He smiled again.

After riding for some time, he decided to once more stop at the river's edge in order that both he and his horse might drink. He dismounted and let loose of the reins. His horse slowly walked to the riverbank and lowered its head to the water. This was the right course of action, and he intended to employ the methods that had worked for him since the beginning. What he was doing now was just the beginning. Last night he had been stymied in his efforts at tracking, but it would not happen again. He would dog them and thus keep them from getting any rest. It was the first and best way to get the witch to confess her sins before her execution.

Now it was time to ride forth and corner her, just as he had done to many in the early days of his career. By 1645 he had become a true expert in witch-finding and never again employed his profession as a lawyer. He had found his true calling. The fact that he was still here and working proved how divine he was. As he remounted his horse, he kept his back straight and his gaze steady.

"I pray for your soul, Matthew Hopkins."

He whipped his head to the side and gasped. "You!"

He had not set his eyes upon this face since 1646. He remembered it as if it had been this day. The man wore the robes of the clergy, which infuriated him now as much as it had on that long-ago morning. That the man would have put on those robes and dedicated his soul to the devil was a disgrace that even the flames that had burned his earthly body could not erase. It should not shock him to see that face this far from his home.

The clergyman nodded, and the trace of a smile creased his lined face. He had not been a young man when Matthew had watched him burn, and he was not one day older or younger now. "I have waited many seasons to gaze upon your face again."

The laugh that roared from Matthew was bitter. These visions of conquests past had no power over him. "You never change. I knew the first time I laid eyes on you that you were the devil's spawn. That you stand before me even now is further proof. I destroyed you and yet here you are. Only Satan could make that happen."

"I stand before you as a child of God."

"How dare you speak of God. You have no right."

"No, Matthew, it is you who has no right, and you never did. You killed in the name of our Lord, but you did so out of malice and greed. Innocents died at your hands, and you profited from their deaths. On this bright and glorious day, you shall atone for your many sins."

Hardly a threat he took to heart, and he laughed. "If my God sees fit to take me home, it will be to heaven. I alone am free of sin." A pure man would also find a home in God's house.

This time the clergyman laughed. "No, Witch-Finder. Be confident of this: it is not heaven that will embrace you. The flames you freely loosed on the guiltless will welcome you to hell."

He didn't bother to go for his rope this time, for he felt certain that, once again, the body he was looking at, speaking to, would vanish the moment he drew close. Instead, he turned his face away and stared in the direction he planned to travel. "We shall see," he said with confidence. "We shall see."

He kicked his horse into a trot and then once more so that they were sailing across the open spaces. This last apparition made him all the more resolved to finish this here and now. On the back of this large and powerful horse, he could cover the distance in no time. Soon he would be on his way back home filled with righteous satisfaction. He was smiling as he rode, oblivious to the dangers of where he went. He failed to see the gaping hole as he prodded his horse.

Suddenly, he was flying off his horse, and when he landed on the ground, all the air was pushed from him. He missed hitting a rock with his head by no more than an inch. It was not luck. It was divine intervention.

Muttering under his breath at the stupidity of the large horse, he stood and brushed dried grass from his clothing. Once more he thought about how glad he would be when this was done and he could rid himself of this tiresome beast. When he brought his head up, he was surprised to see the horse still on the ground.

He walked over to it to where it lay on the ground. Matthew's screams filled the air as he looked down.

CHAPTER TWENTY-FIVE

Despite telling Aquene she agreed with her, Molly really wasn't sure it was the best idea to go back to the cabin if some weirdo was out there hunting them. She also wasn't sure it was a bad idea. She hoped Winnie and Angus would have the same thought and head back there too. If that was the case, they would have numbers on their side. Once they kicked the legs out from under the bastard hunting them, they'd be able to reunite and figure out a way back home. She was pretty sure it would take a village—their village—to find their way to the twenty-first century once again.

At least last night's rain had passed and it was turning into a beautiful day. Their travel should go smooth and quick.

"I think I'll grab another drink before we take off." She'd really like a table at Winnie's restaurant with a tall glass of ice water, a cup of coffee, and one of her famous fluffy omelets. She almost groaned just thinking about the food, which made her hungrier than she already was. Aquene's dried salmon was good, an omelet was better. Maybe if she filled up on water, she wouldn't think about a four-star breakfast.

The water seemed to help. Her stomach stopped growling, and she felt more alert. The little bit of salmon just wasn't a lot of food for the physical effort they'd put out both last night and already today. She stood and turned to Aquene, intending to ask how much farther she believed it was to the cabin. As she did, her foot slipped on the wet riverbank. Before she could stop herself, she tumbled backward and hit the water. It was like she was in a slow-motion movie. She could feel herself going, her arms waving and her feet sliding. Nothing she did could stop her momentum. If somebody were to video her fall, it would surely go viral.

The water was cold when she hit, and she felt like someone had punched her in the gut. It took one hundred and ten percent concentration to avoid full-on panic mode, and that wasn't easy, given where she found herself. She was never much for open-water swims.

Luckily, she hit close to the shore where it was fairly shallow, and the strong river current didn't sweep her away. Thank the good Lord for small favors. Scrambling up, she reached out, and Aquene grabbed her hand, helping pull her to dry ground. Despite the warmth of the sun, she began to shiver. She felt like she'd just stepped out of a freezer dressed in soaking-wet pants and jacket. If she had any question about her jacket being waterproof, she now had an answer. Nope. Nyet. Nein.

"We must get you out of the wet clothing." Aquene was taking command.

Her teeth were chattering. "I don't have anything else to put on."

"You cannot stay in these garments. You will fall ill. We cannot stay here long, but we must get most of the water out of your clothing before we journey on." Aquene wasn't waiting for her to comply with the directive. She'd already pulled Molly's jacket off and was reaching for her shirt. Molly started to protest. A decent person didn't strip down in public. Then she almost laughed. Exactly what public was here to see her? They were in the middle of nowhere in the middle of the nineteenth century. No public. No cell phones to capture video. No internet to upload said video. Yeah, she was pretty safe. She began to strip off the cold, wet clothing, and while the air was cool against her skin, it was infinitely warmer than the ice-cold pants and shirt.

Surprisingly, she wasn't totally uncomfortable once she was naked. The sun was warm enough that, once she was dry, she felt pretty good. It was a little weird standing in her altogether in front of Aquene, but then again, why not hang out in her altogether? They wouldn't see each other again after Molly went home. Besides, she discovered that she wasn't self-conscious in front of her either. Aquene's calm demeanor and matter-of-fact efforts made it all seem just fine.

As Molly sat on a rock with her legs pulled up, Aquene produced a length of cloth out of her magic bag and wrapped it around her shoulders. Despite where they were and the one hundred percent guarantee she could strip without anyone filming her, it was still hard to be completely at ease. She kept glancing over her shoulder, expecting to see some guy with a smartphone taking a video. The cloth didn't cover much, though it did make her feel a lot less exposed. It also smelled a bit like salmon, which made her smile and feel hungry at the same time. "Thanks."

"You are welcome." Someone had not only schooled Aquene in the English language but in the polite customs as well. It was endearing.

Molly was also comfortable in her birthday suit because Aquene wasn't really paying attention to her. She was busily spreading Molly's wet clothing on rocks and hanging them from exposed tree branches, presumably so they would dry faster. It was a good idea, and she felt a little guilty sitting here instead of helping. It wasn't Aquene's fault she'd taken a header into the river, and it shouldn't be her responsibility to clean up her mess.

Molly almost laughed as Aquene picked up her sports bra and studied it with a confused expression. "It's a sports bra," she explained.

Her explanation didn't change Aquene's expression. "A what?"

This time she did laugh. Holding her hands under her breasts, she tried to explain in a little more detail. "It's to give support right here."

The ghost of a smile crossed Aquene's face, as if the idea of such a garment was amusing. She supposed in a way it was. "It is a strange land you live in. Strange words and strange clothing."

"Yeah. Sometimes it is. It's like anything, though. You get used to what you see around you every day." Of course, she was also looking around and thinking it couldn't be much stranger than right here. Seriously, a pale woman sitting naked on a rock in the tall grass with a little scrap of cloth draped around shoulders and a Native American woman wearing the real-deal clothing of her tribe standing next to her didn't strike Aquene as strange? Pretty unusual in any situation, if you asked Molly. Top that off with the serious attraction she was feeling toward said Native American woman, and yeah, it was pretty high on the weird meter.

As Molly watched Aquene twist each piece of clothing to rid it of as much water as possible, she kept thinking how lovely she was. She lacked all the modern comforts that Molly enjoyed, yet her hair was beautiful and shiny, her skin flawless, and her body enticing beneath her garments. Best of all were those moccasins; they were gorgeous and made her legs look the same. All of sudden, Molly wasn't so sure she hadn't hit her head during that fall into the river. Usually in a crisis situation she didn't get sidetracked by a beautiful woman, yet here she was with the urge to drop the cloth and say, "Take me." Definitely must have hit her head. It was the only explanation that made sense.

Except, maybe, just maybe that glint in Aquene's eyes as she looked over her shoulder at Molly said she was feeling a bit of the same thing.

❖

For the first time since finding herself in this altered dimension, Winnie was scared shitless. They'd managed to trek maybe a hundred yards before Angus stumbled. He would have fallen if she hadn't caught him, and that was no easy feat given his size. That she had kept him from crashing to the ground amazed her, and for a second she felt elated. Only when she felt his bare skin did her elation fade. He was hot and clammy.

Her first-aid skills lacked a lot. Like any good chef, she had enough basic skills to get her by until EMTs could arrive. Accidents happened routinely in busy kitchens. She'd even had to practice on herself a time or two when her knife work grew sloppy. But wilderness first aid was a completely different beast. Angus was always the go-to guy for that because he loved hiking, biking, and basic survival. If he had his wallet on him, she'd wager it had an up-to-date first-aid and CPR card in it. He would know exactly what to do and how to do it.

Not so in her case. She was lost, though not enough to be oblivious to the fact she had a problem on her hands. A real big, one-hundred-and-eighty-pound problem. Angus was losing energy and color fast, and they were still a fair distance away from the cabin and even farther away from home, hospitals, and good doctors. What she wouldn't give to hear the obnoxious scream of an ambulance siren right about now. What worried her most was the certainty that it wouldn't be long before he lost consciousness in addition to energy. Then what?

"Pull it together, Winnie," she muttered under her breath. "You can do this." If she approached the situation like she would if someone was hurt in her kitchen, she could figure it out. She hoped.

As if in slow motion, Angus turned and looked at her. "What?" Was it her imagination, or did he slur that word?

She put a hand to his cheek, his very warm cheek. Great, just fucking great. Infection was about the last thing she needed. She forced a smile and kept her voice light. One of them panicking was plenty. "Just muttering to myself, sweetness. How are you doing? We don't have far to go," she lied.

His eyes closed and he shook his head. "Banjaxed," he said quietly.

What did that mean? "You're what, baby?" Probably just heard him wrong.

Her worst fears began to be a reality. His legs began to buckle, and he started to drop. "Sorry," he whispered. "I love you."

This time she couldn't help except to try to keep him from hitting his head as he went down. He crumpled on his bad side to the grass-and-branch-strewn ground in a heap. He didn't move. Kneeling beside him, she shook his shoulder. "Angus," she said loudly. His eyelids didn't even flutter. He was out.

"Oh, God, oh, God, oh, God," Winnie cried this time, and she allowed the tears to flow down her cheeks. "No way are you checking out on me, Angus Farrell. I'm meeting this mum of yours come hell or high water. You hear me, big boy?"

Shifting to take hold of his shoulders, she stretched him out so that the arm he had fallen on was no longer bent beneath his body. Blood seeped from several scratches on the side of his face. Inspection showed they were not deep. That was good. One less problem to solve. She had bigger things to be concerned about. He still had his arm and hand with the snake bite strapped to his body, and that was a relief. The fall hadn't dislodged the makeshift wrapping. There was still a problem, however, and it concerned her a lot. He'd told her it was important to keep the bitten hand below heart level, and the way he was lying flat now, it was definitely not below his heart.

Glancing around she spied a fallen tree nearby, which gave her an idea and not a little hope for at least a temporary solution. She dragged a heavy tree branch over and then slid Angus around until his upper body was propped on it and his injured hand was below his torso. His head sort of lolled, but she was less worried about his head and far more concerned about keeping that injured area below his heart.

By the time she had him situated she was breathing like she'd just run a full marathon at lightning speed. She was huffing and puffing so loud she promised herself that when—and she refused to even consider if—they returned home, she was hitting the gym hard. At her age, she should be able to do better than this. She'd worry about that later. Right now, she had a bigger issue: how to get Angus back to the cabin without killing him along the way. She certainly couldn't carry him, and it wasn't like she could drag him that far.

Or could she? Standing over him with her hands on her hips, she had a thought, and the more she considered it, the more she liked it. In fact, she decided it was the only option that had any chance of success. The fallen tree had given her an idea. It would cost her the lovely jacket she wore. No big deal. If she had to, she'd strip naked, if that's what it would take to get Angus to the cabin.

It took her hours, or at least that's what it felt like, to fashion a makeshift litter out of scavenged tree branches lashed together with strips of her clothing. Once she had it put together, she spent what seemed like another eternity getting Angus up onto it. He was dead weight. She was happy that, at the very least, he wasn't dead. Once again, though, she was panting hard. Yes, indeed, the gym was on the top of her must-do list.

From the look of it, the plan to use the litter to move Angus would work well, until she tried to pick it up and get on the move. It didn't work out quite as easily in reality as it had in her head. She panicked. If she didn't get him back to the cabin where just maybe she could find something to help, Angus could die. Tears sprang into her eyes and her heart thudded. After a few seconds, she talked herself out of panic and back to calm thoughts. She hoped she could find a solution. No, wait. No hope about it. She would find a solution.

It came in the form of the web-style belt Angus wore. It wasn't long, but it was long enough to fashion a strap she could use as a sort of handle. Once she found a way to attach it to the litter, she was off and moving, albeit slowly. She could deal with slow as long as she was closing the distance to the cabin. Her relief when it worked brought her to tears, and though she'd barely held them back only minutes before, now she let them slide down her cheeks as she trudged forward. She was entitled.

The underbrush and grass gave her trouble. At times she had to go wide in order to avoid fallen trees or big rocks pushing out of the ground. More than once she had to detach bushes from where they'd snagged on the bottom of the litter. The effort was grueling and took all of her strength, which wasn't a lot, considering how long it had been since she'd had anything to eat or drink.

She didn't know how long she'd been pulling Angus when she saw that the river wasn't far away. Though she didn't want to stop, she had to. She had momentum on her side and worried she would lose it. On the other hand, dehydration was nasty, and she couldn't afford nasty at the moment. Carefully, she lowered the front of the litter to the ground. The position wasn't ideal, because once again it put Angus prone on the ground, and she really wanted to keep his upper body raised. For a second she thought about picking it back up and continuing. Then she decided against it. It was a risk she had to take.

Winnie ran to the river's edge and kneeled so she could scoop water into her hands and drink it like the parched woman she was. It was the most satisfying drink she could ever remember and gave her an immediate lift. Sure, she was hungry. No solution for that. The water, however, seemed to give her back her life. She glanced over to where Angus lay motionless and wished she had her purple water bottle. He needed it as much or more than she did.

Looking down at the remnants of the T-shirt she wore gave her an idea. It was much shorter than when she'd put it on because she'd ripped off the bottom to help create the litter. She'd already lost her jacket and part of her shirt, and losing a little more of it wouldn't kill her. Lack of water just might kill Angus. She ripped again, pulling a length of the fabric free. Dunking it in the water, she let it soak until it was fully saturated. As she hurried back to Angus, she cradled it in her cupped hands to save as much of the water as she could. She wanted to get a good amount of it down him and at the same time keep it from soaking his shirt. He didn't need to be wet in addition to unconscious.

Kneeling next to Angus, she began to dribble the water between his lips. Much of it seemed to drip down his cheeks. She prayed more of it went down his throat and chose to believe it did. Had to. His eyes fluttered, and he started to murmur. Winnie put her ear closer to his lips. "What did you say?"

"Thank you." It was more of a sigh, but she could still make out the two words, and they sounded wonderful.

She kissed his forehead. "Stay with me, Angus. Remember, we're going to Ireland to meet your mom. So, you hang in there because I'm getting you to help." God, she hoped that wasn't a lie.

For a second, his eyes opened and he met her gaze. "Love you always." Then his eyes closed and he once more stilled.

"Shit," she muttered, frustrated that she'd lost him again. That moment of contact should have given her hope. It didn't. She felt a fear down inside that told her she was truly losing him and suspected those last words meant he felt it too. Hydrated and believing she'd done everything she could, she put the wet cloth into one of the pockets in her cargo pants, picked up the belt handle, and once more began her journey toward the cabin. Tired as she was, she reached deep and called on strength she didn't even know she possessed. Time was her enemy right now, and she was determined to beat it. She moved the litter carrying Angus faster.

CHAPTER TWENTY-SIX

Aquene felt the breath leave her body. Molly was the most beautiful woman she had ever seen. That she was bare of clothing did not disturb her. She had been in that state with her friends many times through the years and knew the female body well.

Except this was different, special. Not once in all the times she had stood next to Alumpum and others without cover had she felt this way. She liked it even if it was not the time to explore what her own body was urging her to do. Looking at Molly gave Aquene a strange feeling deep inside her. She wanted to reach out and touch her smooth, pale skin, to press her lips to Molly's.

As much as she wanted to do those things, she did not, for it would not be right. They were in a war that, if they failed, could cost them their lives. She did not intend to fail, and so she must keep her thoughts on their journey and only their journey.

Tipping her face to the sky, Aquene closed her eyes and felt the sun on her skin. It was warm. That was good, for it would not take long for the wet clothes to dry enough for Molly to put them back on, and then they could be on their way. "We will be able to walk on when the sun is above us."

"Noonish," Molly said to her as she too tipped her head to the sky.

"What is noonish?" She was beautiful, and it made Aquene feel warm all over.

"It means the middle of the day. Does that help?"

Aquene nodded. "Yes."

"You find me a bother, don't you?" She was sitting on the same rock she had been on since removing her clothing, with her knees pulled to her chest and the cloth wrapped around her. Wet hair curled around her face. She was no longer shivering, which made Aquene happy. When someone could not stop shivering, it signaled very bad things. She did not want that to happen to Molly.

"You use many words I do not understand, but I do not find you a bother."

"You find me something, though. What is it?"

How did she tell this woman from another time that she wanted to walk at her side until her last sunset? That she made Aquene feel complete? She had no words to tell her, for it was not to be. Molly was not meant for Aquene's world. Once they had stopped the man who wished to harm the innocents, Molly would surely find her way home. What she felt would have to stay inside her, and she would have to find comfort in the memories of their short time together. It was as it had to be.

She decided to at least share words of truth. "You are not like those I have met in my life. You are better."

Molly said nothing, and Aquene was afraid she had offended her. It was important that she speak only honest words. When she began to try to explain what her words meant, Molly started to speak, making Aquene go silent.

"Thank you, Aquene. I don't think of myself as better than others, but what you said means a lot. My family is different and has been for generations. Many have hated us simply because of that. It hurts."

"Your power."

Molly nodded. "Yes. Power is one word for it. Magic is another. Those who hate us use the word witchcraft."

"Like the man we seek."

"Yes. I believe he would use that word. We have always tried to be a family who sends out only goodness into the world. Never anything black or evil. We adhere to the threefold law of return."

"I wish I understood you more, but I do not."

"It means that whatever we put out in the world comes back to us in threes. If we put out something evil, it will return to us three times as bad. We pledge to put forth only things that are good and will harm no one."

"You would not harm anyone. I do not see darkness in you."

"Thanks. I appreciate that. I try not to harm anyone. But I don't even know what I'm capable of. My powers remain to be seen. I mean,

I think something in me brought us here, and maybe that's what I've been waiting for. I just don't know for sure."

"I heard you speak words of protection. They kept us safe from the man."

"That's true. Remember that I had Hannah's words to guide me. You know, I've always had my family's power to help me while I've floundered in my heritage, not really knowing where I fit in. I followed my own path, indulging by making a career from my love of baking. Then I ended up here, and I'm beginning to believe this is where I'm supposed to be, to find out what the universe has in store for my own bit of power." Her head tilted as she studied Aquene. "I'm a little jealous of you, because you are so solid in your beliefs and in knowing what you're going to do."

She understood much of what Molly said. Her words were born of truth. Aquene still had a question that had yet to be answered for her. Molly felt she was supposed to be here. Did that mean she was supposed to be here with Aquene? Her heart hoped that was true most of all.

❖

It was yet another test. It had to be. Why else would Matthew's horse fall into a hole, breaking both a front leg and its neck? When he had picked himself up from the ground and investigated the cause of the spill, he had been furious by what he had discovered. The horse was dead, as were his hopes for a speedy arrival at the witch's cabin.

At first his fury had been so great, he had been unable to even think. As it abated and he realized it was God testing him again, his calm had returned. Everything happening to him today was some kind of trial, and he had to believe that it was the final one. God was getting ready to bring him home, and that filled him with immense joy.

He took his needed items from the saddle and continued his journey by foot. It would cost him a great deal of valuable time. It would not stop him from completing his job. He would make it to the cabin. He would kill the witch. He would destroy her book.

As he walked, he thought about what had happened thus far today. Matthew should be annoyed by the appearance of two of his conquests; he was not. They could bloody well go back to the damnation he had sentenced them to centuries ago. He could think they were spirits trying to frighten him. That was not how he viewed their untimely appearances. No. They were from the devil, trying to dissuade him from his current quest. It would not be the first time, and it would not be the last.

His mission would not be thwarted, for he would succeed. He had not failed since the moment he accepted this all-important mission as a very young man. His life had been dedicated to protecting the world from the demons that tried to escape the gates of hell. He had read Dante, and he not only understood the circles of hell; he had seen them firsthand. Anyone who had hunted the creatures he did knew it was real and its demons sent to walk the earth. Just as God was real, so too was the devil.

It was up to Matthew to cleanse the world of the scourge of witches and their craft. Others demons he left to others, for he knew one had to stay true to one's craft. He was not just a Witch-Finder. He was *the* Witch-Finder.

As the sun climbed in the sky, he stopped to eat of the provisions he had packed in his bag. It was important to partake of sustenance, for any weakness would hinder him should he be forced to physically restrain the witch. When he was able, he employed the services of strong but feeble-minded individuals to assist him. He preferred those with limited minds, for they asked few questions, and if they sustained serious injury, it was better that it happen to them. He was too important to risk injury. What he liked more than anything was that they did as they were told, collected their rewards, and went on their way.

In the beginning, he had found it curious that she would come here where the lands were difficult, human contact—at least of the civilized kind—was quite limited, and survival could be difficult. Before he followed her here, he had heard stories of the many who began their journey west only to expire under the harsh conditions or at the hands of savages. It still remained a mystery to him why she would risk such odds. In the past, the witches he had hunted preferred the cities, where they could blend in with normal, pious people. They chose the cover of innocents to hide their dirty deeds. Here it was lonely and isolated. With no people for miles around, it was hard for a witch to ply her trade.

Easy for him to destroy her.

CHAPTER TWENTY-SEVEN

It wasn't long before Molly's clothes were dry enough to put back on. She grimaced as she pulled on the damp underwear, followed by the pants that were likewise still soggy. It would take a few more hours before they were completely dry, although they were a far cry better than when she'd slipped out of them after her unplanned dip in the river. Good enough to get them back on and moving in the direction of the cabin.

The silence they shared while they waited for the garments to dry should have been uncomfortable. They barely knew each other, barely spoke the same language, and Molly had been sitting there naked except for a length of cloth. Yes, she should have felt ill at ease. She didn't. It was more like hanging out with a life-long best friend…one she felt incredibly drawn to, as in a kind of I-want-to-jump-her-bones way.

Crazy, that's what it was. Everything had been nuts since she'd touched the grimoire. She wanted to say she was sorry she'd even picked up the damn thing, except it would be a lie. Truth was, this was the most exciting thing that had happened to her in forever. Well, save for the whole fire-in-the-shop thing, but that was a different kind of exciting. This was the kind that made her heart race and her toes curl, and she liked it.

Once she put her clothes back on and gave herself a minute or two to acclimate to the feel of the touch of dampness in her pants and her bra, they began once more to walk in what Aquene assured her was the direction of the cabin. She couldn't swear that's where they were, in fact, heading, as it all looked quite alike to her. If they were back in her century, yeah, she would have been able to say for sure. In her time, she would have had landmarks and power lines and all sorts of clues to tell her the direction of travel. Here, she didn't see anything but fields and trees and the river, and it all looked alike. Without Aquene, she would be lost, which sent a shot of fear up her spine. What if Angus and Winnie were in the same boat? They'd all hauled ass out of that cabin when danger came calling, and she was still convinced it had been the right thing to do.

Winnie and Angus had been running blind, while she'd had a skilled guide with her. She and Aquene had managed to put miles between them and the cabin. Winnie and Angus would have been able to do the same thing if they'd kept moving. God, she hoped her friends were okay. If anything happened to them, she'd never forgive herself. They were only here because of her, and it would be on her if they didn't survive this strange twist of fate.

"Worry not." Aquene's voice startled her out of her troubling thoughts.

"What?"

Aquene took her hand, and the shock of the contact almost made her pull it away. She didn't, because the touch was incredibly comforting. "You worry about your friends."

"How do you know that?" Aquene seemed to be listening to her thoughts. Maybe Molly wasn't the only witch in the group.

"I do not know how it is I can feel what is in your heart. I do, and it is that simple. You worry for the safety of your friends. I tell you they will be well."

If being in her family had taught her anything, it was that nothing was really that simple. The universe had a way of working its magic through threads that tied them together. That same universe had seen fit to bring her and Aquene together, and she knew deep in her heart it was no coincidence. Neither did Aquene, who seemed to be reaching in to draw out her very thoughts. Simple? Not hardly.

She linked her fingers with Aquene's. "We're here together for a reason, aren't we?"

Aquene smiled. "Have I not said that to you since I first looked into your eyes?"

This time, Molly laughed. "Yeah, you kinda have."

"We are to fight this demon together and to end his killing of the innocents. It is why we are here now. We are stronger together."

Molly stopped and turned to stare into Aquene's dark eyes. She saw much life and knowledge inside this beautiful woman, and it made Molly's heart beat fast. She was so attracted to her it almost hurt. More than that, though, she felt honored to be working beside her. She was special in a unique way, and Molly would hold this woman in her heart even after she went home.

"I believe you're right on that one too. We *are* stronger together."

"We are, and it is as it should be."

"We will stop him, won't we?" Fear of a different kind flitted through her, and she squeezed Aquene's hand. If she didn't embrace courage and confidence, they wouldn't just fail to stop him. They would die.

❖

"I can't do this," Winnie wailed to the sky. Her shoulders were screaming, her quads burning with pain. With each step, Angus seemed to grow tens of pounds heavier. He hadn't moved or made a sound since she'd given him the water, and twice more she'd stopped to part his lips, trying to get a little more water down his throat. She wasn't sure her attempts were helpful, but trying made her feel better. He was so heavy on the litter she was certain they were moving only inches with each step, each pull. At this rate, it would take her days to get him to the cabin, and that kind of time she didn't have if there was any hope of saving her man.

When she could see finally see a bit of the cabin through the trees, tears sprang to her eyes. Fear had begun to chip at her confidence and make her believe they wouldn't make it. She was failing, and Angus, well, she didn't even want to think about what was happening to him. Each time she'd stopped to give him water, she was certain his skin had turned a different color: from pale to white and finally to gray. She could handle the paleness of his skin, but when it developed the gray tinge, the panic she'd managed to shove to the background flamed back in full force.

The glimpse of the cabin's roof bolstered her spirits and buoyed the last of her strength. She managed to close the distance in what she considered to be a record amount of time. Carefully, she lowered the litter to the ground and bent over with her hands on her knees. Asthma didn't usually bother her, but right at the moment, she would have paid a million dollars for an inhaler. Her lungs seemed about to burst from her chest. Her shoulders were roaring in protest and her legs quivering. It would be incredibly easy to drop to the ground, curl up in a ball, and sob.

She didn't. Now wasn't the time to feel sorry for burning lungs and an aching body. Big effing deal. Though she might feel like she'd done a marathon at warp speed, Angus was in far worse shape than she was, and that took the sting out of her physical complaints. She could see this through. Standing tall, she pushed open the door. It was just as they'd left it, so no one—translation, the frightening stranger—had been here while they climbed the basalt rocks. Good. She certainly didn't need someone else to worry about. What she needed was to keep her attention entirely on Angus.

Inside, she shoved the table that still lay on its side over to the far wall. That gave her an unimpeded path from the door to the fireplace. It was the best she could do, and she went back outside. Moving her makeshift litter as close to the door as she could, she maneuvered herself around until she had her back to the interior of the cabin. With some effort, she was able to slip her arms under Angus at his shoulders and drag him up and over the threshold.

By the time she had him in the middle of the cabin, sweat drenched her body. She could easily haul a twenty-five-pound bag of flour around the kitchen without a problem. The dead weight of a full-grown man took all her strength. Again, she wished she could lie down beside him and sleep for a year or two.

Winnie not only didn't lie down and sleep, but she also didn't stop moving. The gray color to his skin still scared her. For just a second, she studied him, and his words came back to her: keep the bite below heart level. Okay, so that's what she needed to do now that she had him under some cover. Leaving him prone on the floor wouldn't cut it. Too dangerous.

Glancing around the room, she didn't spot much that might help. This place wasn't exactly a modern home with all the usual conveniences. It provided pure wilderness living at its most basic. Comfortable for what it was, which really wasn't saying much. Only the fireplace could even come close to being considered a comfort item. As she studied her limited options, she decided the overturned table was her best bet. She dragged it back across the room and positioned it with the tabletop close to Angus's head. Then she circled around the table until she was standing beside what would be the underside, if it were upright. Once more she grabbed him beneath his arms and, calling on strength she was surprised she still had left, hauled him to a sitting position, with his head and back against the tabletop. So far, so good.

She stood back and studied what she'd accomplished. Hand with the snake bite beneath his heart, check. Stable position, no check. He looked like he was ready to tip over at any second. That wasn't going to do. All she needed was for him to hit the hard, wooden floor with his head. Snake bite and concussion? Not on her watch.

Once more she had limited choices. There was, however, a narrow bed. Like the table, she dragged it over and positioned it on one side of Angus. Good. It would keep him from tipping over in that direction. Half the problem solved.

The bed had a nasty-smelling blanket on it, and though she loathed to even touch it, in a pinch, she'd do what she had to. Gingerly, she picked it up and took it outside, where she gave it a hard shake. Dust flew like a Nebraska snowstorm, sending her into a coughing fit. A couple more shakes and she figured it was as good as it would get.

Inside, Winnie rolled the blanket and then tucked it next to Angus, with the roll bunched up a bit at his neck to create a sort of pillow. When she stepped back and surveyed her work, she figured it wasn't too bad for a chef stranded in the wilderness with an unconscious man. He was sitting up and semi-stable. Entire problem solved.

If it wasn't such a dire situation, she'd find it amusing. In a way, her support for Angus looked like the framework for the kind of fort her parents had let her and her brothers build in the living room when they were kids. They would move furniture and use any blanket they could get their hands on to create their masterpieces. However, they constructed those forts in a room with heat, running water, telephones, and emergency services only three numbers away. Not to mention a refrigerator stocked with yummy snacks. Oh, what she wouldn't give for a turkey sandwich right about now. Like Pavlov's dog, her mouth began to water.

Once more she put her hand against his forehead, and the feel of his skin against her hand shook her up. He was hot, very hot. The implications felt like a knife to the heart. She reached for her cloth, dismayed to find it almost dry. Now more than ever, she needed the cool, clear river water.

With a sigh she stood up and looked toward the open door. She had two options: stay with Angus and watch him burn up with fever, or run back to the river for water that would keep him hydrated and possibly break his fever. As much as she hated doing it, she decided to go with option two. She needed water, cold water, and she needed it now. The only upside was that, on a shelf, sat a water kettle. Made of black cast iron, it had a narrow curved handle, a small round lid, and a swooped spout. It was sturdy and undoubtedly heavy even when empty. Before she could talk herself out of going, she grabbed it and headed for the door.

With a backward glance at Angus, she felt her heart take a painful lurch. "Don't you dare die on me," she said with a sob. "Don't you dare." Then she was out the door, kettle in hand, running as fast as she could.

CHAPTER TWENTY-EIGHT

Aquene felt uneasy, as if something dark and oppressive pressed against the back of her neck. The spirits were telling her that their time was growing ever shorter. Danger was just beyond their vision, and it was closing the distance between them. Before a new day dawned, everything would change. She knew it with a certainty she could not explain to any other.

If only Tilla were with them now. The ground they must cross was still long, and with Tilla they could fly across it like an eagle. In a way she understood that this was how it was supposed to be. The journey was for her and Molly alone. Why? She did not know why—only that it was meant to be. They would walk the earth and return to the cabin of the woman who had been her friend. They would end this, one way or the other.

She reached out to Molly. It was uplifting, the feel of her hand. In their short time together she had come to understand this woman was in her heart. Molly had always been there, and she had been waiting for her to come. That was why she could not give herself to another. She was promised to only one: Molly.

The sadness that truth brought almost made her drop Molly's hand. She could not turn away from this pleasure. Yet it also brought bitterness, for once the battle had ended, so too would her time with this woman. She wanted to hold her hand forever, and that, she knew, would not happen. Molly would go back to her time, and Aquene would rejoin her people and prepare them for what was to come. That was the way of any great journey.

She did not let go of Molly's hand. "We must hurry," she told her, and she could hear the fear in her own voice. She wished to be strong as a warrior, yet she could not free herself of the troubling knowledge of what followed at their backs.

"What's wrong?" Molly heard it too.

She wished that they could be shown what awaited them. She knew the man chased them. But because she could not clearly picture what pressed at her now, she was afraid. She was certain it was a test, and she hoped she could meet it with courage and triumph.

"He is drawing near, and I am afraid we will have only one chance to stop him. If we miss it, he will destroy others. We cannot allow him to harm any others. It is why we have been brought together."

Molly had started walking with her and now stopped. Turning, she faced Aquene, their eyes meeting. Once more Aquene thought of the power she witnessed in her eyes. She believed deeply that she was the one, the only one, with the power to stop the dark man who walked her lands.

Molly put her hand against Aquene's cheek, her palm warm and comforting. She almost cried. When this day ended, she would to miss this woman's touch. Their lives would be forever changed, and she could do nothing about it.

"I don't know what it is about you, Aquene, but you make feel alive for the first time in forever. It's an incredible feeling that I don't ever want to go away."

"You are alive." Aquene did not understand what Molly meant. She might have walked through time, but she was very much alive. She could feel her breath on her cheek, and Aquene knew that if she placed her hand on her chest, she would feel the beat of her heart.

Molly's smile made her face even more beautiful. She shook her head. "That's not what I mean. My life has been about work and building my business. I've devoted myself to learning my craft so I could be the very best. I didn't have time or energy to be anything except a baker. I didn't have the courage to let my heart feel for another woman, and until I met you I had no idea what I was giving up."

She still spoke strangely, though this time Aquene thought she understood. It was much the same for her, despite the efforts of all around her to match her with young warriors. No one understood where her affections truly lay, and she did not explain. How could she? While her people were more accepting than those who came here on their horses and in their wagons, she still kept her silence. They came with their peculiar ways and beliefs very different from hers, and she did try to understand them. It did no good, for she could not. It was easier to stay quiet and simply listen. She had learned much while remaining true to herself.

"I understand."

Molly's smile grew warmer. "I thought you might. I'm trying to explain, not very well, that you are the most fascinating woman I've ever met. You make my heart race and my blood pump. I look into your eyes and want to spend every day getting to know you better. It's crazy, Aquene, when you consider we come from different worlds, yet it doesn't make any difference at all to my heart."

Warmth flowed through Aquene, as did another emotion she could not quite define, perhaps because she had not felt it before. "I do understand, Molly, for it is much the same for me."

"Really?"

It was Aquene's turn to smile. "It is true. I have never felt this way before." She took Molly's hand and held it to her chest. "I envied my friend Alumpum for the partner she chose and the life they have created together. They are happy, and the tenderness they have for each other is a gift from the Great Spirit. I did not believe that would ever be true for my life."

"Until now."

She nodded. "Until now." Then she pulled Molly into her arms and kissed her.

❖

Excitement raced through Matthew's body. Despite the setback of losing his horse and having to proceed on foot, he was finally nearing the witch's cabin, and everything was coming together; he could feel it deep in his bones. A noise from behind made him pull up and turn around. After what he had seen some distance back, he fully expected to be face-to-face with another of the witches he had sent to eternal retribution.

This time it was not a ghost. Several deer were running from the trees as if they had been startled. He listened for the sound of another, thinking it could very well be the one he was hunting. That would be fitting and would tie up his journey faster than he could have hoped. He heard nothing further. Were the ghosts that seemed to be lining his path now scaring wildlife?

It was of no consequence. Ghosts could not harm him, and knowing that he had always acted in good faith through the years freed him from even a flicker of guilt. He smiled. Guilt was for others, not men like him.

For centuries, he had done God's will, and he would do so again now. The witch was nearby, and he would be ready to once more banish evil to the fires below his feet. Just the thought of it left him feeling as giddy as if he had finished a bottle of French wine all by himself. In fact, once he made it back to civilization, that was exactly what he intended to do. That and find a woman. He had a need to relax, and only a woman of certain talents would be able to assist him in that endeavor. They were easy enough to find in cities and towns alike.

Once he walked away from the river, the landscape became more peppered with trees and underbrush. It also became more familiar. He had followed this path enough times to be acquainted with its look and feel. Soon enough, his faith in his sense of direction was rewarded, for ahead of him, appearing through the trees, was the cabin.

She had chosen well by deciding to stay here, for it had provided cover while situated near enough to the river to provide her with water and fish, and close enough to the cliffs for her to climb for an excellent lookout. He supposed even a foolish woman was entitled to one or two good ideas.

Except in her case, it had also proved to be her undoing. It had not taken him long to track her down once she had left Chicago. She had not chosen well when she stayed in that town. People remembered her, especially the ones who had found her *talents* useful. At first, many had hesitated to speak of her, and he quickly realized they were trying to protect her. He had just as quickly disabused them of that notion. With his particular brand of persuasion, he was able to discern her probable path.

His ability to not just track her but recruit able and willing helpers proved the righteousness of his journey. It had taken weeks of tracking, sleeping outside in the wind and the rain, and hiding from the natives who lived off the land. In the end, he had been successful, although it had taken an arrow in her side and the ensuing trail of blood that had led him and his soldiers to her hiding place. How he had reveled in putting the rope around her neck and hoisting her bleeding body on that tree branch. How he loved the warmth of the flames that had consumed her flesh, breathing in the heady scent that wafted off the blaze. Everything about it had been magnificent, with the exception of one small detail. The wound in her side had taken her life before the flames did. He liked to see their eyes when the flames burned their souls.

He felt the same self-righteous glory now as he walked slowly to the door of the cabin. His hands trembled at his sides. This time there would be no arrow in the side to deny him the satisfaction of seeing her eyes in the flames. No. This time it would be perfect.

For a moment he studied the closed door and then kicked it open with one booted foot. At first glance, the room appeared just as he had left it yesterday. After a more studied examination, he realized it was quite different. Someone had shoved the table into the center of the room, and leaning against it was a man. He had most definitely not left a man inside.

"Who are you?" he bellowed and loved how strong he sounded. His voice filled the tiny room. The power of his words echoed off the walls. He left no doubt as to who was in command.

When the man on the floor neither responded nor even opened his eyes, Matthew stepped farther into the room, stopping only when he stood over him. "I said, who are you?"

He kicked him with the toe of his boot. Only then did he notice the pallor of his skin and the way his arm was bound tight to his body. When he tipped over onto his side, his head hitting the wooden floor with a thump, Matthew wondered if he was already dead. Probably, though he didn't care one way or the other and did not intend to touch his flesh to find out. He did not dirty his hands when it was not necessary. This man might or might not be an ally to the witch. That he was dead, or near dead, and would be able to do nothing to help her meant he was no threat. He did not warrant further attention.

Though he posed no threat, his very presence was intriguing. Why the man on the floor was even here, particularly considering the very strange clothing he wore, was mysterious. Matthew had never seen anything quite like it. Curious, he leaned down to touch the outerwear, though doing so went against his code. It felt strange, the texture quite different from what he himself wore. Something was wrapped around his body, and given how he was lying on his side, Matthew could not make out what it was. His boots were unlike any he had seen before and his pants of a cloth unknown to him. Nothing about the man seemed right.

To expect normal was silly. This was, after all, the home of a witch. Nothing was impossible for those who practiced the dark arts. He had seen it all, and thus this man in the unusual clothing should not be a great surprise. Witches were capable of many things the mind had trouble making sense of. Another reason his work was important. He banished that which strove to confuse and harm.

With one last kick to the unmoving man, he turned and went back outside. He needed to be ready when she came. She was close, so close he could swear her smell was being carried on the wind. It would not be long now. His body hummed from his head down to the tips of his fingers. It was always this way when his work brought him to this point.

Outside, he walked over to where he'd dropped his saddlebag before he went into the cabin and first took his Colt revolver from inside it. He lovingly ran his hand over the modern weapon. One of the beautiful things about living a long life was seeing changes like the wonderful gun he held in his hand. Back when he had begun his mission, he could never have imagined he would possess something so magical. His gun allowed him multiple shots, which meant his quarry had no chance for escape despite their never-ending efforts to elude him. He could easily stop them, allowing him to complete his job correctly each and every time. In those early days when so many of the black arts were roaming the countryside, a weapon like this would have been most welcomed.

The gun was just one of the tools he employed to complete his task. Once he had the witch cornered he really needed only one simple tool, and it lay on the ground next to his saddlebag. He tucked the gun into the waist of his pants at the small of his back and then grabbed the rope he had carried looped over his shoulder as he had walked here. It already had a noose fashioned on one end, for he believed in always being prepared. He tossed the plain end up and over a branch of the same tree he had used only a year ago. It had worked for him then, and it would work for him now. After pulling the rope until the noose swung from the branch, he tied the plain end to the trunk of the tree. He smiled as he looked at the noose swinging from the high branch. Perfect.

His smile grew as the sounds of movement in the trees reached him. She was still a distance off, but she was coming to him.

Just as he knew she would.

CHAPTER TWENTY-NINE

Molly was plunging along determinedly behind Aquene, still feeling the glow that came with the unexpected kiss, when suddenly she stopped. "What?" Molly asked, not sure about why, when she was certain they were close, they would stop. Perhaps a little more lip-to-lip confidence? Worked for her. Oh, yeah, it really worked for her.

One look at Aquene, and she was relatively certain that wasn't why they stopped, disappointing as that was. Her face was dark, as if storm clouds gathered directly above her head. Molly looked up, expecting to see the presence of those black-bottomed clouds that brought the rain, a little surprised not to see a single one. The sky was clear, and though it was beginning to shadow, the day was simply fading into twilight.

"Do you not feel it?"

"Feel wha…" She took in the weight of the air that swirled around them. It was as if it carried a dump-truck load of dirt. Grave dirt. The thought hit her with frightening force. The universe, or perhaps Aquene's Great Spirit, was trying to tell them something, and she was pretty sure the message started with the word *beware!*

"Yeah…I do," she said softly. "And it's scaring me. Like a lot scaring me."

This guy they were chasing, or more likely was chasing them, was close; that much she instinctively understood. What bothered her wasn't so much his proximity as her own feeling of inadequacy. What was she supposed to do? The book tucked inside her zipped jacket gave urgent warnings of his presence and alluded to the idea he'd been walking the earth for hundreds of years. If that was true, and it was kind of hard to believe, how was one baker from a couple of centuries in the future supposed to stop him? She didn't even have one of her sturdy baking sheets to smack him with. One whack with one of those babies would ring anyone's bell.

Then she smiled. It was funny. If she was, as Aquene liked to say, speaking true, she'd have to admit that all along she'd been wondering how he could be an evil entity walking through time while also convincing herself this was just some sort of folk legend. Kind of like people who travel through time are just good plot lines for novels or books. Yeah, just like that.

"Damn," she muttered. "What do we do now to stop this bastard? It would be nice if we actually knew who he was, what he looked like. You know, little details like that."

For all she knew he could be six three and a good three-fifty. Between the two of them he would still outweigh them by over a hundred pounds and would have almost a foot in height over Molly. Not exactly the kind of odds she wanted to go up against.

Of course, the opposite could be true as well. If history could be relied upon and he'd been around for as long as Hannah suggested, chances were they could look each other in the eye, so maybe the two of them could take him down. She wouldn't need that baking sheet.

For a brief moment, she thought about taking a chance that her latter assumption was correct. Then she decided maybe not. Gambling wasn't exactly her forte, and now wasn't the time to start banking on odds going her way. She patted the grimoire and had a thought.

"I want to take a look at the book."

"We do not have time."

"Let's make time." For some reason she couldn't explain, she felt strongly about this. Hannah was going to show her something, and it might very well be exactly what they needed to gain an advantage over this devil.

"We must hurry," Aquene said. "We have little time."

Molly kissed her on the cheek and once again felt the flutter of excitement that happened every time they touched. "Trust me. I'll read fast."

September 30, 1836

The time has come, dearest granddaughter, and the little strength I have left is for you. I carry great hope in my heart that you will survive. My own daughter's life rests in your hands, and by stopping this monster, you will ensure the survival of our family and the magic that rests in each of our hearts. We are good people and always have been. Century after century we heal and we save. We do not take life. Ever.

Until today. Sweet, sweet Molly, you are the chosen one, and I believe you have always known you were special. Your heart is that of a warrior, which is one of the reasons you were chosen for this task. You, with your hand joined to the one you love, will be able to stop him once and for all. You will help change the world. I know I ask of you great things. Do not worry, for it has always been written in the stars. You and the beautiful one who speaks to the Great Spirit will make his madness cease and send him to the hell that will embrace him with open arms.

My strength is yours. My secrets are yours. My time has come to an end, for my blood spills on the floor, and the sound of many hooves herald his coming. I will not see another sunrise, but I go to meet my destiny with my heart free, for I know that one day you will come, and on that day, you will set the world right.

My love to you, Molly of my blood. Blessed be.

Well, if she'd had any doubts that Hannah was her ancestor, she didn't any longer. Any residual denial faded like the daylight. She was in the middle of nowhere reading a grimoire a couple of hundred years old, and it was talking directly to her. Pretty cool.

Even more cool was what else she wrote. A beautiful woman who speaks to the Great Spirit. Molly's eyes met Aquene's, and she had to accept without any lingering reservations that the magic in her family was powerful and strong, Hannah had taken a look at the future. She had known Molly would come, and she had known that Molly, along with Aquene, would stop the madness.

Okay, so she'd just found her destiny. She had to send this guy to the lake of fire, and if she was reading between the lines correctly—and she was pretty sure she was—Granny wanted her to kill the guy. Great, just fucking great. How was that going to play out in the threefold law of return? Mom would definitely not like this.

She thought about Hannah's words and all that she'd been taught.

Her decision wasn't that hard. Sometimes going on faith was the best thing a person could do. How many times had she been told that, when her time came, she'd know it? It was the day, and it was time to meet the monster head-on. If Hannah was right, she was going to put him six feet under. She still didn't exactly know how. Then again…if Granny said she could, well, then just maybe she could.

Tucking the book back into her jacket, she straightened up and held out her hand to Aquene. "Come on. Let's go kick ass and take names."

❖

Winnie almost broke down crying when she realized she'd gone farther into the woods rather than toward the river. It had cost her time, and she didn't have enough of it to lose even a minute. Once she righted herself, she ran as hard as she could. Every muscle screamed, and in the back of her mind she knew she'd be lucky to be able to walk tomorrow.

Trail runners were nuts, she decided after the second time she picked herself up off the ground when she tripped on a fallen tree branch. It was hard enough to figure out how to get to the right spot without having to worry about every single flippin' step. Unfortunately, she didn't have a better choice. At least after she emerged from the trees, the land that spread out before her was blessedly free of thick trees. It made her time getting to the water much quicker.

When they'd stood on the basalt rock cliffs and looked down this way, she'd been able to see both the man on horseback and what she hoped were Molly and Aquene. From all appearances they were heading in the direction of the cabin. Good, at least where Molly and Aquene were concerned. The man was an unknown, and out here in the Wild, Wild West, she wasn't leaning toward helpful savior. She remembered her history lessons, and violence wasn't unheard of, particularly considering many of the early settlers came out here to escape and hide.

Well, she refused to worry about it. She'd deal with the guy if she had to. The most pressing issue wasn't the stranger in the black hat. It was water. She had to get some up to Angus. Besides, as stressed out as she was right at the moment, she felt like she could take on anyone. If that butthead guy showed up, she'd kick the ever-lovin' daylights out of him, and the horse he rode in on, to save her man. She guessed that's what really being in love with someone meant. That and a combination of fatigue, fear, and adrenaline. Especially adrenaline.

Funny, she'd known for a long time that she was falling in love with Angus, and what he'd said to her had made her heart soar. She just hadn't realized until now how deep her feelings went. That she would take on a bear to protect him was enlightening and, well, kind of empowering. For the first time in her life, she felt kickass outside of the kitchen. She was talented with food, always had been, but she'd never stopped to consider that she might be more than a chef. Angus gave her so much more than love, and by God, whatever it took, she was going to make sure he survived so she could tell him.

Carefully she picked her way down the incline to where the water rushed by. The ground was a little unstable, and she tried to make sure her footing was solid. Every year she heard stories of people who went missing in this river, and she didn't want to be one of them. Particularly not in a century that didn't belong to her.

At last she made it safely to the water's edge and was able to fill the kettle. As she retraced her steps, again making sure her footing was solid, she needed to use both hands to lug the heavy kettle up to the grass. She let out a big sigh of relief when she made it to flat, firm ground. Now she just had to get it back to Angus. He needed water in his system and a cool rag against his flaming skin as soon as possible.

Hurrying, Winnie felt confident, even as her arms screamed at the weight of the kettle and the narrow metal handle dug into her palms. If she could drag Angus to the cabin on her litter, she could carry a container of water back there too. Her arms could fall out of the sockets, her hands shredded, and she would still hold on to the precious water. Her determination worked really well too, until she hit another one of those damned downed branches. She sprawled, face-first, toward the ground. Instinct made her let go of the kettle in order to use both hands to break her fall. It worked. Sort of. Pain shot up to her shoulders as her palms collided with the hard earth and her knees smacked the edge of the branch. She didn't have to look at her legs to see if she'd injured herself. She could feel the warmth of the blood as it soaked through her pants.

Finally, she succumbed to tears. The kettle lay on its side, pouring the hard-won water into the ground. "God damn it," she roared up at the sky. "Why? Why would you do this to me?"

Little surprise, she didn't receive a response. God wasn't answering her, and neither was anyone else, because she was alone. As in all alone in the wilderness of nineteenth-century Oregon. If her life could get any more fucked up, she'd be surprised.

With the back of her hand, she wiped away the hot tears and then pushed herself up to her feet. Her knees felt like someone had smacked them with a baseball bat, and her palms were now red and swollen. Where was an EMT when you needed one?

"No time for tantrums," she muttered as she picked up the almost-empty kettle. The handle pressed against her tender flesh, and she winced. The thought of the kettle being filled again wasn't appealing. No time to whine about it. She had to do what she had to do. Her aches and pains weren't important. The life of the man she loved was.

Overhead, the sun was marching toward the west, and that worried her. She was not an experienced navigator in her own century, where apps and GPS devices could help even the most inept to make their way out of a strange place. All she had today was her recollection of the track she had taken to get here, and she wanted the chance to retrace it all in daylight. This time, she ran to the river's edge, slid down the embankment to the water without worrying about her footing, and filled the kettle again. She scrambled back up with no grace at all and began to run as fast as she could without spilling the precious contents. No way was she going to empty it again, and no way was she going to be out here alone once the sun set.

"Hang on, Angus," she said into the cooling air and fading sunlight. "I'm coming."

CHAPTER THIRTY

Though Aquene did not completely understand what Molly said, she did understand what she meant, and it made her heart happy. The warrior inside this woman was strong, powerful, and courageous. What was there not to admire in her? Nothing that Aquene had seen in their brief time together.

"Before we go," Molly put a hand on Aquene's arm, "I want to throw out a little more magic."

"We must defeat him with our hands." Molly's magic was good; she had seen that herself. Now they did not have the time for it, for they, not the magic that Molly was born into or the powers the Great Spirit had blessed Aquene with, must stop this evil being. It was to be a battle of the flesh.

Molly nodded. "I agree it's going to be a very human-style takedown, but I truly believe we must arm ourselves with every weapon available. I don't have much to offer. I plan to use what I do have. For me, it's all about my family's magic. It's really the most important weapon I can bring to this fight."

Those were good words, and Aquene thought them well spoken. "What would you have me do?"

Stretching out her arms, she said, "Take my hands."

It was the easiest thing she had been asked to do since she had left Alumpum and the others. She clasped Molly's hands in hers and felt the immediate flow of power between them. If she lived to be a white-haired elder, she would always remember this moment.

"You feel it too, don't you?" Molly was gazing into her eyes.

"Yes. It is there each time we touch."

Molly nodded. "Good. Now just hold on. I have got to concentrate and remember what my mother tried so hard to teach me. With any luck, it will work."

Holding Aquene's hands tightly, Molly closed her eyes and began to speak quietly. "Now is the time for gathering in the shadows. We have suffered persecution at his hands for our beliefs, and many have died. Yet we have been reborn among our own. I am one of the hidden children, and from generation to generation knowledge has been passed on. In remembrance, I come now to honor the past, the present, and the future. All things are remembered. All things are restored. As it was in the time of our beginning, so it is now, so shall it be."

As before, the winds whirled around them and the air felt heavy. It also felt safe, as though whatever Molly's words meant, they coaxed the world to close around them in the same warm, protective way a hide could keep her from dying when the winter snows came.

Molly's words trailed off and her eyes opened. "We're ready now. It's the best I can do for the moment." She dropped Aquene's hands.

Aquene was not quite ready. "Wait," she said at the same time she took hold of a leather thong that hung from her neck. She tugged on it and pulled the small bag that had been hidden beneath her clothing. Slipping the thong from around her neck, she took it and put it around Molly's neck. The bag lay between her breasts.

Molly's hand went to the bag, and she started to open it. "No," Aquene said at the same time she stilled Molly's hand. "It is the way of my people and the bag is sacred. It must remain tied."

"But what's inside?" She held it out and looked at it.

Aquene shook her head. "I do not know, for as I gave it to you, so too was it given to me. It is not for us to see. We must only accept the gift of the magic and believe that it will protect."

At first she was afraid that Molly would not heed her words. Then she looked up from the bag and what she saw in Molly's face reassured her. "A medicine bag," Molly said. "I've heard of these."

Aquene was satisfied that Molly understood the importance of her gift. Molly had her magic and Aquene hers. Perhaps together it would prove to be enough. "Let us finish this," Aquene said as she turned and began the final trek toward the cabin.

❖

The nearer she came to him, the more Matthew could sense her. It was always that way as a hunt neared its conclusion, which was the main reason he was the only official Witch-Finder. No one else had ever come close to matching his unique ability to track witches. His only regret about his life-long calling was that Parliament had refused to officially bestow his title upon him. Oh, they were grateful enough for his fine work, but the bastards had denied him his due. After his *death*, his chance for validation from Parliament was lost. No matter. The remunerations were plenty and had served him well. Vindication was his in the end. Over the years, his fortune had grown even larger, ultimately far surpassing the wealth of those who had refused to bestow upon him his rightful title.

He would receive no pay for this one and was not sorry. This was personal. The witch who had hung by her neck from this very tree had defied him, even in death, and that could not be allowed to stand. Rest would not come until he had rectified that oversight. He was unable to return to the softer, gentler life that he was due until he put this witch down. He could not go to his heavenly father's side until then. She was the key to stopping this family once and for all, and that prospect held a great deal of satisfaction.

He slipped between the branches of several small evergreens so that he was out of sight yet still could see the tree where his noose awaited her slim, white neck. He knew many ways to catch witches, many ways to prove they were the devil's daughters. He had no need of proof in this case, for he was certain of what she was. He did not need to coax a confession. All he required was to get the rope around her neck and build a fire at her feet.

It would be glorious.

Faintly, sounds began to drift his way. No longer did just a feeling let him know she was coming. Now he could hear her footsteps as well. Good. The sun was beginning to set, and the sky would soon grow dark. He wanted her suspended from his rope with the fire blazing before the sun dropped behind the mountains. That she was so near let him know his plans would be fulfilled.

Just in case, he had his pistol in one hand. He hoped to be able to capture her without need of the gun. Using it could take away from him his greatest pleasure: witnessing a witch succumb to the flames while knowing he was the one who had ended her evil life. Or him, though in his experience, primarily women consorted with the devil. With the exception of a few, men had more sense.

A sound near the cabin made him turn his head. It didn't seem likely that the man inside would rouse himself. In fact, it did not seem likely that the man inside would ever stand again, for death was whispering in his ear. He was not wrong. No one stood in the open doorway, though a rabbit bounced by the cabin, to shortly thereafter disappear into the underbrush. Later, he might very well go in search of that rabbit or its friends. He could use a good, hot meal.

He turned his gaze back toward the tree and smiled. Coming through the trees and into the clearing was the one he had been waiting for. He had no doubt she was the witch, for her face was one he knew well. It was the same face he had watched burn as the woman hung from this very tree a year ago.

CHAPTER THIRTY-ONE

Molly had never been so glad to see a building, as clichéd as that sounded. Seeing the cabin was like setting eyes on the Davenport Hotel in downtown Spokane. Though the Davenport was a gorgeous piece of Spokane history with its marble lobby, flowing fountains, and luxurious rooms, this rough little cabin represented something safe and familiar in a world gone decidedly wonky. Four walls and a roof were comforts from God or, as Aquene would insist, the Great Spirit.

The only problem? Her nerves started screaming so bad she wanted to jump and run in the opposite direction. Like literally want to jump and run. Or throw up. She reached back where Aquene was standing directly behind her and took her hand. Throughout this whole ordeal, Aquene had been steady and pretty damned calm. The hand she held now was shaking just like her own. She should be surprised by that, but she wasn't. The more time they spent together, the more in tune with each other they became. In other words, Aquene was picking up the same thing she was.

"He's here." She wasn't posing a question. Aquene might not have eyes-on, but Molly knew she was as aware of his proximity as she was. He was nearby, a presence so palpable it was like the thick air of a New Orleans summer afternoon. Not seen but felt nonetheless.

Aquene pulled her back several steps so they stood behind a couple of close-together trees. "He is waiting to harm us." Her voice was calm, even though Molly still felt the tremors in her hand.

Aquene was partly right. "I think he's waiting to harm *me*." Well, that wasn't going to happen. She had no intention of letting some creep get the drop on her. "We have to stop him." Today was not the day she wished to die.

"We must stop him," Aquene echoed.

Now that they were finally coming face-to-face, she felt the pressing weight of her responsibility. As Hannah had written, she had to be a warrior. But how? He was hiding somewhere, just as they were now using the pines as cover. How could she go on the offensive if she didn't know where he was? Then it hit her. Use what she'd been blessed with.

She closed her eyes and could swear the odor of unwashed skin, sweat, and hatred overcame her. It was the first time she'd ever believed hatred could manifest in a tangible sense, but there it was, real enough to touch. Keeping her eyes closed, she told herself to relax and silently called on the Old Ways to help guide her. She prayed for the strength of her mother, her grandmother, her aunts…Hannah, to bolster her. It worked.

Before her eyes, a kind of movie played in slow motion. In it she saw the man in his wool pants and overcoat, black hat on his head and an antique gun in his hand. He crouched behind thick shrubs, his eyes on the tree with the burned branches. His face was narrow and, most prominently, mean. His eyes were dark, as if they had absolutely no life in them. She suspected that was true. A slight smile crossed his lips as he watched her step out of the trees and then step back into them. His entire posture changed, and it reminded her of a cougar getting ready to attack. He'd been anxiously waiting for her, and now his wait was over. His excitement smelled acrid.

Molly opened her eyes and knew what she had to do. Taking Aquene's face between her hands, she kissed her quickly. The sweetness of her lips was all she needed for the last ounce of courage. "We have to surprise him if we have any hope of ending this. He's in the group of bushes near the tree. Can you move around that way," she pointed to her right, "while I draw him out from this direction."

Aquene nodded, and Molly couldn't believe how something so simple as a nod could make her feel hopeful. "I will move silently."

"Great. It's going to take both of us to get him down. He's stronger than he looks, especially for a small guy."

In the vision, she'd seen clearly that he was like most men of his era, slight and short. This size was a cover for the monster that unquestionably lay beneath the facade. Seeing his face put everything in the grimoire into focus. It all made sense at a deeply spiritual level.

Or was that at a deeply familial level? She suspected it was most assuredly the latter.

Aquene moved away from her and, as promised, didn't make a sound. Molly gave her a couple of minutes to get around so that she was coming at small, dark, and dangerous from the side. When she felt relatively certain Aquene was positioned well, she threw her shoulders back and walked out from behind the cover in the trees and into the open space with her head held high.

She had only one thing to do once she knew she was in his sights. She thought of her mom and knew that if she were standing beside her now, she'd be proud. Lifting her hands into the air, she said, "Come all together inside this circle, and the secrets that are as yet unknown shall be revealed. True to my belief and as keeper of the Old Ways, I remove all obstacles, for here lies the key to end the cycle of rebirth that has opened the way for evil. I am the spirit of the great ones, and I call upon their wisdom to reveal the truth and the way."

Winnie felt the pressure. Her arms were screaming from the weight of the full kettle, and her legs were objecting to the speed she was trying to coax out of them. She was accustomed to being on her feet for hours in the kitchen. She was not, however, one of those women who aspired to ninja-warrior-type endeavors, so trying to run with a heavy kettle through unfamiliar and uneven ground was totally out of her wheelhouse. It weighed a ton, and that handle was killing her hands. At least she didn't have any more tripping mishaps. The little things made her happy.

The sky overhead was growing darker by the minute. If she didn't haul ass, the sun would set before she got back to Angus. That was not an option. Not at all. So she pulled up her big-girl panties and moved as fast as she could. If only she hadn't had that first crash. Going back to fill the kettle a second time had cost her precious time she didn't have. No sense obsessing over spilt milk...or water...It was time to simply get back to Angus.

God, she hoped Molly was on her way to the cabin as well. She had to be. Where else could she go? It was the only common denominator in this twisted world they'd discovered themselves in. Molly had to show up soon. It scared her to think otherwise, and she had enough other scary things going on to add one more to the mix. If ever she needed Molly and the wicked magic she knew Molly had inside her, it was now. Besides bringing the cool water to Angus, she pinned her hopes on Molly's powers to get them home. She was no nurse and had very basic first-aid skills. She could wrap up a cut with the best of them. A snake bite? Not quite in her skill set. Still, she knew enough to realize that Angus was in trouble. That snake bite would kill him if they didn't get him back to advanced medical care, and soon. As in very soon.

After running and jumping over fallen trees and protruding rocks for at least fifteen minutes, she had to stop even though she knew it was a pretty bad idea. Winnie swore her arms were about to pop right out of their sockets if she didn't give them a rest. Sinking to a fallen tree, she managed to gently set the kettle on the ground despite her shaking arms. Her whole body relaxed once the weight was off, and she closed her eyes. Weariness made her shoulders droop. What she wouldn't do for a bed. The respite was incredible. She could sit here for hours. Throw in a glass of wine and it would be a nice long sit. She wouldn't, of course, but oh how she could. In the distance, a scream cut through the air. Her eyes snapped open, and she jumped up as though she'd been shot. Her heart pounded because the scream came from the direction of the cabin. Angus? God, no. What had she been thinking? She never should have stopped. She started to run again and then stopped herself. After turning, she raced back to where she'd left the kettle on the ground. The water was as precious as gold to her right now. As she picked up the cast-iron container and once more began to run, her muscles protested again. This time she didn't even worry if some of the water splashed out. Her feet flew over the branches and fallen trees, and she ignored the pain in her quads. None of it mattered—not the bodily pain or the protection of the life-saving water. The time to be careful had passed like a flash of lightning.

CHAPTER THIRTY-TWO

Aquene was grateful for the lessons both the men and women of her people had passed down to her. The teachings all had their place, and right now she embraced the role of careful hunter. Molly was right in her thought that they must come at the man from two different directions. She was as sneaky as a predator.

On silent feet, she had moved through the tree cover until she crouched a short distance from him. He had not heard her, as she had known he would not. Her abilities as a hunter equaled those of most men, and of that she was proud, as was her father. Little did she understand that, as she had learned from the most accomplished, she would one day use those skills to hunt a man. She wondered now if the Great Spirit had spoken to her father, for throughout her life he had shared with her the same lessons he would have had she been a male. It seemed to her on this day that all the lessons her father taught and the skills he shared had brought her to this moment and to this man.

In her heart, she sensed that he was no ordinary man, not *only* a man. All her teachers, her father included, had talked of spirits that breached the worlds of both the living and the dead and embraced the essence of either good or evil. As she peered through the brush that separated them, she could see his face. So serene and ordinary on the surface, his expression was designed to trick the unwary. She was not fooled. He was far from ordinary. The blackness that he held inside him was as clear to her as if she could actually see inside his body. He embodied the evil that she had been warned of all her life.

The air around her was charged, as if a storm was on its way, and indeed, it was a storm in its own way. This was the moment she had been waiting for since she had pulled herself onto Tilla's back and ridden away from her friends and family. It was the end of the journey that had been set for her. She did not yet know exactly how it would end, only that on this day, this night, it would.

From the sheath at her waist she pulled the knife she always wore. It was an exceptionally fine knife that she had traded many pelts to obtain, one of her most treasured possessions. A bow would be a more efficient weapon in this instance, but hers was wherever Tilla was now, and that, she felt certain, was back with Alumpum. She could use the knife as well as anyone, and thus not having a bow did not distress her. The knife was effective, and she was comfortable with it.

In their time together, she knew that Molly carried little that would gain her advantage in a fight. Anything of physical strength, that is, for Molly possessed something otherworldly that had its own great power. It could very well be the only weapon that could defeat the monster she could see peering out from the cover of the brush in the exact direction of where Molly hid behind some large pines.

As much as Aquene wanted to charge and take the man by surprise, she also worried that the element of surprise was a false belief. Somewhere inside her was a whisper telling her that he knew she was here, and should she charge him, he would kill her as though she were little more than a deer for slaughter. Molly must head the attack. In every hunt, one warrior would lead the others. Aquene had to be patient and wait, for on this night, that warrior was Molly.

The twilight was charged as though lightning was ready to explode across the sky. The scent of the charred wood of the tree was bitter on the air, making her eyes sting. Overhead, the hoot of an owl sent a chill through her body, for it brought with it the promise of death. His, she prayed. Aquene forced herself to still and wait.

She did not have to wait long. While she expected Molly to come into the clearing with a mighty charge, she was surprised when instead she walked out slowly and raised her arms to the sky. The words she spoke were calm and measured, yet with each word, power gathered around her like a thick, warm cloak. It became so thick and alive that Aquene was surprised she could not see it. It was the most impressive sight she had ever seen.

She continued to remain motionless and hidden, her eyes on Molly. She understood what she was doing. She was calling on the strength of the Old Ones, and they were answering. When her words trailed off, she waited still. Something whispered in her ear: he must make the first move, and then he did. He was smiling as he revealed himself, stepping, as Molly had done mere minutes earlier, into the clearing. He walked like a man who believed himself to be better than others. She had come to know more than one like him.

"At last we meet," he said with a voice that held no fear.

"Now," the wind whispered, and it was the sign Aquene waited for. Her knife held tight in her hand, she moved from the cover of the trees and into the clearing steps behind the man. She focused on her prey and nothing else.

The sound registered in her ears only moments before pain seared through her body. The hand holding the knife dropped to her side and she stopped to stare down at a spreading red stain at her middle. It was not right. How could this be? He was not close enough to touch her, but her body told her differently. It was if he had pierced her body with the blade of a knife, and yet he was many steps away. When she looked up, he was smiling at her, an unknown object in his hand and pointed at her.

"One must appreciate new weapons," he said as he turned it this way and that. "They call it a revolver. Take another step, squaw, and I will demonstrate why." He once again held it steady and pointed at her.

"Aquene!" Molly started to race toward her.

The pain in her body was red-hot. She ignored it as she focused her gaze on Molly. She had to make her understand that Aquene's life was of no importance. It was Molly who must win this battle. "No!" Aquene's harsh word halted Molly. "You must stop him." Darkness began to settle over her vision, but before it went completely black she saw something that made her want to cry. Moving with the speed of big cat, the man had used the moments that Molly was looking toward her and not at him to put a rope around her neck.

It never failed. They were, simply put, not smart enough to escape him. They always made an attempt. They were always disastrous. She came out of the woods with her little spell on her lips, and all it took to disorient her was a single shot right to the middle of a native woman. The ease of it made him laugh. Despite all the time it had taken to ride around the countryside to track the witch, it had been over in a matter of seconds. Oh, there was no doubt, he was the best for a reason. No one escaped the Witch-Finder, despite their continual efforts to do so.

With a hard yank he felt into his shoulders, he tightened the noose around the witch's neck. She stumbled on her feet, which helped to tighten it even more. Usually by the time he got them to the fire, all the fight had been knocked out of them. Not true with this one. Though she stumbled, she righted herself immediately and used her hands to claw at the rope cutting off her breath. She could try all she wanted. It would do her no good. His rope always did its job.

He did not look back at the native. She was of no importance and certainly no threat to him. The shot might not have killed her right away. It would most assuredly stop her. That was all he needed. Once the blood began to flow, it was only a matter of time before her life likewise drifted away. He would like to watch for the sheer amusement. He could not, for he had to deal with the one trying to get the rope from around her throat. She was his true prey in any event.

His swift ability to tie off the rope and get to her side came from years and years of practice. She never had a chance. In a matter of seconds, he had her hands behind her back and secured with a leather thong. Touching her skin without gloves to protect his own hands made his stomach lurch. It was yet another sign that she was the one. No mortal woman would fill him with such revulsion at the mere touch of flesh against flesh. He pulled the leather tight, and her squeal of pain was satisfying.

"You feel the agony of your victims, Witch?"

"Fuck you."

He came around in front of her and slapped her cheek with his large hand open. It left a beautiful red image of his palm and fingers on her pale flesh. He liked that. "I do not tolerate coarse language."

"I'll say it again then. Fuck you."

And again he slapped her, satisfied to see tears form in her eyes. They did not spill down her cheeks. She was a strong one, and excitement raced through him. The strong, defiant ones were always the most satisfying to break. "You are finished, witch, so do not waste your last words on vulgarity."

She spat on him. He used the cloth of his coat sleeve to wipe it away. He kept his eyes on hers the whole time. He would not give her the satisfaction of believing it had disturbed him. Once this was all done, he would be certain to wash away any trace of her on his skin.

He had her hands tied and the noose around her neck. Her little native friend was on the ground bleeding to death and the man in the cabin undoubtedly dead. No need to hurry, for there was nothing, no one, for him to worry about. He moved away from her and to the end of the rope he had tied around the tree. He loosened it enough that he could pull the noose tighter and lift her from her the ground. Only enough that she could still stand on her toes. He did not want her to die. Not quite yet for he wanted her to see and understand what came next.

She was balanced on her toes when he walked back to where he stood in front of her. It felt good, and every time he did this, righteous glory filled him. "Just a little longer, wicked one. You need not worry about the rope, for it will be the flames that take you home."

He was shocked when she smiled at him. "Oh, I'm not worried, but I think you better be." Her gaze went over his shoulder, and he spun, thinking that the native woman had managed to rise to her feet. Like she was going to be a threat even if she did. His shot had hit her, and if she had any life left in her, it would be thin and powerless. Besides, she was a tiny woman, and he could smash her beneath his boot like a bug. That he would be happy to do.

"Yes," she said softly to his back, her voice hoarse from the noose that was tight against her throat. "I'm the witch you've been searching for, but it isn't me the flames will take home. Hell's coming for you."

It was not the native woman, for she still lay where she had fallen. His gaze moved from the body on the ground, and he stared. For the first time ever, he felt fear.

CHAPTER THIRTY-THREE

Yes, her legs were screaming as she balanced on her toes to keep the noose from cutting off all the air to her lungs. It took supreme effort to keep steady. Her throat burned from the noose that seemed to grow tighter by the second. Still she used every ounce of core strength she possessed to keep still and upright. In her mind she was thanking her friend Heidi for insisting on core training. Never imagined she'd end up needing it like this. Her toes screamed as she balanced on them. Still, she was willing to go for it because she was not going to give that bastard the satisfaction of killing her. All she had to do was give karma a minute or two.

That was the essence of the spell she'd cast earlier, and by God, it had worked.

Even though a casual observer might think it was her end, they couldn't see the whole picture like she could. It almost made her smile. Her family had always told her that one day she would come into her true power, and when that day came she would know. Well, guess what, Mom? The day had come, and damn straight, she knew it. Granted, it was a couple hundred years in the past, but damned if it didn't happen just as they told her it would. It was quite the feeling, and the power of it filled her all the way to her fingertips.

Unfortunately, her new-found skill didn't extend to anything physical, like getting free of the leather thong that was cutting off the circulation in her wrists or blowing off the noose around her neck. Now, that would be an incredible power to have at the moment, because without it, she was stuck with pretending she was a ballerina using toe shoes. Dancing never was her thing, and the way her toes screamed in pain, not something she would ever be inclined to pursue.

On the other hand, she had an unobscured view of what her magic had achieved, and it was awesome. The look on the guy's face was worth a million bucks. Aquene and Hannah, as well as the visions that had come to her, all attested to the evil at his core. Even with those testaments, the cruelty she saw now was so much worse than she'd imagined. This guy was a real shit, and he had what was coming to him. If this was the last thing she ever saw, at least it was something magnificent.

At the touch of hands on her wrists, she jumped and nearly lost her ballerina footing. The noose tightened a bit, and panic shot through her until she heard Winnie's quiet voice at her back. "Hold on a sec."

It seemed more like an hour, when in fact it was maybe fifteen seconds before her hands were free. Immediately, she raised them to the noose around her neck. It was hard to get purchase as her fingers had gone numb and now felt as though thousands of needles were shooting through them. Working through the pain, she managed to dig at the rope with impressive energy.

"Hang on," Winnie told her, though it was hard to hear through her momentary panicked response. She had to free herself. Get as far away from the rope as possible. "Molly! Stop."

She did, as soon as she realized what Winnie was trying to do. Her arms were around her waist, and her beautiful, loving friend was lifting her from her feet. It was enough to put slack in the rope, and it gave her exactly what she needed to loosen the noose and slip it from her neck. The relief was immediate and immense. Winnie then dropped her back to her feet. The whole thing took maybe a minute, probably less, and during the entire time, the man paid them no attention as he was still staring into the woods beyond the cabin. Molly knew why.

"Do you see them?" she asked in a hushed voice.

"See who? Aquene? Come on. You need to help her. She's hurt. And I need to get to Angus."

"He shot Aquene. I know. But no, I don't mean her. I mean do you see *them*?"

Winnie was reaching down to pick up what looked like a kettle. Molly didn't understand. Who cared about a damned kettle at the moment? They needed to stop this guy. Nobody needed water. "They've come to help," she tried to explain. "It's amazing. There's so many of them."

Winnie stood holding the kettle in both hands. Her eyes swept over the clearing. "I don't know what you're talking about. I don't see anyone else."

"You really don't?" Molly was shocked. They were so solid. So alive. So pissed off.

"No. I've got to help Angus. You take down butthead and help Aquene."

"Go away!"

Both of them stared at the man who was backing toward them.

"You!" He had spun and was now glaring at them, his eyes black with fury. His whole body trembled visibly.

Molly couldn't help it. She smiled. "I told you I wasn't here alone." By all rights, she should be afraid of the gun he held pointed toward her, and if it wasn't shaking, she might have been. Also, if it hadn't been for the mass of figures closing in behind him, she might have been. This was a new spin on the I've-got-your-back concept. She liked it. Oh yeah, she liked it a lot.

His eyes burned as he stared at her. He fired a shot, and she felt the whoosh of air as Winnie went down behind her. If she hadn't seen the shot go wide, she'd have turned to check on her friend. She was pretty confident it was fear that had Winnie dropping to the ground.

"Call them off or I'll kill you." The gun was still shaking in his hand.

She shrugged. "You were going to kill me anyway, so no, I won't call them off."

"Who?" Winnie had risen back to her feet.

"Them!" He waved his arms. "Every damned witch I ever destroyed. They're all here. All of them."

"This dude is really losing it, isn't he? He's definitely a brick short." Winnie was shaking her head and didn't seem intimated by the shaking gun either.

He didn't give Molly a chance to answer. He did it for her. "I am Matthew Hopkins, Witch-Finder, and you are both going to die. No one defeats me. No one humiliates me."

Molly gave him credit for guts. He ran at her then, the gun still pointed in her direction. She intended to meet him head-on, but Winnie had a different idea.

"Oh, for heaven's sake. I don't have time for this shit." He dropped like a hot rock when the cast-iron kettle Winnie swung smacked him in the head with a satisfying thud.

❖

"I don't know what's going on here, but I don't have time for this arrogant bastard." Winnie let the kettle drop, though she made sure not to let it spill too much water. No way in bloody hell she was going back to the river to fill it again.

"Nice," Molly said at the same time she kicked the gun away from his hand. Winnie was glad Molly wasn't foolish. The kettle might have knocked him silly but no sense taking chances by leaving the gun near enough for him to grab. This one was sneaky enough to play possum.

The man who called himself Matthew Hopkins was facedown on the ground and groaning. Didn't look like such a tough guy right now. "Take that, you piece of garbage." That's what happened when someone got between her and her man. She didn't need magic or a weapon. She was a chef, after all, and her best weapon was something from the kitchen. Worked in the twenty-first century. Worked in this one too.

Molly was still smiling as she looked toward the trees again. Her expression was filled with what? Gratitude? Winnie blinked and then squinted. Still a big fat nothing.

"What are you looking at?"

"You really don't see them?"

Winnie didn't see anything except Aquene and the guy she'd hit with the kettle. "I don't see anyone except the four of us, a noose, and a whole lotta trees. That's plenty in my book."

"Well, let's just say I called in a few reinforcements."

"As in?" The state patrol? The RCMP? Who? She was relatively certain that kind of reinforcement was at least a hundred years in the future. All they had was each other, because the other two were both in bad shape.

"As in every person this piece of shit ever destroyed, and they all showed up for the party. No RSVP required."

Ah, now she got it. Molly had finally whipped up the magic they all knew she had inside her, and it worked. Good deal. "You worked up a little mojo to shut this guy down."

"I did indeed."

"Nice work. I always knew you had it in you to kick some serious ass." Now, Winnie figured at this point, Molly could take care of whatever needed to happen with the guy. She had something far more important to take care of. "I've got to get to Angus."

Molly put a restraining hand on her arm. "Give me a second. I need your help."

"Angus…" She shook off Molly's hand. She'd wasted too much time already.

"Please. I need you both."

There was a note in Molly's voice that made her pause. It was only then that she noticed Aquene had joined them, and she was bloody and unsteady on her feet. It was pretty impressive that she was actually upright. She had an iron will, that was pretty clear. Winnie also realized she was going to need the precious water for more than just Angus.

As much as she wanted to race in and check on him, the plea from Molly was compelling enough that she stayed with a single caveat. She held up her index finger. "One minute, and then I'm in with my man. That's it. One minute."

"It's all I need." This was a new Molly, with something powerful and firm in her voice and her eyes filled with determination. "We're sending Mr. Witch-Finder to the hades that's been waiting a long time for him."

Winnie wasn't quite sure how she could help with that one. Another smack in the head with her kettle? When Molly held out her hand, she figured she might as well play this out. She took her hand. "I need you to let go of that for just a minute."

Winnie still had the kettle in her other hand, and she held on tight. She had fought too hard to get the water here. "I don't know…"

"Please. It will only take a little while. Set it down and take Aquene's hand. Please,"

It seemed as though a little voice whispered in her ear. *Trust her.* No-brainer. She trusted Molly with her life. Carefully she set the precious kettle on the ground and took Aquene's hand. The three of them formed a circle around the fallen man with the goose egg on his forehead. Pretty good whack with her kettle, if she did say so. As soon as the three of them held hands and the circle was complete, she felt a rush through her entire body.

Not just a rush, but suddenly everything changed and they weren't alone anymore. Now she understood what Molly had been asking her because now she could see. Forming an outer circle around Molly, Aquene, and her were hundreds of mostly women. One of the few men in the crowd was a man dressed in a priest's collar. Holy crap, she thought. Holy. Crap.

As they continued to hold hands, Molly started to speak. "By and by all things shall pass, season unto season, year unto year. We have come again, hidden children of time, to harness the mystery of the magic circle that is placed between the worlds of the living and of the gods. We seek justice for those betrayed and those unfairly taken. We seek justice to right the sins of the man at our feet and for the lives he stole. For this, Matthew Hopkins, you shall descend into the Realm of Shadows, where you shall remain for all eternity."

"What the…?" It was like something out of a bad horror movie, and just like in a horror movie, it all seemed to be happening in slow motion. The ground beneath his body opened, revealing what appeared to be a roaring fire. He tumbled in, and as quickly as the hole appeared, it was gone. Gave the devil's flames a whole new meaning.

It took her only a second after the chasm closed for her to let go of Molly and Aquene. Molly had gotten her minute. Winnie wasn't waiting any longer. Since the moment she'd heard the scream earlier, all she could think about was getting to Angus. If something happened to him, she wasn't sure she could go on. She would have to drop down beside him and die in that stupid cabin.

She reached down, grabbed the kettle, and raced into the cabin. What she saw as she charged through the door made her heart stop and a scream pour from her lips.

CHAPTER THIRTY-FOUR

The moment Aquene took Molly's hand, she knew they had the power to end this. It was as the Great Spirit had shown her what now seemed very long ago. The pain in her side was strong, yet she found the courage to find her feet and join with Molly and Winnie. She was not wrong.

The man who had brought such madness and misery to the earth was gone quickly, and it was as if he had never walked the land. The spirits Molly had called upon to join them faded away as well. What had taken so long to come together was over in mere moments. When Winnie raced to the cabin, Aquene's knees gave way, and once more she sank to the ground. Her body ached and discomfort laced her side as hot as a fire on a winter snow-filled night.

Molly crouched next to her. "Let me see." Her touch was tender, though it still sent pain coursing down her side. The man's weapon had been a harbinger of agony. She thought of the owl's hoot and wondered now if it had been meant for her. Was death coming to greet her?

"It's not bad. He was apparently a poor shot, because the bullet left a deep groove in your side but didn't pierce anything. That's good. Come on." Molly stood and helped Aquene to her feet. "We need to get you inside and cleaned up. I'm confident it will heal well before you know it."

"There is much pain."

"Not surprised. It gouged your side pretty good. We can fix you up, and as long as it doesn't get infected, you'll be ready to go in no time."

That was a good thought, as Aquene also wanted to believe she was not mortally wounded. The pain was strong, but it did not steal her breath any longer and she realized the bleeding had stopped. She glanced down at the ground where the man had been. It was not her the owl came for. "We must help the others." She had seen the desperation in Winnie's eyes and instinctively understood her man was in danger. She did not know why, only that they must help.

They had sent the evil one to the beyond that he deserved, but her work was not yet complete. Inside the cabin, it became even clearer that she must use the gifts bestowed upon her to assist these warriors in returning home.

"What happened?" Molly was kneeling beside Winnie, who had Angus's head in her lap and was pressing a damp cloth to his forehead.

"A rattlesnake bite. We climbed the ridge to try to find you, and he was bitten. By the time I got him back here, he was out. He has a horrible fever, and I can't get him to wake up. I think he's dead." The sorrow in her voice was clear.

"He is still alive." Aquene had seen this before, and she wanted to put hope back into the other woman's heart. Gently she too kneeled beside him. For a moment she closed her eyes as the pain in her side threatened to make her vision go black. When the pain passed, she opened her eyes again. She took the cloth binding his arm from his body and unwrapped his hand. It was puffy and red, also hot to her touch. This too she had seen before.

Slowly she stood and searched until she found a cup. Her pouch still hung at her side, only now it was covered with her blood and sticky to the touch. From it she took dried herbs and crushed them into the cup. With a bit of water from the kettle Winnie had brought back from the river, she made a paste. It had a pungent aroma she was pleased to smell. The herbs still held their power. Carefully, she patted the paste onto his hand and then took the cloth and wrapped it once more around the wound.

Expelling a long breath, Aquene sat on the floor and met Molly's eyes. "You must take him home now. My medicine may not be strong enough to save him. I believe that in your time, his life can be saved. Is it not so?"

Molly nodded. "We have medicine that will heal him quickly."

All that could be done here was complete. "It is time for you all to go."

"I don't know how to go home." Molly's face was pale. Sadness tugged at Aquene for what Molly did not say: that she did not want to go home.

Aquene sensed that the danger her friend now faced was causing her distress. She understood, for if Alumpum lay on the floor fighting to stay alive, she would feel great fear. It was only right that Molly think first of her long-time friend and not of the woman she had just come to know.

She now shared what she believed to be the right path. The only path. "It must be the same as when you came. We will do it together." Aquene believed that their touch had brought Molly and her friends here, and it would send them home. Each of them in their own way possessed a piece of the magic that opened the door between their worlds. Together they came, and together they would leave.

"I don't want to leave you." Molly's words were filled with anguish.

She heard what she longed to, and it made her feel happy. "You will not leave me."

Storm clouds gathered in Molly's eyes. "I don't understand. I can't stay, and you can't go."

"Guys…" They turned to Winnie, who was rocking Angus while tears streamed down her face. "We have to leave now. I'm afraid we're losing him."

Aquene stared at Molly and nodded. "She speaks true. He must go and find that which will save him. It is not in this time. I have done all I can to help. We must join again and use our magic to get you all home."

"I can't. I can't leave you." Tears spilled from Molly's eyes.

"You will not leave me," she repeated once again. This too she knew to be a truth, for as Aquene had lain on the ground, her blood flowing out of her, the Great Spirit had come to her one last time and shown her another vision. Her work was not yet done. Sending the evil man to the dark beyond was only the beginning. She now understood her full destiny. "You will not leave me, for I am going with you."

EPILOGUE

Spokane, Washington
Three months later (present day)

Molly stood in the middle of her newly remodeled bakery kitchen and smiled. It was beautiful, absolutely beautiful. She might very well have to change the name of her bakery to the Phoenix, because it had literally risen from the ashes. Once the investigation had been completed and the source of the fire ruled one hundred percent accidental, everything had moved quickly. It had been amazing to watch it turn from a blackened shell to a shining, functioning kitchen once again.

More than just the bakery was remarkable. Just thinking back on what had happened in that cabin still boggled her mind. Having Angus dying on the floor, Aquene shot, and Winnie in crisis had literally been the bleakest moment in her life. Talk about feeling helpless. Except Aquene had turned it into magic. She'd been right when she'd suggested that they recreate the moment that had transported them to the nineteenth century.

Of course, in the midst of an attempted lynching, she'd dropped the grimoire outside. Thank the stars for the little flashlight still in her pocket, because while they'd been inside, it had grown pitch-black. After she'd located the book, she'd raced back inside. Huddled together on the spot where Hannah had hidden it, she and Aquene had touched it as one. To this day, she was convinced Hannah had put a spell on that spot, because nothing else explained how they had moved through time. She and Aquene might each possess a bit of magic, but enough to move them all through time? She would never believe it to be so simple. Nothing would ever convince her that it wasn't Hannah's spirit guiding them every step of the way.

As she and Aquene jointly held the grimoire, again they had experienced wind and sound and darkness. After it all passed, they were back in the twenty-first century, complete with Loba waiting patiently at the cabin door. She could say without hesitation she'd never been so happy to see her dog. The second thing to strike her was that Aquene hadn't been lying when she said she was coming with them, for she was kneeling next to Molly, still clutching one end of the grimoire.

Only after she called for emergency services—which she was able to do because her cell phone, still tucked in the pocket of her pack, now worked—and both Aquene and Angus were airlifted to a hospital in the Tri-cities did she learn why Aquene was able to come through time with them. She explained how the Great Spirit had sent her on her journey at first to help Molly defeat the Witch-Finder and end his reign of terror. After the vision they shared on the bluff in Umatilla, Aquene had begun to understand her journey entailed far more than simply stopping Hopkins. After she was shot and lay bleeding on the ground, the Great Spirit had then shown her what she must do, and it had nothing to do with evil.

All along, Aquene had kept telling Molly that she was the savior of Aquene's people. That wasn't exactly the way it had worked out. Molly was only the conduit. In a world where her language had disappeared, Aquene had come to bring it back. Their hearts and magic joined together, it was Aquene who walked through the shadows to save her people.

Surprisingly, Aquene adjusted fairly easily to the changes the centuries had brought. Each new discovery made Molly smile as she watched Aquene's pleasure. More than that, she was thrilled to be a part of her adventure. Her heart had never felt so full, and the fact that Aquene shared that feeling was the most amazing thing ever.

If anyone had told her a fire in her bakery would change her world like this, she would have called them insane. What a wonderful thing life had turned out to be, and never had she appreciated being from a family like hers more. She would always feel sad about the way Hannah had died, and at the same time she would always feel grateful that her many-times great-grandmother had foreseen her coming and used that knowledge to help Molly reach her full potential. Life was so mystical and marvelous.

Aquene came into the kitchen and smiled. "It is quite beautiful."

So was Aquene, who was wearing white pants, a white blouse, and a beautifully colorful jacket. Molly too had dressed for the occasion in a sky-blue dress. "It is, isn't it? I can't believe how incredible it turned out." The best part, though, was what she had done to christen the new kitchen: bake a wedding cake. Not just any wedding cake. No, she had baked her first cake in her new kitchen for Angus and Winnie.

"We must be on our way. Let us get the cake and hurry, for we do not want to be late."

Angus had been in rough shape by the time they got him to the hospital, and he still didn't have full use of one hand. Time would tell if the nerve damage was permanent. But that hadn't slowed him down a bit. He had recovered quickly and was back at it soon. After what she'd seen during their great adventure, Molly was pretty sure Angus possessed his own bit of magic, and she was betting he'd enjoy a full recovery. She loved that about the man. She loved even more that he was marrying her best friend today.

Kissing Aquene, she went to the refrigerator and took out the cake. It wasn't large, because the wedding was small: only about twenty in all, comprised of family and friends.

An hour later she held Aquene's hand as they watched their two precious friends join their lives. Aquene leaned close, kissed her ear, and whispered, "It is beautiful."

"Yes, it is." And it was. She had never seen Winnie look so gorgeous. Angus, despite his wounded hand, was handsome and clearly in love with his bride. Her heart sang.

"I believe ours will be too."

For a moment, she had to think about what Aquene just said. Slowly she turned her head and stared at her. A small smile played at the corners of her mouth. "Ours?"

"Ours."

Molly laughed softly, squeezed Aquene's hand, and began to think about the perfect place for a spring wedding.

About the Author

Sheri Lewis Wohl grew up in northeast Washington State and though she always thought she'd move away, never has. Despite traveling throughout the United States, Sheri always finds her way back home. And so she lives, plays, and writes amidst mountains, evergreens, and abundant wildlife. When not working her day job in federal finance, she writes stories that typically include a bit of the strange and unusual and always a touch of romance. She works to carve out time to run, swim, and bike so she can participate in local triathlons, her latest addiction.

Books Available From Bold Strokes Books

Beauty and the Boss by Ali Vali. Ellis Renois is at the top of the fashion world, but she never expects her summer assistant Charlotte Hamner to tear her heart and her business apart like sharp scissors through cheap material. (978-162639-919-8)

Fury's Choice by Brey Willows. When gods walk amongst humans, can two women find a balance between love and faith? (978-162639-869-6)

Lessons in Desire by MJ Williamz. Can a summer love stand a four-month hiatus and still burn hot? (978-163555-019-1)

Lightning Chasers by Cass Sellars. For Sydney and Parker, being a couple was never what they had planned. Now they have to fight corruption, murder, and enemies hiding in plain sight just to hold on to each other. Lightning Series, Book Two. (978-162639-965-5)

Summer Fling by Jean Copeland. Still jaded from a breakup years earlier, Kate struggles to trust falling in love again when a summer fling with sexy young singer Jordan rocks her off her feet. (978-162639-981-5)

Take Me There by Julie Cannon. Adrienne and Sloan know it would be career suicide to mix business with pleasure, however tempting it is. But what's the harm? They're both consenting adults. Who would know? (978-162639-917-4)

Unchained Memories by Dena Blake. Can a woman give herself completely when she's left a piece of herself behind? (978-162639-993-8)

Walking Through Shadows by Sheri Lewis Wohl. All Molly wanted to do was go backpacking...in her own century. (978-162639-968-6)

A Lamentation of Swans by Valerie Bronwen. Ariel Montgomery returns to Sea Oats to try to save her broken marriage but soon finds herself also fighting to save her own life and catch a murderer. (978-1-62639-828-3)

Freedom to Love by Ronica Black. What happens when the woman who spent her life worrying about caring for her family finally finds the freedom to love without borders? (978-1-63555-001-6)

House of Fate by Barbara Ann Wright. Two women must throw off the lives they've known as a guardian and an assassin and save two rival houses before their secrets tear the galaxy apart. (978-1-62639-780-4)

Planning for Love by Erin Dutton. Could true love be the one thing that wedding coordinator Faith McKenna didn't plan for? (978-1-62639-954-9)

Sidebar by Carsen Taite. Judge Camille Avery and her clerk, attorney West Fallon, agree on little except their mutual attraction, but can their relationship and their careers survive a headline-grabbing case? (978-1-62639-752-1)

Sweet Boy and Wild One by T. L. Hayes. When Rachel Cole meets soulful singer Bobby Layton at an open mic, she is immediately in thrall. What she soon discovers will rock her world in ways she never imagined. (978-1-62639-963-1)

To Be Determined by Mardi Alexander and Laurie Eichler. Charlie Dickerson escapes her life in the US to rescue Australian wildlife with Pip Atkins, but can they save each other? (978-1-62639-946-4)

True Colors by Yolanda Wallace. Blogger Robby Rawlins plans to use First Daughter Taylor Crenshaw to get ahead, but she never planned on falling in love with her in the process. (978-1-62639-927-3)

Heart Stop by Radclyffe. Two women, one with a damaged body, the other a damaged spirit, challenge each other to dare to live again. (978-1-62639-899-3)

Undercover Affairs by Julie Blair. Searching for stolen documents crucial to U.S. security, CIA agent Rett Spenser confronts lies, deceit, and unexpected romance as she investigates art gallery owner Shannon Kent. (978-1-62639-905-1)